KEEPING SCORE

CATHRYN FOX

COPYRIGHT

Keeping Score
Copyright 2021 by Cathryn Fox
Published by Cathryn Fox

ALL RIGHTS RESERVED. Without limiting the rights under copyright reserved above, no part of this publication may be reproduced, stored in or introduced into a retrieval system, or transmitted, in any form, or by any means (electronic, mechanical, photocopying, recording, or otherwise) without the prior written permission of both the copyright owner and the above publisher of this book.

This is a work of fiction. Names, characters, places, brands, media, and incidents are either the product of the author's imagination or are used fictitiously. The author acknowledges the trademarked status and trademark owners of various products referenced in this work of fiction, which have been used without permission. The publication/use of these trademarks is not authorized, associated with, or sponsored by the trademark owners.

Discover other titles by Cathryn Fox at www.cathrynfox.com. Please sign up for Cathryn's Newsletter for freebies, ebooks, news and contests: https://app.mailerlite.com/webforms/landing/c1f8n1

ISBN 978-1-989374-37-5
ISBN Print 978-1-989374-36-8

ROCCO

Hate is a pretty strong word.

It's not one I use frequently, or even flippantly. I use it only when I mean it. When it's justly deserved, and when no other expression fits. Like that time when I was sixteen, and one of my foster parents dragged the new kid into the bathroom and flushed his head in the toilet because he didn't eat the broccoli on his plate—because getting a serving of fresh greens once a week was a privilege, not a right.

Hate.

That's the only word to describe what I felt for that cruel bastard. He deserved the ass kicking I gave him for hurting a fellow foster kid, but I didn't take joy in hurting him, or in all the hating—and there was a lot of hating. That stunt landed me in a new foster home, with a whole new set of problems.

But that's not what I'm thinking about at the moment. I'm thinking about the only other person I can truly say I hate, and I'm currently sitting across the table from him, my legs relaxed, my feet kicked out in front of me, as beads of sweat trickle down Cochrane Montgomery's too perfect face as he stares at the cards in his hands.

I don't hate rich folks as a rule. Hey, whatever hand we're dealt is the hand we have to play, right? I learned to deal with poverty and violence early on, but Cochrane here, he's had it good up until now, which is why he's having a hell of a time dealing—or rather laying his cards down.

Am I taking enjoyment in his misery? Would it be awful if I said yes? Horrible if there's this satisfying pleasure washing over me as he squirms? I might have grown up on the mean streets of Chicago, and learned to use my fists for survival, but I like to think I'm a civilized human being—thanks to my sophomore year gym coach. He saw potential in me, and taught me to use my hands for something other than crime. He even gave me his old 1969 Honda CB 750 motorcycle.

No one has ever given me anything before, other than an ass kicking that I probably deserved. That bike has been with me since I graduated high school, when Coach handed her down to me—a ride for college, he'd said with pride, knowing he was a big part in shaping my future. I didn't want to take her, but he insisted. In return, I promised I'd take good care of her and now she's my pride and joy and I wouldn't trade her for the world. Sometimes I think it's the bike—Coach's belief in me—that gave me the motivation to make something more of myself and make him proud of me. That's why I'm here at Kingston College on a football scholarship, staring at the rich fuck who made my freshman year miserable by making sure I, as well as everyone else in our house and on campus, knew I was trash from the wrong side of the track.

He licks his lips, and his head lifts. I almost laugh as he tries to play it off, play it cool, like I can't see right through him. Christ, I'm a hood rat, and can read a room, a situation, an opponent with my eyes closed, and if he thinks I'm not aware of his stress, of every muscle twitch in his body as he tries to beat me at poker, he's out of his fucking mind. I guess he figures a baller like me, a kid from the streets, must suck at math. He'd be wrong. Cards come naturally to me. Joining in the monthly underground secret game at Wolf House, however, was not my thing...until tonight.

"Are you going to play or look at them all night?" I taunt, shifting a little deeper into my seat, not at all worried he's going to win. I have a straight flush, and he's shit out of luck, in more ways than one. Rumor has it Daddy cut him off, put him on an allowance, because he'd been draining his account. The truth is Cochrane—I prefer to call him Dick, a play on his name, but mostly because he hates it—has a gambling problem.

But it's not the douche bag's money I'm after. Rich boy just needs to be taken down a notch or two for treating me like trash when we roomed together first year. Guess he's not the cock-of-the-walk tonight. Back in our freshman year, he's lucky I didn't give him a Burnside beatdown—that's what we called it back in our Burnside neighborhood—but my scholarship to bigger and better was far more important to me. Plus, revenge really is a dish best served cold, and while I'm quoting proverbial phrases...Karma is a bitch.

"Yeah, yeah," he mutters and swipes at his face. He might be rich, and tall and good looking, and might know how to charm the girls, but everything about him rubs me the wrong way. There's more to him, something insidious lurking beneath his perfect exterior. Maybe the girls are too dazzled by his perfect white teeth to see it.

"Come on, Dick. We don't have all night."

He glares at me through beady blue eyes and I grin. My confidence is shaking him to his core and I almost—almost—give a shit.

"The name is Cochrane," he seethes through clenched teeth.

I glance around the basement of Wolf House, at the other intense, and illegal, games going on around me. I turn to our dealer, Andrew, as he waits for Cochrane to make a move. Andrew was the one who told me Cochrane was broke and looking to win back some money. He's really one of the good guys. Rich, but treats everyone equally. We bonded my first year at Wolf House, when I was roommates with Cochrane. I have no idea who made that mix-up. Putting a scholarship baller in with the captain of the college's elite rowing team? Obviously, someone mixed the papers up or had a brain tumor. I suffered through freshman year at Wolf House—I never belonged there to begin with—then switched houses during sophomore year, going off campus with a few of the guys I met on the football team. It was a much better fit, and I never looked back, until Andrew, the only guy I ever liked from Wolf House, sent me a message about tonight's game. He never was much of a Cochrane fan either.

"So, where's that girl of yours tonight?" I ask, knowing it will just rattle him. "Such a sweet thing." Reagan might be sweet to look at, the perfect California blonde and a killer body, but I don't like her much either. I don't hate her. She doesn't deserve that harsh label, but she is one of the rich girls, following in her folks' footsteps. Truthfully, I don't begrudge her that. Good for her for having the grades and ambition to aim for the senate like her parents. I don't know why I know that about her, only that I do. Really, she means nothing to me.

Then stop thinking about her, Rocco.

"Where she is and what she's doing is none of your business." He turns his attention back to his shit hand, and the table begins to vibrate with the nervous shaking of his foot.

I go silent, and just smirk at him. He takes a fast breath, and I'm pretty sure he's throwing up a silent prayer to God, which makes me laugh. Where the fuck was the mighty being when I was getting the living shit kicked out of me when I was barely a teen? Never mind that, where was my mother? Oh yeah, I remember. She fucked off when I was a toddler, leaving me with a mean bastard of a father, who resented everything about me and blamed me for her departure. When I got older, he used to like to show me how much he hated me, either with his fists, or his belt. He said it was to toughen me up, make a man out of me. He used to say that's what his father did to him, and he turned out just fine. Wrong. He did not turn out just fine. I was taken away in my early teens, and have no idea where he is today. I don't care.

He plays his hand, and I stare at the pair of kings. I exaggerate my movements, slowing everything down to drag out the moment as I lean forward and lay my hand out, showcasing a gorgeous straight flush. Cochrane goes so silent, I think he might be having an out of body experience, and not a good one. His head lifts slowly, and his nostrils flare. He stares at me for a long moment.

"Pay up, buddy." I say, breaking the silence between us as the other games go on in the basement.

He glares at me, his blue eyes hard, and almost...pleading. Man, it really shouldn't give me pleasure to see the guy who taunted me, went out of his way to exclude me—make me feel less, especially in front of his girlfriend—called me gutter trash, and every other derogatory name under the sun, because I wasn't born into a prominent family, squirm. He got away with it because I couldn't fight back and risk losing my scholarship. Guys like him, with powerful fathers, would get me kicked out of college. I had a future to focus on. Still do, which is why showing up at this illegal game is out of character for me.

"Again?" He glances down, reaches for the cards, but I put my hand over his to stop him. His head lifts, his perfectly styled blond hair a little mussed from running his shaky hand through it. "Double or nothing?"

"No time." I pick up my phone to check for messages. "I have somewhere to be." I don't, but I'm not playing him again. I'm sure I could beat him, but taking his money isn't the point here.

"Listen, I can't—"

"Can't what?" I ask, and take my coat off the back of my chair as I cast Andrew a glance, wondering if he's going to step in. Looks like he's going to let me handle things my way and that's fine. I give him a nod to let him know I've got this and he steps away, leaving us to battle it out.

Cochrane leans in, and steals a glance around. "I can't get the money to you tonight."

I give a low, slow whistle. "That's against the rules, bro."

"Yeah, look, can you give me a week or two?"

I click my tongue and give a slow shake of my head. "Don't think so. There's a new ride I've had my eyes on." I put my hands out, and mimic the action of revving a motorcycle. Yeah, he owes me a shitload of money. I lift my hand, like I'm about to gesture the private security guard over, and Cochrane pushes his chair back.

"Don't."

I drop my hand. "Don't what? Don't tell anyone you can't pay?"

"I can pay, it's just going to take me a while."

I shrug into my Falcons coat, and fold my arms. "I'll wait while you call Daddy."

He curses under his breath, and pulls his phone from his pocket. He scrolls, but he's stalling.

"I want my money, Cochrane. Tonight." I bite back a chuckle, and decide to let him squirm just a little while longer. The truth is, I already won. I don't need his money, or a new motorcycle. My old one serves me well.

"Look." he leans closer, all conspiratorial like. "My girl..."

Okay, now he has my interest. "What about her?"

"You like her. I know you do."

I don't. Sure, I was nice to her when I shared a room with Cochrane. Why wouldn't I be? But all right, let's see where he's going with this. "What does that have to do with any of this?" I wave my hand over the disarray of cards. "You want me to play her or something? I mean, if you're desperate for me to take her money—"

"You can take *her*."

I sit there, my ears buzzing with the hum in the basement, positive I'm not hearing him correctly. Cochrane did not just offer his girlfriend up in exchange for money, right? No way, no how did he mean that. If he did, I might just have to beat the shit out of him once and for all.

I stare at him, trying to regulate my breath, slow the pulse at the base of my neck as I wait for him to continue, and he finally does.

"I don't have the money right now," he lowers his voice and continues with, "Reagan, maybe you can...I don't know..."

"Fuck her?" I blurt out for shock value, and his nostrils flare as he scrubs his face.

He shakes his head. "No, I don't mean that." He tugs on his hair, clearly digging himself in deeper and it's going to be fun to watch him try to come out of this with a shred of decency left. Who offers up their girlfriend? "I just, maybe you can hang out with her or something. I'm not suggesting sex. It's not on the table."

"Yeah, because that would make her a whore, Cochrane."

"She's not a whore. She's just the only thing I currently have of value."

Holy fuck.

My heart beats a little faster against my chest, and as my shock ebbs, rage takes its place. To think this guy would actually use his girlfriend for payment...I mean...I can't even wrap my brain around that. I always knew he was a dick. I just never knew he was this big of a one. Reagan does not deserve a douche bag like this for a boyfriend, one who is willing to trade her to cover his own ass.

Speaking of asses. Reagan has the sweetest ass I've ever set eyes on. The sweetest everything...but I am not going to take her in exchange for money. That is fucking ludicrous.

I crack my knuckles. "What the fuck would I want with Reagan?"

"She could maybe help you with your homework."

"I've got straight As, dude." I gesture to the cards. "I'm good in sciences and math."

"Yeah, okay, well. Maybe she could...cook for you. She's a great cook."

"Keep going."

He sits up a little straighter. "You could—"

"Show her what a loser you really are? Spread a little of this Rocco charm and take her from you, make her my own?" I'm just egging him on. Reagan is a nice looking princess, but a princess nonetheless, and we don't belong together. Not in this world or any other.

He snorts. "Yeah, like she's going to choose you over me, Rocco."

"You sure about that?"

"Yes. She's smarter than that."

"Maybe I'll prove you wrong."

"Not going to happen."

I glare at him, and don't like the gleam in his eyes. "Listen, you fuck with me, I'll fuck with you."

"How?"

"By getting sweet princess Reagan to fall for me, to prove you wrong." I'm bluffing. I'm not an ass who goes around playing with other people's feelings.

"You can't."

He obviously wasn't worried about that when he put her name on the table. Now though, as he averts his gaze, I catch a small hint of worry. I can't help but think she should see what a disrespecting douche he really is, ready to hand her over to bail himself out. Anything to save his own ass. Fight your own battles, dude. Christ, if I had a girl I loved—and I'm questioning Cochrane's love for Reagan—she'd be on a damn pedestal, and I'd fight tooth and nail to protect her.

"You can't touch her. She doesn't deserve that."

I snort. "She doesn't deserve any of this now, does she? But here's what I'll agree to. I won't touch her, unless she wants me to."

"She won't," he bites out harshly.

That's fine by me, I don't want to touch her either and I am one hundred percent sure Reagan is going to shut this shit down. Although there is another part of me, a small part that sees the obedient daughter, the doting girlfriend, the strait-laced college student who might do whatever it takes to save her boyfriend's balls, as little as they might be.

I crack my knuckles. "If she says no, we'll have to find another way to make you pay." I've been keeping score of all the hateful things he said to me, all the cruel pranks to make me look like a loser to his buddies at Wolf House freshman year. Yeah, it was Cochrane who had a huge end of year bash at a posh downtown hotel and invited everyone from Wolf House—everyone but the loser from the wrong side of the tracks. He did love to flaunt his money, and drive home the fact that I didn't belong. I can't help but think there was more to it though, that there were other reasons he hated me. Maybe it was because his girlfriend was always nice to me, and I was always nice to her. Maybe on some level he felt threatened. Or maybe not, and I'm not even sure I care.

He gulps. "She'll agree."

I tap my fingers on the table. "If I agreed to this, we'd need to set rules."

"Yeah, of course," he quickly agrees, a measure of relief registering on his face.

"You owe me a shit ton of money. Reagan is going to have to work that off for as long as it takes."

His throat gurgles as he swallows, hard, and he tugs at the collar of his shirt as his gaze drops to my knuckles. Is he suddenly realizing the error of his ways, the precious cargo he's putting in the hands of a guy who was dragged up on the streets? Oh, what would senator daddy think of this? Yeah, like Reagan, he too is following in his father's footsteps.

"What are the rules?" he asks.

"She's mine for one month."

His body stiffens. "You...want her for one month."

"Yeah, I think that sounds about right. One month to work off *your* debt." I press my thumb into my bottom lip, like I'm considering what she might taste like.

"You can't touch her. It's not like that."

"Like I said, I won't, unless she wants me to."

"She won't." He shakes his phone. "Can you give me a minute to talk to her? I need to run the whole month thing by her."

I grin. I don't want Reagan—don't want to fuck her. I'm not into high maintenance princesses, but his comment about her never wanting me pisses me off enough to say, "Sure, but don't blame me if it's my dick she wants when the month is all over."

2

REAGAN

I take one fast breath and then another as I stare at my boyfriend and take in the worried, almost pleading look in his eyes. I briefly pinch my eyes shut, sure I'm dreaming and he didn't just show up late at night to tell me he sold me in a poker game. A hysterical laugh crawls out of my throat, because that's insane, right? Yeah, it is. This is all just a dream. I'm really in bed, all snuggled beneath my blankets, and Cochrane isn't here offering me up to the notorious, big bad football player who sort of scares the shit out of me.

We had a run in once, or twice, or a dozen times. At least, I think we did. It was freshman year, the night was dark, foggy, and I could barely see where I was going. I'd tried to call campus security for an escort back to my place, but they were working overtime due to the recent rash of events on campus and I couldn't get through. Cochrane said he was in group study and couldn't get out of it to walk me home. I had no choice but to hightail it myself, despite the warnings that no female should be out alone after dark. There was a stalker on campus, and a girl had been attacked. She was okay, thank

God, and while walking alone wasn't my smartest move, I couldn't stand outside the lecture hall all night.

Keys in hand, I ran in the fog until the rumbling sound of a motorcycle engine reached my ears. My step stilled as my heart beat faster and through the haze I was sure it was Rocco Gianni, following me on his bike. Was he the stalker? I never found out, and after that I changed paths, taking an even longer way home. Nevertheless, over the years, late at night when I was all alone, I was sure I could still hear his bike, smell his scent—a mixture of freshly soaped skin, motor oil and leather. It's lived inside my brain since I first met him at Wolf House freshman year.

"Reagan, did you hear me?" Cochrane's whiny voice pulls me back, and I open my eyes. Blood drains to my toes because no matter how much I want to believe I'm hallucinating, I'm not. Cochrane is standing in my kitchen, begging me to save his ass by handing mine over.

"I heard you," I say softly, quietly, as I back up until I fall into a kitchen chair. I lean forward, brace my elbows on my knees and bury my face in my hands. "Can't you just ask your dad for money?"

"He cut me off, you know that. If I ask, he'll tear me a new one, and maybe even investigate. If he does and realizes I've been gambling illegally, here at Kingston..." His voice goes quiet and I spread my fingers to peek at him. He puts his finger to his throat and makes a slicing motion. "Lots of heads will roll and it probably won't look good for you, either, you know since we're a couple and people will think you're guilty by association."

"My God, Cochrane. How could you drag me into this?" I hate conflict, any kind of conflict, and here I am being dragged into the middle of a horrible situation. I hug myself to stave off the cold that always lives inside me, more so tonight.

He hurries up to me and sinks to his knees. He takes my hands in his, his blue eyes wide and imploring. "You'll won't have to do much. It's not like you have to sleep with him or anything."

My heart jumps into my throat. I hadn't even considered that sex could be part of the re-payment plan. But what if it is? What if Rocco, a brutal guy with those rough and tough hands, wants me in his bed? A strange shiver goes through me. Would he touch me brutally, tear at my clothes and force-fully devour my mouth? Or would he caress with gentle hands, a slow easy seduction that would shake the ground beneath me and send me soaring into outer space?

Which do I want more?

Wait, what? I don't want either. That is not going to happen in a million years. A billion, even. Not even if we were the last two people on earth and mankind depended on us.

"Reagan?"

"No, just no. I am not something that can be traded for currency. I can't even believe that crossed your mind."

He points to his face. "If you want to see this in one piece again…"

My jaw drops open. "He threatened you?"

"Not with words, but he cracked his knuckles and stared at my face."

"My God, Cochrane. We need to go to the police. Wait, wait…" Another thought hits. "There's a guy threatening you with physical violence and you still thought it was a good idea to put me up for trade."

"He won't hurt you, Reagan. He likes you."

My head rears back. "Likes me? He doesn't even know me, and..." I pause as a shiver goes through me, memories of him watching me from the fog stealing the air from my lungs. I guess if he wanted to hurt me, he would have, right? Then again, maybe it wasn't him following me those dark nights, keeping his distance until I locked myself in my house, and then revving his bike as he took off, me safely behind my door until the noise faded into the night.

"Please, buttercup. Do this for me, for us. We can't let anything stand in our way of becoming senators, getting married, having the family we always wanted."

I swallow the lump in my throat. Right, can't let anything get in the way of those plans—plans that had been carefully laid out for me by my parents. I think they were grooming me to follow in their footsteps the second I was born. I've done everything right, followed all the rules, been the good daughter and the good girlfriend, but this...this is over the top.

I fold my hands on my lap, the fight going out of me. "What do I have to do?"

"Whatever I tell you to."

The deep voice at the door has Cochrane jumping to his feet, and me nearly falling backward on my chair. I grab the table, trying to stop myself from toppling over when Rocco is right there, catching the back of my chair and righting me before I fall—while Cochrane stands there doing nothing.

"You okay?" he asks, those translucent blue eyes of his locking on mine with genuine concern. He hovers over me, all brawn and muscle and smelling like wind and leather, like he'd just taken a long bike ride. Everything about him overwhelms me, frightens me...does weird things to my insides.

It's a struggle to find my voice, but when I finally do I smooth my hand over my nightie, instantly realizing how thin it is. Oh God, he can probably see my nipples. I cross my arms over my chest to hide my body from his eyes, even though they haven't strayed from my face. He's not interested in me sexually, otherwise he would have looked, so I guess that's good news.

"I am now, thanks," I say.

"What are you doing here?" Cochrane asks.

Rocco doesn't turn, not right away. Ignoring Cochrane, his worried gaze moves over my face, like he's making sure I'm okay, and his closeness starts messing with my brain and body.

I push back my chair, needing a reprieve from his closeness and he finally straightens to his full height and turns. That's when I notice the big black bag on the floor by the door.

"Why wouldn't I be here?" he says to Cochrane as he picks his bag up and hikes it over his shoulder, letting it dangle down his back in that rough and tumble masculine way that teases parts of my body I didn't know existed before.

He turns to me. "So you're cool with this, Reagan? Cool with Dick here selling you to me for one full month?"

"A full month," I yell and jump up, but instantly wish I hadn't because Rocco is right there again, my body almost flush against his, my nipples now a tiny bit harder. He dips his head, not to see my near naked body, but to meet my eyes, like he's checking in on me. My entire body quivers.

"There are rules," Cochrane pipes in, and I inch back, needing to put a measure of distance between us.

"Rules?" I squeak out.

Rocco smirks. "Yeah, I'm not allowed to fuck you."

My throat tightens at his vulgar words, the world closing in on me a little. "I'm not...doing that."

"That's okay. I don't want to fuck you either, Reagan."

What the hell? Why am I so offended that he doesn't want to fuck me? What's wrong with me? Oh God! What am I even saying?

"But you are mine for the next month. I just have to figure out what it is I want to do with you." He looks past my shoulders. "First, I guess we should figure out where I'm going to sleep. Do you have a spare room, or will I be bunking with you?"

"My...roommate."

He angles his head, and his thick dark hair falls over his eyes. "You want me to sleep with your roommate?"

I give a fast shake of my head. "No, I mean. I have to clear this with her. We share this house."

He glances around. "Pretty big house for two people. You girls probably won't even know I'm here, anyway."

"Oh, I'll know," I squeak out.

His brow raises. "What's that?"

"Nothing," I say, trying not to sound as breathless as I feel.

Rocco is staying at my place for one full month!

What did I ever do to deserve this?

I lift my eyes to his. "What was that you said about rules?"

He jerks his head toward Cochrane. "Your boyfriend said no fucking. I guess you and me will have to figure out the rest come morning." He stretches, acting and looking like he's always belonged in my house. "Do you want to show me the way, or should I just fall into the first bed I find?"

My heart is crashing so hard, I'm sure the guys can hear it. "There's a spare room, second door on the left. You can sleep there tonight. We'll figure the rest out in the morning."

He nods, and walks around me. "Night."

As he stomps off, I turn to find Cochrane leaning against the kitchen counter, rubbing his chin hard, worry all over his face.

"This was a mistake," he murmurs. "A stupid fucking mistake."

I plant my hands on my hips. "You think?"

He swallows, and pushes off the counter. "I shouldn't have."

"Goddamn right you shouldn't have." It's not like me to swear. Good Lord, proper manners have been pounded into me since I was a child. I'm sure every strand of hair on my mother's head would fall out if she heard me. But under the circumstances, with my blood boiling in my veins, I can't help myself. Apparently finding out I've been sold has reduced me to my worst.

His eyes are wide, like he's too shocked at my outburst, as he reaches for me. "I'm sorry, buttercup. If I could take it back, I would."

I shake my head. For some reason, I'm not so sure I believe him. "Yeah, well, you made your bed, Cochrane, and now Rocco is lying in it."

"Reagan—"

"Out," I snap and point to the still open door.

He hesitates but I stand my ground. "Leave."

He turns and sulks to the door, his slow movements grating on my last nerve. He looks back over his shoulders. "I can come back tomorrow to help you set the rules."

"I'm a big girl, I can do them myself. I think you've done enough already."

He nods. "I really am sorry. The month will go fast and he's only sleeping here tonight to piss me off. We don't really like each other. He'll probably leave come morning, and you'll never have to deal with him again."

"And if he doesn't? If he's underfoot for a whole month, what am I supposed to do then?"

He snorts and gives a humorless laugh. "I don't know, just don't fall for him."

I stand there for what feels like ten minutes staring at Cochrane, completely dumbfounded. I shake my head to pull myself together. "That's what you're worried about?" I ask, my voice bordering on hysteria. "You sell me to the scariest motherfucker on campus, and your biggest worry is that I might fall for him?" He takes a step toward me. "Go." I practically shove him out the door and lock it behind him, then lean against it, trying to catch my damn breath.

What the hell just happened, anyway? Maybe I really am dreaming all this.

Boots shuffle in the upstairs hall and a growl crawls out of my mouth. Nope, not dreaming. Rocco Gianni, the toughest guy on the football team, a guy who is full of scars and bruises from a brutal upbringing, now owns me for one full month. The floor upstairs creaks again, and I wonder if he's lost.

I shut off the kitchen light and dart up the steps, coming to a resounding halt when I find him dressed only in a pair of jeans, his hand on my bedroom door handle.

"What are you doing?"

He turns to me, and I try hard not to let my gaze drop to take in his hard chest. "I thought I'd take a shower before bed. I hope you don't mind."

"Over there," I say and point to the door to the left. "That's my bedroom and it's out of bounds."

"You a Falcons fan?"

"No. Why?"

He shrugs. "You just used a football term." He hovers over me and my damn knees weaken. "In football when we go out of bounds, there's a penalty." He glances at my bedroom door. "What kind of penalty would I get if I crossed that threshold?"

He's teasing me, playing with me, trying to get to me, and he's doing a damn fine job. I guess his hatred of Cochrane extends to me simply because we're a couple, but I've never done anything to him.

"Just don't go in."

"Maybe you meant to say it's off limits."

"Maybe I did." God, this guy is throwing me off big time. I point a shaky finger. "Shower's right there." He turns, his chuckle reverberating through me as he walks down the hall, looking as good going as he does coming.

Yeah, there's no way I'm not going to know he's here.

3

ROCCO

I wake up early, like I always do, and the second my eyes open, I jackknife up in bed. "Where the hell am I?" I mumble curses under my breath as I take in the room, the frilly blankets I'm under, and wonder why there isn't a body beside me. I might not want a long-term relationship, but that doesn't mean my Saturday nights are spent in my bed alone. I rub my eyes, and memories of last night, the card game—Reagan—and what she said to her douche bag boyfriend when I left the room, floods my brain in a whoosh.

Scariest motherfucker.

I honestly hate the idea that she's afraid of me, and for the life of me, I don't know why or what I did to frighten her. Hell, we've talked when I lived with Cochrane, and we even shared a class our first year. But she never really paid me much attention. Fuck, maybe I should just call this all off. None of it's her fault, and Dick never should have dragged her into it. I showed up last night just to piss him off. I grabbed an equipment bag full of my shit, but I wasn't even sure I was going to stay.

Why did you?

I don't know but I'm sure it had nothing to do with that flimsy nightie Reagan was wearing. It can't be that. I don't want her and she doesn't want me and that's just fine. I probably should have left last night, but seeing Dick on his knees begging his girlfriend to let him throw her to the wolves roused the beast in me and brought out the protector. I can be like that, overprotective at times—always fighting for the underdog.

A loud noise outside my door drags my focus and my body tenses—always in fight mode. The noise is followed by a round of muffled curses. Who the hell is up at this hour on a Sunday morning? I throw the covers off, and dressed only in my boxers, I pad across the wood floor and tug open my door. The second I see the vision before me, I nearly bite off my damn tongue.

"Having trouble?" I ask as I try not to stare at Reagan's ass, barely covered in that sexy nightie from last night—the same one that invaded my dreams.

Yeah, sure, you don't want her, Rocco.

Down on her hands and knees, Reagan turns my way. Shit, she looks so adorable, and seeing her on her knees like that takes my mind in a direction I don't want it to go. Yeah, that's it. I'm getting out of here while the getting is good. Before I'm tempted to take her in my arms and show her how she should be treated.

"Oh, sorry did I wake you?" she seethes, a fire in her eyes as she glares at me.

As her gaze hits like a slap, I take a step back, and really, I shouldn't be shocked at her angry outburst. She doesn't want me here, and I can't blame her. "You need some help?"

"I don't need anything from you and perhaps you should go back to your own place if you don't like to be woken up early." She gathers up the laundry she dropped and shoves it back in the basket. That's when I notice the open, double closet doors across from my room, exposing a stacked washer and dryer. A grin turns up the corner of my mouth. Oh, I get it. She's up at the crack of dawn to do laundry to drive me from her house. I kind of like her tenacity.

Gorgeous hazel eyes narrow in on my near naked body, and she gazes at my scars, a mixture of fear and...is that concern? To be honest, last night I was hoping she'd tell Cochrane to go shove it, to clean up his own messes, but I should have known better. She jumped in to save him, despite the predicament he put her in. I shake my head. The rich protect the rich, and would go to extreme measures to help those they love. Or maybe she likes being treated like shit.

So much for me showing her how a girlfriend should really be treated. Not that I've ever had a steady girlfriend. I'm too focused for that, and to be honest, I've never loved anyone, or been in love. The only people I care about on campus are the guys on my team and the ones I share a house with. It does make me wonder what I'd do, how far I'd go, to protect a loved one.

I make a turn to gather up my stuff and get the fuck out of her place when she barks out, "Do you think you could put some clothes on?"

I spin back around, and her chest is rising and falling quickly as she tries to avert her gaze. "Actually, my clothes are dirty, since you're doing a load..." I gesture to my equipment bag and her face twists.

"You want me to do your laundry?"

"You do have a debt to pay off, Reagan." I slide my thumbs into the elastic of my boxers, and her eyes go wide. "You can start by washing these." I'm goading her, simply to get a rise out of her, although I'm not sure why.

"I am not touching your...junk."

I laugh. "It's not my junk I'm asking you to touch, Sunshine."

She stands, and huffs. "Don't call me that."

"Hey look, I wouldn't be here if Dick hadn't sold you out."

"That's not his name. Don't call him that, either."

"Would you prefer it if I called him Cock?"

Her cheeks go the prettiest shade of pink. "Don't call him...him...that."

"Cock? What, can't you say it?"

She starts shoving clothes into the washing machine, grumbling something under her breath. She fills it with liquid detergent, and pounds on the start button, but nothing happens. She curses some more, mumbling something about the broken button and stupid washer.

"I'm sorry, Sunshine. Can you speak up? I can't hear you."

She turns, and her face is completely flushed when she says, "I don't know how you beat Cochrane."

I lean against the door jamb and cross my feet, curious as to where this is going. "Are you saying I'm stupid?"

"No, I'm just…" she bites her lip. "He's good at cards, and you…"

"What about me?"

She waves her hand. "You're just…you."

I grin. "Did you ever stop to think that maybe I'm good at cards too?"

She folds her arms and leans against the machine, her eyes full of accusation. "Maybe you cheated."

That almost makes me laugh. Yeah, I'm the one who cheated. Freshman year, Cochrane and I were in math together, and he cheated off everyone. He never cheated off me, though. He just assumed I was a loser, here on a football scholarship, and probably couldn't add two plus two. Does she not know her boyfriend at all? One thing is for sure, she sure as shit doesn't know anything about me, and dammit, I shouldn't want to change that.

I take a step toward her and she stiffens. "I don't cheat."

She swallows, and lifts her head, her hazel eyes a bit darker as they lock on mine, unafraid…but afraid. "Yeah, well that's what you would say."

She's a tiny girl, clearly frightened of me—not that I'd ever hurt her—yet her shoulders are squared as she's standing before me holding her own. It makes me like her a little bit more. Her chest rises as she draws in a fast breath and that's when it hits me. She might be a pampered princess, living in this big ornate house with only one roommate, but there's this innocence about her, a vulnerability. There's also a fire in those hazel eyes of hers, a fire that could burn bright, but she, or someone, keeps it smothered.

"That's what I know," I counter, and make a split-second decision to stay around a bit longer. I'm not really sure why. I don't need to prove to her I'm an honest guy. I don't need her approval for anything.

I step closer, crowd her, and don't miss the quiver traveling the length of her body. I reach out, and she gasps. "What are you doing?"

I slide my hand around her and press the start button on the machine. It instantly starts, and her eyes go wide.

"Starting the machine. What did you think I was doing?"

"I...I don't know. How...how did you do that?"

"Right touch, I guess." I say and step back, the air between us changed, and her body vibrates against the washer and she searches the hall, like she wants to look at anything and everything except me. "Reagan." Her focus returns to me.

"What?"

"I know you hate me, but this..." I wave my finger back and forth between the two of us. "It's not on me. It's on your boyfriend."

"I never said I hated you." Her voice is low and I have to strain to hear it over the washing machine.

"You didn't have to."

"I...I don't know why you and Cochrane hate each other so much, and obviously, your hate for him extends to me too, otherwise—"

"I don't hate you. I don't even know you. Just like you don't know me." Dark lashes fall slowly over those gorgeous eyes of hers and her head bobs slowly as she glances down, like she can't figure out why I'd want to stay and make her miserable just to get back at Cochrane. But I'm not sure I do want to make her miserable. In fact, I'm not really sure about much at the moment—what the hell am I doing and why am I doing it —and while there's very few fucking things that scare me, that uncertainty does. "But we've got a whole month to rectify that, don't we?"

"I...listen if you want to toss your laundry in with mine, you can." I reach for my boxers again and she holds her hands up. "Don't."

I laugh. "You know I'm just messing with you, right?"

She laughs, an almost airy, light sound that curls around me. "Yeah, okay. But we do need to set some rules on what can and can't be worn outside the bedroom."

"Does that go for you, too?"

Her eyes go wide, like she's just realizing she's still in that sexy, almost see-through nightie from last night. She folds her hands over her chest. "Oh, I..."

"It's okay, I don't mind."

"I'm not used to guys staying overnight."

"Are you telling me Cochrane doesn't stay over?" My God, there is no way this girl is a virgin. She's been with Dick since freshman year, and maybe even before that.

Before she can answer, another door opens, and I turn to find a girl standing there in a T-shirt that barely covers her ass. Her shirt lifts, as she rubs her sleepy eyes, and I catch sight of her pink underwear.

"What the hell is going on out here? I'm trying to..." Her words fall off when she finds me standing in the hall beside

Reagan. Without any shame or embarrassment, she lets her gaze go from my face, down a slow, leisurely inspection all the way to my toes, and back up again. "If this is a dream, do not wake me."

"It's not a dream," Reagan huffs out, her shoulders stiff. "Miranda, this is Rocco. Rocco, Miranda. Rocco will be staying with us for the next month. Some things went down last night, and I didn't want to wake you, but I hope you're okay with it."

"Okay with it, why wouldn't I be okay with it?" She continues to gaze at me, her smile reaching her eyes as she appreciates my battered and bruised body. "And you don't have to tell me who he is. Everyone knows the Falcons bad boy, Rocco Gianni. He's the best tight end the team has ever had, and I mean that in more ways than one."

Reagan's face turns blood red as Miranda steps closer and pokes me with her finger. "What is it they call you... Rock Hard Gianni?"

"He's real, Miranda, and you can't just touch someone without asking. It's called consent."

"Oops, sorry," Miranda giggles and presses her finger to her bottom lip in a cutesy, innocent way. I don't think there is anything cutesy or innocent about her, but I like her. Hard to believe she's roommates with Reagan. They seem so different. Maybe that's what makes them good together. They do say opposites attract, and you can't get much different than Reagan and me. Not that I'm attracted to her. Well, okay, yeah, I'm a red-blooded male, and there's no denying she's gorgeous. But she's not mine, and never will be, and I'm okay with that.

"How would you like it if he just touched you...never mind." Reagan groans, exasperated and already knowing the answer to the question, much like I do. For a brief second, I wonder how Reagan would like it if I touched her.

Stop!

"She's right," I tell Miranda. "You can't touch without permission."

She chuckles. "If I ask for permission, will you grant it?"

"Ohmigod," Reagan says and holds her hands up to cut off her friend off. "Enough. Go back to bed, Miranda. There's nothing to see here."

"Then you need glasses, girlfriend." Miranda looks me over again. "I should probably ask why you're staying here for a month, but I'm not even sure I care."

Reagan frowns. "He's...I'm..."

"She's helping a guy out," I explain, to save her from the embarrassment of explaining that Dick the Douche Bag sold her out.

"Helping a guy out, huh?" Miranda wags her brows playfully. "Is the guy helping the girl out too? 'Cause girlfriend, you've been so uptight lately, it would do you good to find yourself between a rock and a hard place."

Reagan takes a breath, like she has one last nerve and her friend is close to fraying it. "It's not like that."

"Oh yeah, well that's too bad," Miranda says and spins, an exaggerated swing of her hips as she goes back to her bedroom and closes the door, leaving us alone in the hall, my body hyper-aware of the woman next to me.

I turn back to Reagan and grin. "She seems nice." Her eyes fall shut and she's murmuring something under her breath about Miranda being her *ex*-best friend, and I can't help but think Reagan *is* super intense and maybe Miranda is right.

Maybe she could use a little rock and a hard place.

4

REAGAN

"You know you do that a lot."

I lift my head as Rocco strolls into the kitchen like he's lived here his four years of college. I can see why his nickname is Rock Hard Gianni. Everything about him draws my attention, overwhelms me in the strangest ways as his muscles bunch and shift with each easy movement.

He still hasn't put a shirt on, but at least he has sweatpants on as he stretches his arms like he's getting ready for a run. And no, I am not going to think about the way his pants hang low on his hips, showing a dark line of hair that trails downward, drawing my gaze like I'm some dimwitted moth. I force my head up, and that's when I see the long purplish scar on his chest. I caught a hint of it in the hallway earlier, but now I can't seem to stop staring at it.

"This?" he says and points at it.

I pull my gaze away, and toy with my ponytail. "Sorry, it was rude of me to stare."

From my peripheral vision, I catch the way he rubs his scar. "No worries," he says, and doesn't explain how or why he got it. Not my business anyway.

"What do I do a lot?" I mumble, my eyes back on my laptop, but my focus now shot.

He steps closer, almost in front of me and rubs his chest with those big, stupid hands of his, and I'm going to kill Miranda. A rock and a hard place. God...

"Huh?"

I take my eyes off the statistical equations I can't figure out, and lift my head. My God, I hate statistics. Hate it! I have no idea why it's a requirement for a Bachelor's of Business degree. "When you walked in here, you said I do something a lot."

"Oh, yeah, you mumble under your breath when you're pissed off about something." He comes even closer and glances at my laptop. My first instinct is to slam it shut. I don't want to come off as stupid because I suck at statistics, and have been struggling through my courses for the last three years. But I force myself to keep my hands on my lap, not wanting to rouse his suspicions by reacting. "Why are you pissed off?" He does some lunge thing to stretch his legs as he strains to see my screen.

With a little nudge, I ever so slightly slide my computer to the right, and through gritted teeth, say, "Didn't we just discuss rules about you wearing clothes?"

"I don't really think it was a discussion."

Lord, how can he stay in that lunge position so long. I did yoga once and couldn't move for a week.

"What's the problem anyway?" he asks as she swipes at his brow. "It's ridiculously hot in here."

"It wasn't hot."

"Wait, are you saying…" I glance at him to find his lips curl at the corners, and I shake my head.

"I'm not saying anything." Truthfully it wasn't hot until he walked into the room. Usually I'm freezing, even in summer, so this insane hot flash means I'm either going into early menopause or…or… Never mind, I don't want to think about it.

I'm about to tell him to go get dressed when my phone pings. I don't need to look at it to know who's calling. My boyfriend has his own special ring. Rocco leans in close, and I smell my grapefruit body wash on him. I should be angry, to think he was in my shower, using my things—it feels far too intimate— but I can't think about that right now. Not with Cochrane calling, and I'm not even sure I want to talk to him.

"Aren't you going to get that?"

I blow out a breath, and fist my hands on my lap. "I don't really want to speak to him right now."

"Can't say as I blame you."

My head jerks up. "Hey, don't say things like that." As soon as the words leave my mouth, I briefly close my eyes. Look at that, always the good girl, always jumping in to defend family and friends, because it's been ingrained into me.

"It's great that you stand up for your people, Reagan. Admirable, really."

I glare at him. He wants to say more, I can feel it, but instead he crosses his arms, and goes silent. But maybe he should say it. Maybe I do need to hear what a horrible thing my boyfriend just did to me. If his father ever found out...if my father ever found out. They're best friends, and I can imagine they'd come to blows over this, and Cochrane could possibly get kicked out of college...Rocco too.

"Just...don't say bad things, okay?"

"You're right. He's your boyfriend, and I shouldn't talk trash about him. That's not really my style."

I get what he's saying. It's Cochrane's style, not his. I've heard Cochrane mutter a few things about Rocco. I never stood up for Rocco because I didn't really know him, but that didn't stop me from being nice, considering he was always nice to me whenever we met in passing.

"Why do you two hate each other so much anyway?" I get up, pour a mug of coffee and his eyes widen in surprise when I turn and ask, "Milk or sugar?"

"Black is good."

I step up to him, and take in his blue eyes in the overhead light, and wait for him to answer my first question. When he doesn't, I press, "Why do you hate him?"

"That's a question you should ask him." He winks at me. "I did just agree not to talk trash." He holds three fingers up. "Foster Mom number three always said, if you don't have anything nice to say, don't say anything at all." He gives a humorless laugh. "Of course, she was coaching me before my social worker showed up for her monthly check-in." He takes a sip of coffee, and turns, a scowl on his face like he said too much. I'm not about to probe, his past is his past and not my business, although it does sound like he had a horrible upbringing. Freshman year, rumors went around that he had actually killed someone. Pair that with him being a beast on the field, and everyone learned pretty quickly he wasn't a guy to mess with.

He angles his head and says, "Although, come to think of it, I don't want you to ask him. For the next month, I don't even want you to see him."

My mouth drops open, hardly able to believe what he's suggesting. I sink into my chair. "You can't do that. That takes us into Thanksgiving, and we usually spend that with my parents."

"Not this year."

"Rocco—"

"It's like this, Reagan." He sits in the chair across from me, sets his mug down, and shifts so our knees are lightly touching. "He's the one who should be paying his own debt. Why should you be stuck with me, and he gets off easy, never having to take responsibility for his actions." I shift closer. "I think not talking to you for one full month is just what he deserves."

Okay, breathe, Reagan, breathe. He's just a guy, nothing special, and there's no reason for you to be breaking out in a sweat just from his proximity. "You do?" I ask, somehow managing to put those two words together and push them from my lips.

"Hell yeah, if you were mine, and I couldn't talk to you or touch you for a month, I'd probably end up killing someone."

My heart beats like I'd just downed a triple espresso and before I realize what I'm doing, I reach for his mug of coffee and take a mouthful. The second I set it down, he picks it up and drinks. Here I thought him using my bodywash was intimate…suddenly that's nothing. Drinking from the same mug sends shivers skittering through me, like his mouth wasn't on the mug, but instead on my body. What the hell is going on with me?

"You…you would kill someone?"

"In my world, I either fight or fuck, and if I can't fuck, I'd have no choice but to fight."

I brace both hands on the table, my brain and body too fired up to respond, and he casually turns my computer his way, and carries on like he hadn't just been talking about…fucking.

"Stats giving you trouble?"

"What…huh?" I blink, and try to unscramble his words in my brain.

"Stats. You were cursing at your computer when I came in remember?"

I shake my head. "Yeah, I just…it's not my thing."

He links his fingers and cracks his knuckles. "Lucky for you, it's mine."

"Don't you have somewhere to be?" I take in his half-naked body.

"Let's do this first. Then I have to go for a run and you have a phone call to make."

He grabs the pen and paper in front of me, and jots down the equation. I stare at his big, scarred hands. "Phone call?"

"Sure, you have to break it off with Cochrane for the next month."

"Break it off? You said you didn't want me to talk to him, not to break it off."

Without missing a beat, he starts solving the equation, and says, "Changed my mind. If you're going to pay off his debt, it means no contact with him, at all, and you have to come to my games to cheer me on, and hang out with me instead."

"Rocco, you can't do that. I'm...we're supposed to get engaged after college, supposed to go to Harvard Law together...supposed to..."

He angles his head, and my heart races. Oh, God, why is he looking at me like that, like he can see right through me?

"You have it all planned out, I see."

"Well...sort of." I shift, uncomfortable under his close inspection. "Why are you looking at me like that?"

"Like what?"

"Like I'm some sort of big joke." He might not be looking at me like that and I could be projecting. I'm in business, and I feel like a fraud as I struggle through it, knowing it will take my parents' pull to get me into law school—the path they expect me to take.

"I don't think you're a joke, Reagan. Not at all. It's great that you have a plan, that you know what you want, and are going for it. It's not always easy to know what we want at our age, and it's admirable that you do, and have this whole plan set out."

"That's the second time you said you admired something about me."

"I guess it must be true," he teases. "I like that you know what you want, that's all."

"Don't you know what you want to do?" I ask, twisting the subject before he delves in a little bit deeper, and I end up spilling secrets that are lurking in my darkest corners. He is not the kind of guy I'd tell my hopes and fears to.

"Yes, I want you to break it off with Cochrane for the next month."

He's knows I'm talking about the future—his future—but he's circling back around, and backing me into a corner.

I blink slowly. Cochrane is going to lose his mind. He should have considered the consequences last night. "Is that what you want?"

"For now."

I shake my head, my ponytail swishing over my back. "You must really hate Cochrane," I say, mostly to myself.

"Yeah," he responds, his gaze dropping to my mouth and another thought hits. Maybe he doesn't *hate* Cochrane as much as he *likes* me. A ridiculous quiver goes through me. I don't want that and of course he doesn't *like* me. He might not hate me, but he doesn't like me—or want me. We don't really know each other. Sure, I know things about him. Rumors run crazy on campus, but this...this is all about getting back at Cochrane. Before I even realize what I'm doing, I wet my lips, and meet his eyes, to find him staring at my mouth, like I'm the lamb he's about to slaughter.

I sit up a bit straighter. "So...statistics."

"Okay, here's how to solve this—"

I hold my hand up to stop him. "Talk slowly, like I'm a baby with a cookie."

He laughs. "I take it Dr. Seth is your prof."

"How did you know?"

"He's a brilliant man, but not only is he hard to understand, he talks a million miles an hour. When I had him my freshman year, he told us we all had to go home and spend the weekend musuring."

"Musuring?"

"Yeah, exactly. It took me forever to realize he was saying measuring. Brain blown." He puts his hands on his head and pulls them apart, mimicking an explosion. I laugh out loud and whack him, instantly wishing I hadn't when my hand connects with a wall of hard muscles.

Rock and a hard place.

"You're making that up," I blurt out.

He laughs and shakes his head. "True story. Scout's honor."

I snort. "Yeah, right, like you were a scout?"

"You don't know my life," he teases and I take a breath, a new lightness and ease blossoming between us.

"You're right, I don't." I shrug easily, like it doesn't matter one way or another, although I'm not entirely sure I really feel that way.

He winks at me. "Like I said, one month together will rectify that."

I nod, and although I can't quite figure out what kind of game he's playing or what he's out to prove, I have to say one month doesn't seem quite as bad as I thought it would be.

You have to break up with Cochrane.

Right, there's that.

He spends the next half hour going over my homework questions, and I sit there in awe of his teaching skills and his intelligence.

"If you don't make it in football, Rocco, you'd make a great prof."

"Thanks. I had a great coach in high school, and he told me I should always give back when I could." He nods, but a frown tugs down the corners of his mouth.

"What?"

"Why did you wait until fourth year to take stats?"

I shrug. "I hate it." I glance at him, and I have no idea why, but I confess, "I hate business."

His frown deepens. "Then why are you taking it?"

"I'm...it's expected." Oh God, what am I doing? Why would I say that? He goes quiet, too quiet, and I realize I might have crossed a line into the personal and maybe he doesn't want to hear that.

"I'm sorry, Reagan."

I shut my computer and blow out a breath. "I have no idea why I just told you that. I shouldn't have."

"Your secret is safe with me." He smiles to reveal that one crooked front tooth. The funny thing is, it makes him who he is, and it doesn't detract from his looks, it enhances them. Who would have though imperfections could be perfect if they were on the right person?

"It's not like me to do that."

"I guess you must trust me."

"Trust? I don't know about that. Trust doesn't come easy to me." I grew up privileged and I appreciate all I was given, but I never knew who wanted to be my friend because of what I had or because they liked me.

"Me neither. I guess we have that in common, and you probably shouldn't trust a big scary motherfucker."

Heat flashes across my cheeks, and I cover my face with my hands. "You heard that."

"Yeah." He takes my hands and slowly removes them from my face, and the second my eyes lock on his, catch the warmth in his eyes my breath stalls in my lungs.

"I don't want you to be afraid of me, Reagan. Your boyfriend, yes, I want him to shit his pants when he sees me coming, but not you."

"Okay." I swallow. "I'm not much into shitting my pants."

We both laugh, and it quickly dies off. A second passes, and then another, and it's like the oxygen has been sucked out of the kitchen because I can't seem to breathe. I finally break the silence and say, "I owe you an apology."

"We all make judgement calls." His eyes narrow in on me. "Our first impressions are based on our experiences and upbringings, whether they're right or wrong."

As I take in his intensity, I can't help but think he's talking about himself, and that he might have been judging me in return. What must the boy who came from nothing, and secured himself a football scholarship, think of the girl born with a silver spoon in her mouth? Maybe that's none of my business.

"I'm sorry I accused you of cheating." I toy with the hem of my T-shirt and pluck at a string. "That was wrong of me."

"It's okay."

He's wrong. It's not okay. I never should have accused him of cheating. To be fair, none of this is his fault. This is on Cochrane. He's the one who thrust us together because of his gambling problem, and then what does he do? Warns me not to fall for Rocco. Unbelievable! Never in a million years is that going to happen.

Totally ludicrous, right?

5

ROCCO

It's Monday afternoon, and I'm on the football field for practice. I scan the bleachers and find Reagan sitting there with her roommate, both with their laptops open, but they're not working. They seem to be in deep conversation, and from the looks of it, a very intense one. I wish I could hear them, but I'm too far away. Yesterday, and again this morning over breakfast, I sensed that Miranda wasn't a fan of Dick, but I could be wrong.

As if feeling my eyes on them, they both turn my way and we stare for a long time, until Levi hits me in the gut to get me moving as the team takes position for our mini-scrimmage. I walk across the field, and take up position opposite Levi, our offensive lineman, and he gestures to the stands.

"What are you doing with Cochrane's girl?" Everyone on campus knows Dick. His grandfather funded the new wing many years ago. Cochrane is the kind of rich you don't fuck with. Then why am I fucking with him?

"Hanging out," I say and give a casual shrug. I like Levi, he's a good guy, but the less people know about the illegal games at Wolf House, the better.

"He doesn't look happy about it."

"What are you talking about?"

I turn my head just as the coach blows the whistle, and Levi pushes past me, taking me to the ground. Coach Myers blows the whistle again, and I jump up and pull myself together. I should have been ready for that, instead of letting Cochrane distract me.

"Get your head in the game, Rocco."

"You got it, Coach," I say, and tamp down the rage welling up inside me as Cochrane stands in the bleachers, hovering over Reagan. We all line up again, and this time I channel that rage into my play and take Levi to the ground. I smack his helmet and grin at him as the play continues on around me, then I jump up and rush down the field as our running back cuts toward an opening in the defense. He's chased down and gets tackled by Joshua and Coach blows his whistle. I lift my head and find Cochrane glaring at me, and I glare back. He stands there for a second, then stomps off.

Coach calls us all over as Reagan and Miranda get up and leave. I jump around, shake my hands and work to block everything from my mind and get my head into the scrimmage. We have a big game coming up, and we need the win.

"What's going on with you?" I turn to Alistair, my closest friend and roommate as he stretches out his legs. "You didn't come home last night."

"Sorry, Dad," I snicker, and he smacks my helmet and laughs.

"Are you in some kind of trouble?" He looks me over. "You actually look like you want to murder someone."

My gaze strays to the stands, where Cochrane was only moments ago. "I'm good."

Alistair follows my gaze, but it comes up empty. "You sure about that?"

"I'll explain it later, okay?"

"Sure." He grabs my helmet and gives it a little shove into my midsection. "Head down, buddy. Nothing or no one is worth blowing your scholarship over and fucking up your career."

"You're right." He is right, and as I put my helmet back on, I realize it's not the first time I've asked myself what kind of stupid game I'm playing with Reagan. I honestly don't know the answer. If that's a lie and if I do know the answer, maybe I just don't want to examine it.

We spend the next couple hours doing drills and I'm exhausted, and hungry by the time I finish. After we shower, I walk back toward our off-campus place with Alistair. I lift my face to the late day sun as my stomach grumbles.

"Talk," Alistair says, and I grin at him.

"You're not going to believe it."

"Try me."

As we stroll home, I fill him in on everything. As I talk, the line in his forehead gets deeper and deeper, and I can't help but think I'm also getting myself in deeper and deeper. I should have bailed Sunday morning. Hell, I should never have gone to her place Saturday night. But it's a little too late to turn back now and let Cochrane win this thing—whatever it might be—between us.

"One month." Alistair rubs his face as he slowly shakes his head. "You're fucking crazy, you know that?"

"No other explanation." I laugh.

"Keep it in your pants, Rocco."

"I'm not going to fuck her," I shoot back as my dick twitches, wanting to be the one calling the shots.

"Yeah, you just keep telling yourself that."

"This is just payback. Cochrane had it coming, and don't forget he's the one who sold her out, not me."

"Just be careful. I hate that fucker as much as you do, and I just don't want to see anything happen to you."

"Yeah, I know," I agree, unease eating a path through my gut. "What can he do? He was at the game, he sold his girl-friend out. He opens his fucking mouth, and this is on him."

"It should work that way, but..."

He lets his words fall off. He doesn't need to say anything else. I get it. The rich live by different rules than the rest of us. When I get a big NFL contract, I'm not going to be an asshole like the rest of them. Guaran-fucking-teed. I'm going to do good things with my money and fame, mainly help the kids with no one to turn to.

We reached the house and I forage through the fridge, looking for something to eat. I shove some leftover chicken into my mouth, and pack a bag full of fresh clothes. After a quick shower, I stop outside Alistair's bedroom door, about to knock, when I hear giggling. I grin, leaving him to which-ever girl crawled into his bed. It's not unusual to come home and find our beds occupied, and I have to say I'm glad mine was empty today. Maybe everyone sensed my shit mood during practice and decided to steer clear.

"Later, bud," I call out and take the stairs two at a time. Outside, I hike my bag up, and the sun is still high in the sky this late October day as I make my way to Reagan's house closer to campus. I left my bike at her place earlier, parked beside her bright red Volkswagen bug, and jogged to the football field, since it was so close to her place.

As I walk, the hairs on the back of my neck begin to stand on end, a familiar sensation when trouble is about to find me. I rub my neck and slowly turn to find a sports car back a bit, driving slow, like it's following me. I do a quick scan, and I'm pretty sure there are four guys inside.

Not a fair fight, but what in life is fair, right? I consider calling Alistair for backup. He'd be here in a heartbeat, but I think I'll give it a minute to see how it plays out first. I drop my bag onto the sidewalk and turn to face the car. My fingers curl into fists at my sides, and while I can't see the occupants' faces, as they all have ballcaps pulled low—Kingston rowing team caps, actually—I'm pretty sure it's Cochrane and the members of his rowing team. They're big, strong, but I'm sure to get in a few good punches.

The car slows to a stop, and I take a few deep breaths, waiting... But chicken shits that they are, they press on the gas and speed by. I hold my hand up and give them the middle finger.

"That's what I thought," I yell, and pick up my pace. I want to know what Cochrane said to Reagan today. Worry worms its way through my veins. Maybe I never should have put her in that position. What if Cochrane got angry with her, or threatened her somehow? Shit. I jog all the way to Reagan's house, and hurry up the stairs. The door is unlocked, which surprises me. Maybe they were waiting for me to return. They haven't given me a key yet. Inside, the house is quiet, the lights low as evening settles in, and I set my bag down, and head to the kitchen, my nose following all the delicious smells.

The second I enter and glance at the kitchen table, my heart squeezes tight, a kind of warmth I've never before experienced, flooding my bloodstream. I swallow, and pick up the note. I don't really know what Reagan's handwriting looks like, but this can only be from her.

Dinner is in the fridge.

Isn't it crazy how five simple words can mean so much? Fuck, I have no idea why they hit me harder than my father's fists, sending me backward a little with the force. This hit hurts, but in a different way. In a way I'm not equipped to deal with. I set the paper down, and the house is so quiet, I find myself tiptoeing to the fridge. Where are Reagan and Miranda? The more important question is, why did they make me dinner? A guy could get used to this. I sure as shit shouldn't.

Inside the fridge, I find a white bowl with ravioli, and not the kind you need a can opener to eat. I take the plastic off the bowl and breathe in the delicious smells. A quick two minutes in the microwave, and I'm headed up the stairs to eat in my room. I walk slowly past Reagan's room, and her door is slightly ajar. Yeah, her room is off limits, but I'd like to thank her.

"Reagan," I say quietly, and nudge the door just a bit with my foot, just enough to give me a peek into her private space. What the fuck? All around her room she has artwork, paintings of flowers, scenery, and a few of people. I call out to her again, and a movement on her bed draws my attention. My God, is she under some makeshift blanket tent? Like I used to make in one of my foster homes? Her blankets lift, and I take in the flush of her face as her eyes meet mine.

"Hey." I lift the bowl. "Thanks."

She smiles but then it falls from her face, and her eyes pinch tight. "What are you doing in my room?"

"Technically, I'm in the hall."

"You can't be in here." She pushes from the bed and dressed in comfy pajama shorts and a T-shirt, she comes toward me, no doubt about to slam the door in my face. Honest to God, the girl is all contradictions. Nice to me one minute by making me dinner, the next looking at me with murder in her eyes.

"Did you paint all these?" I poke a ravioli and shove it into my mouth, and she hesitates. She goes still, and it's easy to tell she's debating her next words. "You're very talented. You could sell those."

Something comes over her pretty face. Gratitude? Pleasure? Pain? I'm not sure, but at least she isn't introducing her foot to my balls and sending me packing for being out of bounds. She backs up a bit and stands before one of her paintings.

"What do you like about them?" she asks, so quietly I can barely hear her.

I take a small, tentative step inside, and count to ten, giving her time to shove me back out. When she doesn't, I set my bag on the floor and my dinner on her dresser. I step up behind her, and don't miss the shift in her breathing, the tightening of her shoulders. Is she still afraid of me, or is this reaction something altogether different?

Don't go there, dude.

I take in the picture of the forest, and the clearing where there's this lone cabin. It's not a perfect cabin, and it doesn't have perfect flowers in the window boxes, but everything about the scene she's depicting is perfect. "This one feels like sanctuary," I murmur quietly

She spins so fast, her eyes so big, I step backward at her strong reaction. She reaches out and puts her small hands on my arms. "Sorry," she says.

"Was it something I said?" I ask, in no hurry to move. I like her hands on my body. Probably too much.

She frowns. "Would you mind..." Her voice trails off and her brow pinches as she continues with, "...telling me why it feels like sanctuary to you?"

I pause and take a breath. I'm not so sure I want to dredge up the past, take a painful walk down memory lane, but the pleading in her voice has me opening up. "I grew up in Chicago, pavement everywhere. You couldn't really get away from it. I was out one day, found myself on the other side of the tracks, you know." I pause and she nods as her arm falls, and I immediately miss her touch. "It was getting dark, and I probably should have been home." I give a humorless snort. "Not that anyone would have known, but I knew better than to be out on the streets after dark. I was cutting through paths, and saw this big treehouse in someone's backyard." I spread my arms. "It was huge, like a fucking house."

She laughs at that. "Exaggerate much."

"Let's just say it was big, and I was little." She smirks and I angle my head. "What?"

"I don't know. Just picturing you little. I bet you were cute."

"What do you mean were? I still am," I joke and straighten a bit, trying to pull a smile from her.

"Go on." She waves her hand to give me the floor again and I glance at her painting.

"Safety wasn't something I felt often, but I climbed into that treehouse, in some stranger's backyard, and found comic books and games and blankets and pillows. I loved it. I stayed there all night. Small places, right? They have this weird sense of safety and security." I glance at the blanket she'd been under. "Come morning, I got up bright and early and high-tailed it home."

She touches my arm. "Were you in trouble when you got there?"

I shrug. "Nah, no one even knew I was gone."

She frowns. "I'm sorry, Rocco."

"It's okay. I'm not looking for pity—"

"I know you're not, but I am sorry, and I love that you found comfort in that treehouse."

"I went there a lot. When I found out social services were coming for me, I took off. I spent days in that treehouse." I snicker. "I really gave them a run for their money."

"Did they eventually find you?"

I rub my stomach. "No, I eventually ran out of food."

She grins, and picks my bowl up and hands it to me. I assume she's about to end our conversation and kick me out, but she says, "Eat," and turns back to her painting. "I like that this painting brings out strong emotions in you." She puts her hand over her heart. "That it gives you comfort."

I fork a ravioli into my mouth as she picks the painting up. "Let's hang this in your room for while you're here."

"Yeah?"

She nods, and gestures to the door. "Lead the way."

I scoop up my bag, and eat as we walk down the hall, and she follows me into my room and sets the picture down. I glance at my bed, and turn to her.

"Hey, I thought you said you didn't want to touch my junk."

⑥

REAGAN

"**W**hat?" I ask when he turns to me, the cutest grin on his face. Before I can help myself, my gaze drops to his...junk. *Stop staring, Reagan*. I shake my head. "What are you talking about?"

He jerks his thumb over his shoulder and points to the pile of neatly folded clothes on his bed.

I let loose a breath. "Oh, I had to throw a couple things in, so I tossed in yours, too. You said your room wasn't off limits, so I didn't think you'd mind."

He sets his bowl on the small desk in the room. "You folded my boxers?" he asks incredulously, amusement all over his face as he steps a bit closer to me, overwhelming me with his close proximity.

"You don't?" I ask, my nose crinkling as I set the painting on my feet and rest it against my legs.

He laughs. "You have to show me your dresser drawers, Reagan. I have to see if you fold your—"

"Junk," I say, cutting him off because I know he's going to say panties, and for some strange reason hearing him talk about my underwear does strange things to me. It's private and weirdly intimate to be standing here talking about such things. "I'm sorry, I just thought—"

As if realizing my sudden embarrassment, he goes serious. "Thank you. I really appreciate it, and I like the way you folded my shorts. I didn't even know they could be folded."

"You're welcome."

"You think there was a fight?"

I glance at him, having no idea what he's talking about but he's grinning. "A fight?" I consider my run in with Cochrane on the bleachers. He sure looked like he wanted to murder Rocco.

"My things, your things, battling it out in the washer. They probably didn't like sharing the space..." His voice falls off and his gorgeous eyes are moving over my face.

"I did have one shirt complain. Something about cooties."

He stands there for one second, then he bursts out laughing. He makes a fist and nudges my chin. "You're hilarious."

"I'll be here all week," I tease.

"And I'll be here all month." As my body quivers in the strangest way at that reminder, he glances at the painting, and stands back to admire it. "Next load of laundry is on me."

"Okay." I take down an old picture, and put mine up, making a mental note to keep my underthings in a different pile, so he's not touching them.

"Perfect," he whispers, and I turn back to find him looking at me. A second passes and then another.

"I'll let you finish your dinner before it gets cold.'"

His voice stops me before I can leave. "What did Cochrane want today?" He picks his bowl up and starts eating again, but his eyes are trained on me. "If he said anything to upset you…"

"He wasn't very happy with your demands."

"Demands? Is that what we're calling them?"

I take a fast breath, and I have no idea why my brain is racing, picturing myself on the bed that's less than three feet away, Rocco demanding things of me, dirty things. God, I'm practically a virgin. Cochrane and I have done stuff, but we've not gone all the way. Even though it's the twenty-first century, good girl that I am, I do what's expected of me by my parents, and that means waiting until I'm married. I have to be a proper young lady. Cochrane has never pressured me, which I have always appreciated.

"He wasn't happy." I sigh and throw my arms up. "But he made his bed and now he has to lie in it." My gaze goes to Rocco's bed again.

"More like he made his bed and now *you* have to lie in it. You're the one taking the punishment, Reagan."

"Yeah, you're right."

"Did he upset you?" He makes a fist like he's preparing for a fight.

"He was upset, naturally, and he said he wasn't going to stay away."

Rocco cocks his head. "Are you planning on seeing him behind my back?"

"No," I say quickly, and it's incredibly weird that I'm not that upset. But it's not just that, there's this whole sense of...freedom. I've been with Cochrane since the end of high school. Our parents are friends, and we've known each other since we were little, and when Mom and Dad pushed the relationship before I went off to college, it was the sensible thing for me to do.

But is it what you wanted?

"Are you upset with me?" he asks.

"It's like this. You're right. I'm the one taking his punishment." I don't bother saying that it's not so bad. "And when you said he has to be held accountable, you were right. Maybe Cochrane and I shouldn't see each other for a month."

"As long as he doesn't take it out on you. If he wants someone to fight over this, you tell him to come find me."

I nod, and ignore the stupid thrill going through me. Cochrane would never let anyone hurt me, but there is something about this tough as nails guy going all alpha to keep me safe.

He takes his last bite of ravioli, and sets the bowl back down. "Reagan," he says softly.

"Yeah?"

"Why were you under the blanket?"

I laugh, but it's tortured. "Old habits."

"I don't get it."

I debate on saying anything, and before I can change my mind, I capture his hand and give a tug. He follows me to my room and before we go in, I ask, "You won't tell?"

"Who am I going to tell? We don't have the same friends."

"You're right. Come here." I flop on my bed and pat it. He sits beside me and the mattress dips under his impressive weight. I lift the light blanket and shake it to get air. It falls over us, and I reach for my phone and turn on my flashlight app.

"What's all this?" he asks, and picks up my sketches.

"My drawings. I'm secretly taking an art class."

"Secretly? Why the hell is this such a big secret? You've got talent." He picks up my sketch pad and starts flipping through it. His hand stills when he comes to the one of the football field. He points. "Is that me?"

I go to snatch it back, but he holds it out of my reach. "Is that me, Sunshine?" he asks and this time I don't bother to correct him, don't tell him that's not my name.

Oh, and why is that, Reagan?

I like it.

"I was sketching the other day, it's no one specific."

He takes my flashlight and holds it over the drawing. "Was this when you were with Miranda today?"

"No." He waits for me to explain, and I simply say, "It was a while ago. Something I needed for class."

"Okay, but why a secret, Reagan?"

The seriousness in his tone catches me by surprise as he shifts to face me. His knees bump mine. My God, what the hell am I doing? Why would I show him these things, invite him under my blanket? Everything about the way we're breathing the same air feels far too intimate, and I'm far too aware of his body, his freshly soaped skin. I breathe him in, filling my lungs for later. His big hand lands on my knee, and he quickly pulls it back.

"Shit, sorry, I didn't mean to touch you."

I grow warmer under the blanket, and perspiration breaks out on my skin. "It's okay...I don't mind."

"I guess what I'm wondering is why you hide all this?"

I groan and consider my next words. How can I possibly say them without offending him, or making him look at me like I'm a princess throwing a temper tantrum because I was forced into doing something I didn't want to do? "I don't want to complain about my parents, and I don't want to complain about my upbringing...you know."

"Because mine was shit?"

My body tightens at the way he tosses it out there so casually, so flippant like it was nothing, but I get it's not nothing. He had it hard, and yet here I am going to complain because Mommy and Daddy want me to be in politics, like them. God, I am so pathetic. This time I put my hand on his knee. "I didn't mean it like that."

"Listen, I know what my upbringing was like. We don't have to dance around that, but I think what you're trying to say is this. Just because you grew up with things I didn't have, doesn't mean your life was perfect. Rich or poor, we all have problems. We just have different problems."

"That makes me sound horrible, though. I was given so much."

"It's not horrible. I don't hate rich people, Reagan."

"You hate Cochrane. You never did tell me why."

"I know."

I sit there for a second to see if he's going to finally open up about that. He doesn't, and I can't even ask Cochrane. I'm not supposed to be around him for the next month.

"Are you changing the subject on purpose? If you don't want to talk about this, we don't have to." He lifts his arm like he's going to push the blankets off, and I stop him. It's odd, I don't want him to go just yet. I like being under my blankets with him like this.

"Painting is my passion, but my parents told me early on that I'd never be able to make a career at it, and I should focus on business."

"Fuck them." My head rears back. "I'm sorry. They're your parents. No trash talking." He gives an almost bashful grin. "I'm better with my hands than my words." He picks up the sketch pad again. "But seriously, these are so good."

"Not good enough to sell or anything."

"How do you know that? Have you tried?"

"Well, no."

"I'll take two."

"Stop it." I laugh and whack him on the arm. He captures my hand, and brings it to his mouth. It hovers close to his lips and his warm breath trickles over my flesh. "I hide under the blanket, because it's habit. It's what I used to do when I was young. I actually find it quite comfortable. Small places," I say, and he grins, knowing I'm talking about him and his treehouse.

"Yeah, I do kind of like it in here. Mind if I lay down?"

"I guess not."

He stretches out and I keep the blanket up as I remain sitting. "It's tough, Reagan."

"Tough?"

He turns to his side, and crooks his elbow and braces his head on his hand.

"Not being able to have what you want."

The way he's looking at me steals the breath from my lungs. He can't be talking about me. While I know that in my head, my stupid body warms all over. But I don't want that. I don't want Rocco Gianni wanting me. We're very different people, and I have a boyfriend out there...sort of.

"Do you not have everything you want?"

"I don't want for much, really. I'm happy with the little things, like my football, my bike..."

Before I realize what I'm doing, I flop back onto my pillow and exhale slowly. "Your bike looks pretty old."

He grins. "That old girl. She's going to run forever."

"Is that right?"

"Yeah?"

I turn to face him. "What if she breaks down?"

"These hands." He holds out his big palm, a grin on his face. "I just told you I was good with them. If you don't believe me, ask your washing machine."

I laugh at that. "Do all the guys on the team have an ego as big as yours or are you just special?"

"I'm not special, Reagan." My throat dries at the pain buried in those words and I go quiet, even though I think he's wrong. But I didn't live his childhood, one where he was neglected, forgotten and had to find comfort in a stranger's tree house. Without thinking too much about it, I put my hand over his, give a small, supporting squeeze. He's breathing quietly, but his chest expands and collapses like he's just finished running a marathon and is struggling for air. His mood shifts so quickly, I'm pretty sure I'm going to have whiplash.

He pushes the blanket off us, and while I welcome the rush of fresh air, I instantly miss the warmth and coziness in our little fort. "Come on, grab a jacket and let's get out of here."

"I don't know about this," Reagan says, her hands on her hips as she looks at my bike.

I take my spare helmet and ease it onto her head, and my fingers brush her soft skin as I tighten the straps and latch it. I ignore the shiver sliding down my spine.

"What is it you don't know?" I ask.

She crinkles her nose, and puts her arms around herself in a protective manner. Then again, she could be cold. She always seems to be cold. "Is it safe?"

I arch a brow. "You've never been on a bike?"

"Nope."

"Ah, a virgin," I tease. Her eyes go wide, and once again I get the feeling that, while she's had a long-term boyfriend, she's inexperienced and innocent in many things. "A bike virgin," I clarify.

She relaxes slightly. "I suppose you could say that."

I kind of like the idea of doing a 'first' with her. I let my hands linger on her straps. "Do you trust me with your bike virginity, Reagan? Will you give me the honor of popping your cherry, so to speak?"

She puts one hand on her cheek, looking all demure. "When you word it like that, all sweet and romantic, how can I possibly say no?" She grins at me and I burst out laughing, because we both know I'm being corny, and she's mocking me.

I put my helmet on and secure it. "You're kind of funny, you know."

"Funny, stupid, a fine line, don't you think?"

"If you're scared, we don't have to do this. But I promise you I'm an excellent rider, and even more cautious when I'm carrying precious cargo."

She rolls her eyes, and hugs herself again. "I think you were lying when you said you weren't good with your words. You seem to say all the right things. It's no wonder all the girls on campus are quick to hand over their panties." As soon as the word panties leave her mouth, a flush crawls up her neck.

"What do you know about the girls on campus and their panties?"

"Nothing."

I have a feeling she knows more about me than she lets on. "Unless..."

"Unless nothing."

I smirk at her response. While I like teasing her, I let it go, wanting to get to my destination before the sun sets. "Okay." I tap the seat. "It's your call, but I'd love to show you something. I think you're going to like it." She eyes me, and I laugh. "Don't worry, it has nothing to do with my junk." Wait, is that disappointment in her eyes? "Unless..."

"Unless nothing." She eyes the bike. "How do I even get on this thing?"

I put my leg over the seat, and tap the back. She climbs on, and I say, "Put your arms around me, and your feet on the pegs." She does as I ask, and I tap her hands, and give them a squeeze to let her know she's safe with me. I turn my focus to my bike and start it, but it's so damn hard to keep my concentration on my driving with her thighs hugging my body and her hands wrapped around my chest. I drive out of Kingston and take the windy roads along the shore.

The fresh smell of the briny ocean fills the air, and I breathe it in. The night sky is lit, a mixture of pink and purple as the sun sets, and I lean into the corners. Reagan leans with me, her body following mine. Would our bodies move in perfect sync like this if we were between the sheets? I suspect they would, but I shouldn't be thinking like that. I am not going to fuck her. Nothing good could come from that. After a long while, when I find my favorite spot on the highway, I pull off the road and turn the bike off.

"It's gorgeous," Reagan whispers in awe as she looks at the setting sun over the water. She smiles at me, and my breath catches a little. Cliché, I know, but she really is beautiful. "You're right, I do like it."

"Good." I kick my leg over the bike and hold it so she can get off. "There's more," I say.

"Really?"

"Yeah, come on, I'll show you."

She looks over her shoulder, at the road behind her, and then at the guardrail. "Where?"

"You're going to have to take my word on it."

She hugs herself again as a cool night breeze washes over us, and I step up to her and zip her jacket to her chin. She eyes me. "What are you up to, Rocco?"

"You'll see." I step back and gesture with a nod, but she doesn't budge.

"You're not some crazy kind of stalker weirdo, are you?"

"Stalker weirdo?" I tease. "Can't I just be one without the other?"

Her lips quirk. "No, that's how it works."

"Fine then, no, I'm not a stalker weirdo. Not since the restraining order, anyway." I grin at her. "Are you coming or not? You know you're safe with me."

"Do I now?"

"You wouldn't have let me into your blanket fort if you weren't."

She shakes her head at me. "I bet you were an annoying kid who always got his way." She frowns, and opens and closes her mouth, like she's trying to backtrack.

"Come on," I say, and she blows a breath, relieved that I'm letting it go. She takes my hand when I hold it out to her. "I better not regret this."

"Life is too short for regrets, my friend." I close my big palm over her tiny hand. She's so delicate, I'm afraid if I squeeze too hard I'd break her bones. It brings out the protector in me, and I have to tamp down my rage when my mind circles back to her douche bag boyfriend who sold her out.

"Friends, huh. Is that what we are now?"

"Yeah, I like the idea of us being friends. Do you think Cochrane would hate it?"

"Yes."

"Good." She laughs as we climb over the guardrail, and I keep her close as we go down the jagged embankment, almost all the way to the rocky shore below. Before we get there, I tug her into a crevice in the rock.

She gasps as the rock closes in on us, and she touches the solid, damp wall as if to test it. "What is this place?"

"Sit." I brush the ground and she drops down next to me, our bodies close, but not touching. She stares out the mouth of the little cave.

"Wow," she gasps her eyes wide as we take pleasure in the scenic view through the hollowed-out hillside. "Listen." She cocks her head to the side. "It's like putting your ear next to a big shell."

I nod, and like the way she's describing the sound. I never thought of it like that before. "Strange, isn't it?"

She hugs herself again, and I unzip my coat.

"It is, but I like it. How did you ever find this?"

I shrug out of my jacket and put it over her shoulders. "I don't want you to get cold."

"What about you?"

"I'm never cold," I tell her. She looks like she's about to protest when I answer her question. "I was exploring one day by myself and came across it. You know what's funny? I grew up in a concrete city and I love all the big open spaces here in Southern California, yet I still find myself searching for the comfort of the tree house. This kind of does it for me."

She shifts, and moves closer to me, and I put my arms around her, like that's where it's always been meant to be. She takes a big breath, and puts her head on my shoulder. "I don't ever want to leave."

"I thought you'd like it."

"I don't."

I glance at her, find her looking up at me, her features hidden as the sun dips below the horizon. "What?"

"I love it," she says with a chuckle and turns from me to stare out through the opening, the sound of the waves lapping like a soothing balm to my soul. She takes her phone from her pocket and captures a few shots. I do the same, and we both fall quiet again for a long time. She breaks the silence, "Do you come here often?"

She's asking a question, but there's another question lingering below it. I learned early on how to read people, not from their words but from the way those words are said, along with body language. It kept me out of trouble in most of the foster homes. Why does every mean bastard in the country end up caring for foster kids, anyway?

"Not as much as I like," I answer. "School and football keep me busy. But I always come alone, to clear my head and get away from the world."

She goes quiet for a very long time. "Thanks for sharing this space with me."

"Yeah," is all I say, not even sure why I am sharing it with her. Maybe because she invited me into her space under her blanket and shared something personal with me. Maybe not. The only thing I do know is I like her being here with me. We sit like that for a long time, until the cooler night air sends a chill through our bodies.

"Rocco?"

"Yeah."

"Do you know there is a rumor at school that you killed a guy?"

"They got it all wrong, Sunshine."

"Yeah?"

"Maybe there was more than just one."

She arches her perfectly shaped brows. "Oh, really?"

I wink at her. "Nah, but if there had been, they would have deserved it."

"I'm quite sure." She takes my hand and runs her fingers over my knuckles. Warmth floods my blood. "Maybe it has something to do with all these cuts and bruises you have. But everyone is scared of you."

"Are you?"

"I don't think so. Not anymore." She glances up at me. She wants to say more, but is hesitant.

"You can ask me whatever you want, as long as that works both ways."

She nods, her brow furrowed, and then falls silent. I guess she's not going to risk me asking her something she doesn't want to answer.

Another little chill goes through her body, and it vibrates through me. "You're getting cold. We should head back."

She nods. "As much as I hate to leave, we should."

"We can come again, Reagan."

Her smile curls around my heart. "Thanks. But yeah, we should go. I have some studying to do."

"Under the blanket?"

She chuckles and the sound carries in the night as I slide from the cave and hold my hand out to her. We make our way back to the bike and I help her with her helmet. She takes my coat off and hands it to me for the ride home. I tell her to keep it but she refuses, so we climb on and thirty minutes later I'm killing the ignition in her driveway. Stars light up the night sky and the streetlamps give sufficient illumination for us to find our way to her front door. She uses her key and I follow her in.

"I guess I should get you one of these, huh?" She holds up the shiny key for me to see.

"Unless you want me climbing in and out of my bedroom window."

"It's on the second floor."

"Is that a challenge?"

She laughs. "Nope, I'd be wise not to put anything by you, Rocco." Her chest expands as she yawns. "I should get up to bed, and get some studying done."

"Same," I agree, and I follow her up. We hesitate in the hall. Neither of us are in a hurry to separate.

"Thanks again," she adds.

"Sure." I turn and go to my room. I close the door, lean against it, and take a few deep breaths.

What the hell are you doing, dude?

I bend forward and put my hands on my knees as that inner voice berates me. I know better than to get close to a girl I have no right getting close to. The problem is, I really like being around her. I kick off my boots and flop on my bed. I lay there for a long time, until the world goes silent around me, both girls asleep in their beds. I turn and check the clock. Shit, it's past midnight, and I have early practice before classes tomorrow. Sleep won't come, no matter how hard I try. Every time I close my eyes, I see Reagan. She's smiling and laughing, those gorgeous plump lips waiting for my mouth.

"Fuck," I curse and throw my legs over the bed. Maybe a hot —or rather cold—shower will help cool the heat inside me. I tiptoe quietly to the bathroom, shut the door and turn on the shower. I strip and climb in, bracing my hand on the wall as the hot water pours over my near trembling body. I turn my back to the shower, as my hand creeps down to wrap around my thickening cock. I tug once, twice, and go perfectly still when the bathroom door creaks open. I quickly turn the water off, prepared. Always prepared for the worst. That's what a life on the streets will do to you. But what I'm seeing isn't the worst. Nope, I'd probably classify it as the best. Either way, worst or best, I'm still fucked.

8

REAGAN

With my body still shaking from a dream that should be classified as a nightmare, I push from my bed, and take a few deep breaths. How can I be shaking when my clothes are drenched? Oh, probably because I just had a ridiculously hot dream about the man sleeping one door down from me, and deep in my soul, I'm shaking because I know it's wrong.

I walk quietly across the room, leaving the lights out, not wanting to wake anyone in the house, and head to the bathroom. I'm not sure whether to splash my face with hot or cold water. Maybe a warm shower will do the trick to calm my body down. I walk to the sink, and look at myself in the mirror. My heart stalls. The mirror is foggy. But that's not the only thing sending warnings to my brain. Nope, something—or someone else—is in the bathroom with me.

"Hey," I hear, and turn toward the shower to find Rocco standing there, the shower doors open, and he has a big towel wrapped around his waist.

My entire body quivers, from the hair on my head to the tips of my toes. I hug myself and a strange gurgling sound crawls out of my throat. Within a second, he's right there, standing in front of me. All big muscles full of protective instincts and worry.

"Are you okay?"

"No, I don't think so."

"Shit, you're shivering uncontrollably." His brow furrows. "I never should have taken you to the ocean. You caught a chill." He pulls me to his warm body and I melt against him. His big hands run up and down my back, creating heat with friction. But that's not what's really warming me as I become acutely aware that he's nearly naked and I'm dressed only in a T-shirt and pajama shorts.

"I...I..." I close my mouth. Really, I have no idea what I'm trying to say.

"You need a hot shower."

He drags me backward, keeping my body anchored to his, and turns on the spray. Before I even realize what's happening, I'm in the shower—with him.

"My clothes," I say, but the protest is feeble, even to me.

"I didn't think you'd want me to take them off you."

He'd be right.

He'd also be wrong.

"But they're see-through now."

"I know what a woman's naked body looks like, Reagan."

I nod, and a strange pang of jealousy grips my stomach. What the hell is that all about? He's a player and I have a boyfriend. Sure, we're broken up this month, but we're going to get married someday.

"Why...are you in here with me?"

"You actually looked like you saw a ghost. You're so shaken up, I didn't want you slipping and cracking your head open."

My throat tightens at the way he's touching me, nurturing me. For a boy who had no one, no role models to learn from, he's sure doing a great job of caring for me. I guess it must just come naturally to him.

"Oh, okay."

He pulls me tight to his body and puts me under the spray, gifting me with all the hot water. I shift a little, pulling him in with me, and at first he's hesitant, and it's so strange, the way his thoughtfulness gets to me. I grew up with loving, caring parents, and have a boyfriend, yet everything in the way this guy from the streets touches me, fills me with a different kind of comfort. I slide my arms around his waist, the towel wet and heavy around his hips. I wouldn't be surprised if the knot let go and his towel fell. What would I do with a naked Rocco in the shower with me? Another stupid sound crawls out of my throat.

Rocco inches back, his gaze moving over my face. "You want to talk about it?"

"I had a bad dream. A nightmare, really."

He nods in understanding and pushes my wet hair from my face. My heart flutters a little in my chest as his big hands touch me with such tenderness. His rough calluses that could cut skin, caress lightly, carefully. I put my face on his chest, listen to the pounding of his strong heart. The chills subside, Rocco's heat creating another kind of storm inside me.

"Better?" he asks.

"Yes, thank you."

He turns the water off, and we step from the shower. I begin to shiver again, until he wraps me in a big fluffy towel. He turns me so I'm staring at the door, and my body reacts to the sound of him changing towels. I resist the urge to turn around and admire his hard body.

"Okay, let's get you back to bed."

He keeps me close as we make the short trip to my room. "You need to get out of those wet clothes."

I nod and step up to my dresser, and pull out a clean shirt and pajama shorts. I turn to find Rocco staring at me, his upper body damp, his eyes locked on me and I take a fast breath at the intensity in him—the tent in his towel.

"Can you turn around?"

"Yeah." He stands there for another second, the air between us charged, and I'd have to be an idiot not to realize there's something fierce and powerful arcing between us. He finally turns, and I struggle to get out of my wet clothes. I pull my shirt up, and get my arm tangled over my head. My God, I'm twisting and contorting, and ouch, I think I just pulled something.

"Reagan."

His voice is soft, and labored and far too close.

"What?" I ask, and try to get air.

"Stay still."

I do as he says, and his big hands are on my body again, his knuckles brushing over my rib cage as he slides his hands up and peels the wet shirt from my body. I stare at him, find his eyes closed, and appreciate the privacy he's giving me.

I quickly tug on my dry shirt. "Thank you."

He opens one eye, his gaze on mine. "Do you need any help with the shorts?"

The thoughts of his hands touching me anywhere, especially below the waist, sends heat sparking through me. I'm glad I'm not near anything combustible. Don't sound breathless. Don't sound breathless.

"I think I got it."

Dammit, I sounded breathless.

He nods and turns and as I switch into a pair of dry pajama shorts, he goes to my bed and fusses with the bedding. Once I'm done, he looks me over slowly, takes a huge breath and tears his gaze away.

He holds the blankets up, the warmth of my bed inviting. "Get in," he tells me, and I slowly walk to my bed, my arms wrapped around myself to hide my hard nipples. *He's seen nipples before, Reagan*. Probably hundreds of nipples. That still doesn't make me any less self-conscious.

I slide into the bed, and shift to the far side. I expect him to drop the blankets and leave. Instead, I hear a rustling sound, like he's drying his body, and the other side of the bed dips, as he crawls in and pulls the blankets up over our head, cocooning us in. His towel brushes against my body and I'm glad he's tied it around his waist again, I think.

"What are you doing?" I ask quietly.

"Just keeping you warm."

"Rocco…"

"We're friends, and this is what friends do."

That's news to me and I should argue, I want to argue, but the words won't come out. He drags me to him, the little spoon to his big spoon, and smooths my hair down, allowing him to rest his chin on the top of my head. His heat wraps around me, the rhythm of his strong heartbeat pulling me under, despite the fact that my body is hyper-aware of his.

"Sleep," he orders, like he can hear my mind racing.

My lids fall shut, and the next thing I know, a noise at my window wakes me. My eyes open, and I'm no longer under the blankets. I turn over, and disappointment bursts inside me when I find the other side of the bed empty. I reach across, find it warm to the touch, and my heart speeds up. Rocco spent the night in my bed, and I'm not even upset about that. Angry words from the driveway below reach my ears, and my throat tightens.

Oh no.

I jump from my bed, and hurry to my window to find Cochrane and Rocco standing there. Rocco is dressed only in a pair of jeans. I quickly scan my room, and spot his towel on the floor. Did he leave it on all night, or did he toss it and sleep with me naked?

I look back outside, and Cochrane lifts his head, his eyes connecting with mine, and like a kid getting caught with their hand in the cookie jar, I jump back, hiding behind the curtain. What am I doing? I'm in my room. Alone. Sure, I slept in the same bed as Rocco, but Cochrane sold me to him in a damn card game. There is no need for me to act weird and childish. Guilty.

I straighten my shoulders and move back to my window, wanting to hear what they're saying, but Cochrane is leaving, and Rocco is looking up at me. His body is tight, everything about him hard and unwavering. He backs up, out of my line of sight, and I press my face to the glass. Should I be afraid of him? Was I a fool for letting him care for me last night? Rocco Gianni is tough and brutal, a guy not to be messed with. Yet he touched me with such tenderness. Does he touch all girls like that?

Oh, Reagan, stop thinking you're anything special.

Last night he told me he'd seen numerous naked women. Mine is just one of many, and in one month, life goes back to normal. To the way it was meant to be.

I don't need to turn to know Rocco is at my door. I sense him, feel him staring at me. I slowly turn, and my God, the man is gorgeous. He eats up my doorway, and I can't help but let my gaze fall over him. Neither of us speak. We both just stand there, looking our fill.

"What did he want?" I finally ask.

"You."

"What did you tell him?"

"I told him you were with me, and if he didn't like it, then he should come up with the money he owes me."

His words hit like a slap, a hard reminder that I'm a pawn in a game. I have no idea why I'm about to say what I'm about to say, but can't help myself. "I guess you'd prefer the money over having to stay here for the next month."

"I can only assume it's what you'd want."

I slowly nod, hardly able to believe that I'd need time to think that over.

He pushes off the doorframe. "That's what I figured. I have to get ready for practice." He seems thoroughly pissed as he walks back to his room, his door closing with a hard click. Does he want to stay for the month? Would he prefer being here over taking the money? That can't be right. This was Cochrane's idea, not Rocco's.

I stand there, perfectly still as he bangs around in his room. A second later, he passes by my door, a big duffle bag over his shoulder. He doesn't glance in and he's moving so fast, all I see is a blur.

I don't have class for a while, but there's no way I'm getting back to sleep now. I pick up my cell and note a dozen or so texts from Cochrane, all apologies saying he doesn't know what he was thinking, that he panicked. I shake my head. He panicked all right and, in a bid to save his ass, he sold mine. I toss my phone and head to the shower to clear my head and settle my body. After I shower, all the while trying not to think about Rocco being in here with me, I dress, and go to the kitchen and find Miranda at the table sipping coffee. She stops scrolling through her phone and has a wicked little grin on her face when I enter, and our eyes meet. I brace myself.

"So, you and Rocco, huh?"

"There is no me and Rocco." I grab a mug and pour a much-needed cup of coffee.

"That's not the way I see it."

"What's that supposed to mean?" I grab the cereal, pour it into a bowl.

"I heard the fight between Rocco and Cochrane in the driveway this morning."

"I heard bits of it, too."

She eyes me. "Did you hear the bit where Rocco said you were his for thirty days and if Cochrane tries to talk to you, he'll personally see about shutting his mouth...with his fist."

I exhale. "This isn't about Rocco wanting to be with me. It's all to do with a bet. There's more going on than I can say, but I'm not Rocco's and he's not mine."

"A bet?" she asks.

I take a quick second, debating on what to say. I trust Miranda. We've been friends for a very long time. The card game, though. It's illegal and the less who know the better. I can't let Rocco get into trouble. I mean, Cochrane. Yeah, I can't let Cochrane get into trouble and risk his future.

"Let's just say, Cochrane couldn't pay up, so now I'm stuck with Rocco for a month."

She waves a finger back and forth between the two of us. "I think you mean *we're* stuck. You're not the only one who lives here."

My stomach clenches and I give her hand a little squeeze. "I'm sorry, Miranda. I know I put you in a bad situation, too. I promise to make it up to you, okay?"

"Nah, it's okay. Honestly, why would I be upset? The view is as good coming as it is going. I gave him a spare key. I thought you'd want that, so we don't have to leave the door open for him. I mean, we have no reason to wait up at night, right?"

I nod. "Thanks." I keep my voice light, when I ask, "Did he say anything to you?"

"About what?"

"Oh, I don't know." Maybe that he liked being here, and it wasn't about the money, which is crazy. I take a bite of cereal, and milk dribbles down my chin. I'm a little jittery since waking up.

She leans toward me. "You want to know what else I think?"

"No."

She laughs. "I think Cochrane was an asshole to do this to you." I'm about to agree when she adds, "And that something good can come from something bad."

I shake my head. "You sound like a bad country song."

"Yeah, not at all like the hot noises I heard coming from the bathroom last night."

My heart jumps. "It's not like that."

"The real question is, do you want it to be?"

9

ROCCO

My body is still buzzing like an angry bee by the time I make it to the field, partly because of my run-in with Cochrane. What the fuck was he doing throwing pebbles at Reagan's window first thing in the morning? I ran to my room to grab pants, then bolted down the steps and outside to stop him before he woke her. He's not a guy to put her needs first, obviously. The second reason my body is buzzing? Oh, just that I slept with Reagan in her bed, pressed against her warm body as she melted into me, accepting every last drop of warmth and comfort I was offering.

It was a big fucking mistake. I know it. She probably knows it. Hell, anyone with a half a brain knows it. I guess that's why this morning I turned it around, made it all about the money. The problem is, if Cochrane came at me with the bucks, I might tell him to shove those dollars right up his ass. Hanging with Reagan, no one can put a price tag on that. And that, my friends, is a major fucking problem.

I jog to catch up with Alistair, and he frowns. "What?" I ask and stretch my arms out like I don't have a care in the world, but I'm not fooling him.

"You have that..." he pauses to do air quotes around, "'just got fucked look' about you, and not in the good way."

"I'm fine. Had a run in with Dick today, but it's nothing I can't handle."

Alistair glances around the bleachers like he expects to see the douche watching us. "You sure about that?"

"I can handle him, Alistair."

"Yeah, but can you handle his girl?" he asks.

"There won't be any handling of Reagan. She's innocent in all this, and I plan to keep it that way."

He slaps my back. "Good, because Dixon house is having a party this Friday night after the game, and Jaclyn has been asking about you."

Jaclyn and I have hooked up a couple of times. She's a nice girl and we had a nice time, but I'm not interested in hooking up with her again. Alistair must read that on my face.

"Are you kidding me? Jaclyn is hot, and you're snarling at the idea of sleeping with her."

"I'm not snarling." I wipe the snarl from my face. "I like Jaclyn, but we're not a couple, or anything. We hooked up a couple times, that's all."

He stands there staring at me for a moment longer. "Dude, you'd better get that head of yours on right, before a pretty little princess fucks you over."

I nod, and for a quick second I think about defending Reagan, but I shut my mouth. The coach blows his whistle, and we all hustle across the field. For the next hour, we practice passing drills and get in a little scrimmage near the end. Every now and then I find myself scanning the bleachers, and every now and then I realize how disappointed I am that Reagan isn't up there watching me—sketching me. Crazy, I know.

But the idea of her always having to hide her creative side pisses me off. No one should have to hide under the damn blankets. Unless you're in a foster home and someone is chasing you with a belt, of course. That's the time someone needs to hide under the blankets, better yet under the bed, but that wasn't her situation at all.

After practice, with Reagan still on my mind, I head to the locker room and shower. Once done, I toss my bag over my shoulder and since I have an hour before class, I head back to Reagan's place, a key to her house in my pocket.

I use it to open the door, and hope to find Reagan inside, but she's long gone. The house is quiet, the hum of the fridge the only sound. I make my way down the hall, and with hunger driving me, I step into the kitchen, and...holy fuck.

A grown-ass man comes from around the corner and jumps me, doing his damnedest to take me to the ground. There's an intruder in Reagan's house! That thought fills me with fear. What if she or Miranda had been home? Fight or flight kicks in and since I'm always ready for a fight I let the burst of adrenaline fill my veins. I grab the guy by the collar, and raise my fist, but something in the back of my brain jingles....and before I pummel him, I take another look at him—and his very expensive suit.

"Who are you?" I ask.

"Who are you?" he asks in return.

"I'm Rocco."

"That's not much to go on, Rocco. Why are you sneaking into my daughter's house?"

My blood drains, and I let go of his suit jacket. He runs his hands over the lapels to smooth out the wrinkles. Fuck me. Even if I had a chance with Reagan, even if we wanted to build something, which we don't, what I did right here would have ruined it.

"I'm sorry," I say quickly. "I thought you were an intruder."

He stares at me long and hard, and for a second I think he's going to call the authorities on me.

"What are you doing here, Rocco?" he asks again. I hesitate. What the hell am I supposed to tell him? "It's not that hard of a question."

I scrub my face. "Yeah, I know. Sorry."

He looks at the big hockey bag over my shoulder. "If you're not here to rob the place, why are you here?"

I glance around and try not to look as guilty as I feel. Honestly, Cochrane sold her out, but I'm the douche who decided to stay here. "I'm kind of staying here for a while."

His eyes narrow in on me. "With my daughter, or Miranda?"

"Neither." I wave my hand back and forth in front of myself. "I'm in the spare room. It's all platonic. They're helping me out."

His eyes soften, the fine lines around them smoothing out as he relaxes. It's a reaction I wasn't expecting.

"You needed a place to stay?" he asks, no judgement in his tone.

I nod. "Something like that."

He glances at my bag again, which has our team's name on it. "You're a student at Kingston?"

"I am. Science student, actually." I open my mouth, about to tell him I've helped Reagan with her stats, but I don't. She probably doesn't want anyone to know. "I just finished football practice and I'm dropping my stuff off before class."

He smiles at me. "That's very nice of my daughter helping you out like that."

I instantly like this guy. He's not judging me for having no place to stay, for not being in his social class. I think he could be one of the good guys. Although, they are pushing Reagan into a career she doesn't want. That doesn't mean they have ill intent. They could just be looking out for her best interests, and let's face it, starving artists are called starving artists for a reason.

"She's a very nice girl, Mr. Ellison. You and Mrs. Ellison did a great job raising her."

He beams at me, and I'm about to leave the kitchen, until he looks at his watch and then back at me. "Call me Stewart, and how about we grab a bite to eat?"

Wow, this guy is full of surprises. "Oh, I..."

"You have class right now?"

"In an hour."

"Isn't that your stomach I hear grumbling?" he jokes, then rubs his own. "Okay, okay, I admit. It's mine."

I laugh at his humor. I guess Reagan must get her wit from him.

"Of course, if you don't want to."

"No, it's not that." He doesn't need to be spending his money on me, and I'm not sure how Reagan would feel about me having coffee or lunch with her family. "We can just eat here. Reagan keeps a stocked fridge."

"Nah, let's get out. I want to hear more about your football."

"Were you a player?" I ask, and set my bag down at the foot of the stairs.

"With these knees," he jokes and wobbles his legs.

I laugh at that, any tension from earlier long gone. We step outside. I guess the Mercedes parked on the sidewalk should have alerted me that someone was visiting. If I'd been looking. I'd been too caught up in hoping Reagan was still home to consider my surroundings. That's so unlike me, and I should be worried.

"We could head to the Coffee Shack. They make great sandwiches. It's just a short walk."

"Lead the way," he says, and stops in the driveway when he sees my bike. "Is this yours?" he asks, his eyes wide and full of childlike wonderment.

"She's a real beauty, huh?" I say.

"1969 Honda CB 750." He gives a low slow whistle of appreciation and I like him even more that he knows his bikes. "Where'd you get her?"

I run my hand along the chrome. "My old high school coach. A gift for college. He's the one who helped me get into Kingston on a football scholarship."

He slaps my back. "Good for you, son."

Son.

My chest tightens, right around my heart.

"Do you mind?" he asks with a raised brow.

"Hop on."

He throws his leg over the bike and balances it. He pretends to rev the throttle.

"You used to ride?" I ask.

"Oh yeah. Believe it or not, I was the neighborhood terror." I laugh at that, because no way can I picture this perfectly put together man tearing up the streets.

He smiles at me. "I bet she's fun to ride."

"Yeah, she is. She's a bitch on carburetors, though. I'm constantly rebuilding."

"Football star and mechanically minded. Impressive."

I don't need his praise or compliments, but I do find myself standing a little taller.

"You're welcome to take her for a spin, if you like."

He laughs. "These old bones. Not what they used to be."

"Yeah, don't be too hard on yourself. You just about tackled me to the floor ten minutes ago."

He chuckles. "True, but I couldn't get you there. You must be one hell of a football player. I think I'm going to have to come to a game one of these days."

"We play Friday night, home game. Come watch."

"I might take you up on that." He rubs his hand along my shiny handlebar.

"Reagan never mentioned that you rode." Then again, why would she?

"She never mentioned that she had a football player staying at her place either."

I laugh at that. "I guess we're both on a need-to-know basis."

He climbs off the bike and we start down the sidewalk. "How long have you known Reagan?"

"Since freshman year." It's not a lie. I definitely noticed her freshman year, and it wasn't just because she was dating my roommate. We might not have talked a lot until recently, but I've been aware of her for a very long time now. Since Stewart was at the house looking for her, I ask, "Want me to shoot her a text and ask her to meet us after her class?"

"That's a great idea."

I pull my phone out and fire off a text. I'm a bit worried about how she's going to take this, though. What can I say, her dad wanted to take me out for a meal, and you know... food. I hold my phone and as I wait for her to answer, Stewart unbuttons his jacket.

"Are you in town on business or just to see Reagan?"

"A little bit of both."

We reach the coffee shop and I open the door and gesture for him to enter. Delicious scents fill the air, and my stomach rumbles as I inhale. At the counter, we both order smoked meat sandwiches and coffees. I try to pay for mine, but Stewart is having none of that.

My phone buzzes and my blood runs cold when I see Reagan's panicked answer.

"Was that Reagan?" Stewart asks.

"Yeah, she's getting out early and is on her way."

"How nice," he says. I'm not so sure it is, though. Maybe Stewart is just humoring me until Reagan gets here. Maybe he's super pissed that she has a guy staying with her. I guess I'll find out soon enough. In the meantime, I'm starving and plan to eat. Sandwiches and coffee in hand, we find a table for four and sit. "Where are you from, son?"

"Chicago," I tell him. "Burnside."

He stills for a brief second, absorbing that information, then takes a bite of his sandwich. I dig into mine, my manners, or lack thereof, not really on my mind at the moment.

"Are your folks still there?"

Truthfully, I have no reason to lie to the man, or try to charm him into liking me. After today, I'll never set eyes on him again, so I decide to tell him the truth and when I'm done, he sits there thoughtfully, his head nodding slowly.

"With no family, I take it you'll be having Thanksgiving alone."

"Yeah, it's okay. I don't mind. I can find a turkey dinner somewhere in town."

"Like hell you will," he says, and I stiffen.

"What?"

He gives a hard nod, like he's just come to some great conclusion. "You'll be having dinner with us." Just then Reagan steps up to the table, her eyes wide, her head bobbing back and forth between the two of us.

"I'm sure Reagan would love for you to come home with her for Thanksgiving. Isn't that right, Reagan?"

"What's that now?" I ask as I lean down to give my father a kiss on the cheek. Clearly, he's been bonding with my new roommate, and I'm not too sure how I feel about that. It's nice they like each other. Rocco probably never had a father figure in his life, but Thanksgiving? That's going too far. Dad pulls me in for a hug, and when he holds me like this, it reminds me how much I love him, how much he's done for me, and everything I would do to make him proud.

"It's okay, Stewart. Reagan is doing enough by letting me stay at her place for a while."

Thank you, Rocco.

I break the hug and stand up straight, flashing Rocco a grateful smile as Dad gives him a dismissive wave. "Don't be silly. We'd love to have you. Right, pumpkin?"

Rocco grins when Dad calls me pumpkin and heat rushes into my cheeks.

"Yeah, uh right." I take the empty seat next to Dad. "If he wants to." I tried to inject a bit of enthusiasm into my voice. I mean, why wouldn't I want to invite him? I'm sure that's the question going through Dad's head, considering I'm letting Rocco stay at my place, right?

I'm pretty sure Rocco is excellent at reading people, and can see the clenching of my jaw. He smiles at my dad. "I appreciate the invitation, thank you. I'd like to bring something, of course."

"We can discuss those details later." Dad turns to me. "Now, why didn't you tell me Rocco was staying with you?"

Oh crap.

"It happened quick, only a couple of days ago, and I didn't have time to mention it. I hope you're not upset."

"Upset? Are you kidding me? Rocco nearly busted my nose, and I'm quite fond of this nose." He lifts his chin to showcase his nose. The Ellison nose, as he calls it. Wait, what? Rocco nearly broke his nose.

"You nearly broke his nose?" I glare at Rocco. "What did you do?"

His eyes go wide as he holds his hands up palms out. "Nothing, I just went back to our place, let myself in, and found your father there."

Our place?

"And you tried to break his nose?"

Dad laughs. "He thought I was the intruder, I thought he was. I tackled him, but come on..." Dad laughs and points at Rocco. "What chance did I stand?"

Rocco grins. "Give yourself some credit, Stewart. You almost had me."

I sit there dumbfounded as they trade compliments, a real-life bromance in the making. Did I just enter the twilight zone or something?

"Only because I caught you by surprise," Dad counters. "Seriously, I didn't expect to see a six-foot, muscular guy come around the corner of the kitchen, Reagan. A head's up would have been nice, but I'm not upset. I'm glad he's staying with you."

"You are?" Rocco and I both say at the same time, and then grin at each other.

"He's great protection. You know, I never did like two young girls living in that big old house. Having Rocco around is bound to scare off any intruder."

"That's true." I glance at the long line building at the counter. "I'm desperate for coffee." Rocco being Rocco slides his cup of coffee across the table. Dad's eyes shift from Rocco to me, and I cringe inwardly. Rocco's gesture is a simple one, but an intimate one, and Dad is going to think there is more going on. He's clever like that. Wait, no. There isn't anything more going on, and this weird little guilty feeling mushrooming inside of me is insane. Dad makes a small noise, and I don't miss the ever so slight nod he just made, like he's putting two and two together, but this time it doesn't equal four because nothing is going on. And yes, I *am* trying to convince myself of that.

Rocco must have realized his mistake because he says, "You can have it. I didn't touch it." He stands. "I'll go grab another cup. It's the least I can do for a friend who's helping me out."

My smile is full of gratitude as I look at him, but my father still has that know-it-all look on his face. Rocco looks back at me. "Sandwich?"

"Just coffee, thanks."

Rocco leaves us alone, and Dad says, "He's a nice guy."

"Yes, very nice."

He takes a sip of his coffee and wipes his mouth with his napkin. "How are things between you and Cochrane?"

I resist the urge to roll my eyes. Leave it to Dad to jump right into things. "Good," I say. "We're both very busy."

He arches a brow, a million questions dancing in his eyes. "He's okay with Rocco staying with you?"

I almost snort. "He's sort of responsible for the whole thing." Not a lie.

"Really."

"What?"

"Interesting." I'm about to ask him why that's so interesting, but he speaks again. "If the two are friends, and it was his idea for you to help Rocco out, I guess he won't mind Rocco coming for Thanksgiving." He leans in conspiratorially—and believe me, I know he's fishing—and says, "If I were Cochrane, I wouldn't want a guy like Rocco staying with my girl."

"He has nothing to worry about," I say. "I don't think Cochrane can make it this year, Dad." He raises his brow. "I'll check with him, though," I add quickly, not wanting to raise more suspicions, or give him time from now until Thanksgiving to delve into our relationship troubles. "What are you doing here, anyway?"

"Can't a father drop in to see his favorite daughter?"

I laugh and put my arms around him for another hug. "Anytime, Dad."

"I was in the vicinity and thought I'd see if you wanted to come out to lunch."

Rocco comes back with his coffee and sits. He takes a huge sip and, as if being drawn by a greater force, I look past his shoulder and find Cochrane on the sidewalk staring at us all, with murder in his eyes.

Oh, God.

I throw up a silent prayer: Do not come in here! He disappears and my heart settles, and I note the way Rocco is watching me. He slowly looks over his shoulder, not doubt to see what just stole all the air from my lungs. He turns back to me, his eyes questioning. His question is soon answered when Cochrane steps up to the table.

"Stewart, what are you doing in town?" he asks and thrusts his hand out.

"There you are. We were just talking about you." Dad stands, and in that manly way guys greet each other, they shake and hug at the same time. "Have a seat. Let me grab you a coffee."

"He can't stay," Rocco says, his voice hard and flat, his eyes laser focused on me as the muscles in his neck twitch.

"Not even for a minute?" Dad asks, a little surprised by that announcement.

Cochrane stands there, his gaze on me, his nostrils flaring. I fold my arms and stare back, anger bubbling up inside me. Rocco is right, he shouldn't be let off the hook so easily.

"He has class," I say. "Can't be late for Finance. Professor McAllister locks the door if you're a second late. Isn't that right, Cochrane?"

"That's right," he says through clenched teeth. "I'll see you soon."

"Thanksgiving, I hope," Dad adds. "Rocco will be joining us this year."

Cochrane's eyes go cold, and in all the years we've been together, I've never seen that look on his face before. I guess he shouldn't have put me up as payment in a game he never should have been playing.

"You've got to be kidding me." The muscles in his jaw are so tight, I'm afraid something is going to snap.

"Like I said," I pipe in and face Dad. "Cochrane might be busy, but we'll talk about it and let you know."

"Well then, we'll leave it at that," Dad responds, clearly aware of the tension in the room. "It was nice to see you, Cochrane. You're looking well."

Cochrane nods, and tears his gaze from me. "Thanks. Enjoy your day. I'll talk to you later, Reagan." A deep warning growl crawls out of Rocco's throat as Cochrane practically pushes people out of his way as he stalks out the door.

My dad takes a sip of his coffee, and doesn't bring up the tension, and for that I'm grateful. "How are classes, pumpkin?" he asks.

Rocco finishes his coffee, and stands. "I'm going to let you two catch up. No need for a third wheel. Thanks for lunch and the invitation to Thanksgiving, Stewart. I really appreciate it."

"You don't have to go," Dad says. "We're just getting to know one another. Any friend of Reagan and Cochrane's is a friend of mine."

"I'd love to stay longer but I have class too, and I hope to see you Friday."

"What's Friday?" I ask.

"Home game," Rocco tells me. "Your dad is going to try to get up for a game."

"Oh..." I say for lack of anything else. "That would be fun."

"I had plans to head to the cottage to check on it. I have to bring the dock in for the winter and drain the fuel from the boat. I could push that to the next weekend."

"I miss the cottage," I say with a dreamy sigh.

Dad frowns. "Although I am kind of busy next weekend. Still, I really hate to push the closing of the cottage too late."

"I could always go do it. I can study there next weekend just as well as I could study here, and I have a stats assignment to get done."

"You sure you don't mind? It's a bit of a drive for you."

The idea of getting away very much appeals to me. "Just a couple of hours. I'd actually enjoy the break from campus." I don't need to look at Rocco to know he's staring. Does he think I'm looking for a break from him?

"Perhaps Rocco could go with you. Keep you company. Do you like boating or canoeing?" he asks Rocco.

"Can't say I've done either of those things."

"It's settled then. Rocco will keep you company, and you can introduce him to the lake."

"Okay," I concede, just to appease Dad, although for the life of me I can't understand why he's instant besties with Rocco. Sure, there is a lot to admire about him, and Dad would appreciate any guy who dragged himself up, and despite the odds, is headed in the right direction to make something of himself.

"Sounds like a plan," Rocco agrees, and I stare at his back as he leaves. Dad happily bites into his sandwich, and when he's done, we spend the next little while talking about school, and my future, and he eventually walks me back to my place, giving me a hug and a kiss at his car before he leaves. I wave him off, and as soon as he disappears around the corner, I spot Cochrane and his friends cruising down the street in his car. Not wanting to talk to him, I dart into the house and lock the door. I still my racing mind, and pray he doesn't come knocking. I'm still so angry. The best thing he can do is leave me alone for the next month. Time heals all, correct? Maybe after one month, I'll be happy to be back in his arms.

Or maybe I won't.

A groan slips out of my throat and I push off the door. I head to my bedroom, grab my blankets and cover my head. A text message comes in and my heart races, but it slows quickly when I see that it's from Cochrane. I toss my phone onto my bed, and flop down onto my pillow, but then I reach for my phone again, and a smile touches my mouth as I scroll through the pictures I took at Rocco's private cave.

My heart settles as I find my happy place. After going through the files, a thought hits, and it fills me with joy. I grab my sketch pad, and for the next hour, work on something I'd like to paint. Before I realize it, my hour is over, and I have to get back to class.

I hurry across campus and slow before walking into my lecture hall. From my peripheral vision, I spot a bunch of members of the rowing team, a group of girls all over them. There's nothing unusual about the sight. Cochrane isn't in the mix. He was never one to soak up the attention from other girls. He could have any girl he wants, but he's not a cheater. I used to worry about that, especially after I told him we could fool around, but that I didn't want to go all the way. My mom always told me to save myself for the man I love. I'm doing that but I guess I want to be married first.

Or maybe Cochrane isn't the man you love.

Oh God.

I turn and run straight into a brick wall. "Ouch," I groan and rub my nose.

"I'm sorry," Rocco says quickly, and puts his hands on my shoulders. He gives a slight squeeze, but the strength in his touch, combined with the raw tenderness in his eyes, travels through my body and settles deep between my legs.

"What are you doing here?" I ask.

"Trying to break your nose. Just like I did with your dad."

I laugh. "You were almost successful."

"I called your name, but you didn't hear me." He looks over my shoulder to see what had me so distracted.

"Look," he says, a line in his forehead as he frowns. "I want to apologize. I probably shouldn't have said Cochrane couldn't sit with us. Your dad didn't deserve that."

"It's okay. I didn't want him sitting there either."

He goes quiet for a second, his head down, thoughtful, like he's trying to find the right way to tell me something."

"What?" I ask.

He glances up, his blue eyes dark and deep when they latch on mine. "I've been giving it a lot of thought. While I want to punish Cochrane, I realize I'm punishing you too, and that's not fair." Catching me by surprise, he takes a strand of my hair between his fingers and rubs it. "I guess if you want to see Coch—"

"I don't," I blurt out and his brow raises. "You're not punishing me."

He steps a tiny bit closer, heat emanating from him in waves and rushing over me like a tsunami. I can hardly breathe. "Are you sure, Reagan?"

"I'm sure and look, you can't move out now." I'm trying for casual, but my body is shaking and my stupid words are breathless. I force a smile. "My father likes the idea of you staying with us and keeping us safe."

He nods slowly. "I suppose when you put it that way, in a weird, twisted way I am kind of doing you a favor."

I grin and shake my head. "How's that for logic at its worst?"

"It's still logic and I think that means..." He angles his head and points his finger at me. "That you might actually owe me something in return."

I put my hand on his chest to shove him. "Wow, I think your twisty skills are wasted on football. You should be in politics." He doesn't budge, but he does take my hand in his and lightly rubs my wrist.

"I like your dad."

"He likes you, too."

Breathe, Reagan, breathe.

He brushes his knuckles over mine. "I won't go to Thanksgiving dinner if you don't want me to."

"I want you to."

"To get back at Cochrane?"

"Umm...yeah."

He stares at me for a long moment, and for a quick second I think he's going to kiss me. He doesn't. Instead, he makes a fist and lightly nudges my chin. "Remind me never to piss you off."

I laugh, and he adds, "Your father is wrong. You're strong, Reagan. You can take care of yourself."

"Then why did you always follow me home late at night when I was walking alone?"

Surprise registers in his eyes, holds there for a moment, and then he quickly blinks it away. His eyes narrow in on me and a moment passes. "Who says I did that?"

His reaction tells me everything I've always wondered. But it doesn't answer the question as to why he followed me on his bike, keeping his distance as I trekked home alone late at night. "I do."

"Were you afraid?"

"Yes."

The blue in his eyes deepens. "Are you still afraid?"

"No."

He grins at me. "Maybe you still should be, pumpkin."

11

___

ROCCO

___

She should be afraid. She should be very afraid. Those words ring as loud and clear in my brain today as they did three days ago when I first said them to her. The truth is, staying at her place, seeing her every morning and again every night, it's been hard in numerous ways. I'm not sure I can be trusted to keep my hands to myself much longer. It's taking every ounce of my strength not to touch her, kiss her, crawl into her bed and just hold her. Put my cock in her.

The thing is, I have this deep gut feeling that she wants me to touch her. Whenever we're close, I notice the quiver in her body, the slight parting of her full lush lips, but Jesus, I can't think about that. Not when we're all lining up for a game against Anaheim that we have to win. Not just that, Reagan and her dad are out there, and while I normally play for the team, for the win, there is something deep inside me that's compelling me to impress them. What I should be focused on is me, and the NFL. What the hell happened to my no distractions rule?

Turning everything and everyone out, I get my head into the game for the first play of the night. We huddle and get our play instructions. I take up position, ready to run it and run hard, because the ball is coming to me. The second the ball is in action, I cut down the line, turn to find it zinging my way. Fighting Anaheim's defense, I jump, touch and run. The crowd goes crazy as I get twenty-four yards on a touch and run, scoring the first touchdown of the game.

I hold the ball up and do a little dance as I search and find Reagan and her father, both standing and clapping. I spot Miranda beside them and I'm glad douche bag is nowhere to be found. The ball is handed off to Spade for a conversion, and I stand back as he kicks it, getting us an extra point.

The Friday night lights shine down on us, on the field, our mood high as everyone slaps me on the back. Using our adrenaline rush, we reposition and continue our winning streak. The second half of the game, Anaheim comes back strong, but we end up winning twenty-one to seventeen.

The cheerleaders jump on our backs as we head into the locker rooms, and I'm hoping Reagan and her dad are headed to the Growler to celebrate our victory. Coach Myers gives us a talking to in the locker room, and we all hit the showers.

Alistair turns on the water beside me. "Nice moves out there, bro. You were playing like your life depends on it."

"It kind of does, don't you think?"

"Yeah, I do. Just keep that head in the game."

"Always." I soap up and lift my face to the nozzle, letting the cool spray rush over my hot skin. My mind instantly goes back to Reagan's shower, and how I warmed her body when she couldn't get the chill from her bones. I quickly extinguish those thoughts. No need for a boner in a room full of men showering.

Alistair glances at me. "Hitting up the Growler?"

"You know it."

"Is Reagan coming?"

I turn to him, water sluicing down my face. "I don't know, why?"

"Just curious." He puts his face under the spray. He gets it. I like her. "You coming to Dixon house later?"

"Dunno," I say.

"You know what, buddy? You seem a bit tense. Maybe you need to get laid."

"Why don't you tell me what you really think?"

"You're not ready for that."

He's probably right. I turn the shower off, and head to my locker. The guys are all razzing one another and talking about which girl they plan to 'bag' tonight. It's kind of disgusting, but who am I to talk? Not that long ago, I would have joined in the conversation. Tonight, however, I'm not in the mood for it. We won the game, I played great, but I'm not much in the mood for partying, which is crazy. I put on a smile as the guys all rerun the plays, especially the killer one I ran during our first play.

We all dress and head outside, the night air warm on our faces as car horns blare going up and down the campus streets. Alistair catches up to me as we make our way to the bar, and two cheerleaders come up and jump on our backs.

"Let's go, boys," Melody says as she bucks against me, her body warm, and hot as she slides her arms around me.

I grip her legs, and Alistair grips Clara's and we both take off, a running race to the Growler. It's a fun game, one we play often, but Alistair, a crazy fast wide receiver, just can't keep my pace. We're all laughing by the time we reach the crowded bar, and I step inside, instantly looking for Reagan. My heart sinks a little when my search comes up empty.

I shake Melody off, and she disappears into the crowd. A cold beer is thrust into my hand and I take a long pull. Numerous girls come up to talk to me. A pretty usual occurrence after a kick-ass game, and while I should give them attention—fuck, I should take one of them to bed to help me get my mind off Reagan—I can't seem to summon the enthusiasm. I spot Miranda, and push my way through the crowds.

"Hey," I call to her and her eyes light up when she sees me.

"Hey," she answers and throws her arms around me. Not in a sexual way, but in a friendship way. "Killer game, Rocco. You did good. Reagan and her dad were so impressed."

"Yeah?" I ask, my chest swelling even though I wish I didn't care so much and goddammit, there's a little gleam in Miranda's eyes as she watches me. I try to keep it cool, and lower my voice when I ask. "Have you seen them around?"

"She walked her dad back to his car at our place." She checks her watch. "She's there with him now and said she'd make her way over here afterward."

I nod. "It's dark. She shouldn't be out walking alone."

"Maybe you should go meet her, make sure she gets here safely."

I nod and scrub my chin. "That's a good idea. I have to watch out for my girls." I say and give her chin a slight nudge.

My girls.

God, neither of them are my girls. Still, I don't like Reagan walking alone at night. Especially on game night when everyone has been drinking. I make eye contact with Alistair, and gesture toward the door. Then I yell, "Back soon." He nods, and I push my way outside as more and more people push in. I circle around and take a shortcut to her place, going through a wooded path that she should never take alone, but I want to get to her house quickly.

By the time I get home, the place is dark and locked up and her father is nowhere to be found. Shit, maybe I missed her. Maybe her father gave her a ride to the Growler. I jog back and pick up my pace. I enter the pub, glance around. My phone pings, and I snatch it from my pocket.

Reagan: Great game tonight.

Me: Where are you?

Reagan: Party at Wolf House.

What the fuck? Why is she going to Wolf House? Did she decide to go back to Cochrane after all? I can't blame her. What I asked of her was wrong. That's still not preventing me from losing my shit. I'm just about to when another text comes in.

. . .

Reagan: I'm just walking Miranda. I'm not going.

"Thank fuck," I say out loud. I turn, about to bolt for the door when Jaclyn comes up to me a beer in her hand. She holds it out to me. "Great game, Roc," she says.

"Thanks." I accept the beer. She's a nice girl and I don't want to be rude to her.

"Are you okay?" She follows my gaze to the front door. "Are you waiting for someone?"

"No, there's somewhere I have to be." I take a big drink from the bottle and hand it to her. "Thanks for that. I needed it."

She smiles. "You're welcome. I hope to see you later tonight at Dixon House."

"Not sure," I say. I don't want to lead her on. I don't want to hurt her feelings either. "Talk soon, okay?"

"Okay." She frowns, but she'll be all right. I can already see my buddy Jared headed her way.

I head outdoors and pick up my pace, wanting to make sure Reagan doesn't have an unwanted run-in with Dick. If he says one word to upset her, I'm going to introduce my fist to his face. Yeah, fighting can get me in trouble, and I have a scholarship to worry about, but I'm not going to stand back and let him hurt her more than he already has.

I'm winded by the time I reach Wolf House, and I spot Reagan and Miranda on the top step. I hurry up the stairs, and Reagan looks shocked.

Her big eyes are curious, wide with delight when she sees me and my pulse jumps a bit. "What are you doing here?"

"Out for a jog," I say, playing it off. "Just happened to see you."

She glances the length of me. I'm in my jeans, and my football jacket. "Jogging in your jeans now, are you?" She touches my coat. "Doesn't this weigh you down?"

"I like to mix it up, and the extra weight is good for fitness."

I catch Miranda grinning. "Enjoy the Growler, *friends*," she says, accentuating the last word. What, does she think we're more than friends? She opens the door, and because of my height, I can see over her head. Miranda goes perfectly still, and she turns back to us so fast her head must be spinning. Her face is pale as she slams the door shut, blocking the image playing out before me. We both stare at one another, because we both saw the same thing.

Reagan looks back and forth between the two of us. "What?" she asks. "What's with the secret messaging going on here?"

"Um..." Miranda stands there like a deer in the headlights.

"What's going on, Miranda?" she asks, her voice a little less playful.

Miranda puts her hand on Reagan's shoulders and is about to turn her. "We should get out of here."

Reagan roots her feet, and reaches past Miranda for the door-knob. "Don't go in there," I bark, the force in my words stopping her cold.

"Rocco," she whispers, angling her head to see me, reading the worry on my face. My heart jumps and all I want to do is pull her into my arms and protect her from the cruel world she's not ever been a part of. But what she's about to see will hurt her, and I'm not trying to get her out of here to protect Cochrane. I'm doing it for her. I reach for her, ready to take her back to her place, but my plan blows up when the front door is flung open and a drunk frat boy comes out to throw up in the bushes.

Reagan spins, and the second she spots Cochrane dry humping some girl on the sofa, his tongue halfway down her throat, she falters backward.

"I've got you." I pull her to me, and Miranda reaches for the door to close it again when douche bag's eyes open and stray our way. He jerks upright, knocking the girl from his lap, and swipes at his mouth as he adjusts his pants and screams at Reagan to wait.

She's hurt and I hate that. "Let's get out of here." She nods, and I lead her down the steps and Miranda follows us. Cochrane bursts from the house, and in sock feet runs down the stairs and through the parking lot to catch up to us. I place a shaky Reagan behind my back as Miranda stands tall beside me.

Douche bag is breathing hard when he whines, "Reagan, wait, hear me out. It's not what you think."

Miranda folds her arms, and together we build an impenetrable wall—both of us protecting Reagan. "Go back inside, Cochrane."

He tries to reach around me, but I shift to block him. "Get the fuck out of my way, Rocco."

"Make me."

"This isn't a fight you want to take on."

I shrug. "Try me."

He glares at me, his nostrils flaring as sweat beads on his forehead. "Come on, Reagan. Let's go inside and talk, buttercup. It's not what you think." His voice is softer now as he changes tactics. "You know you're the only girl for me. We're going to get married someday, remember. A power couple, like our parents. That girl, she's nothing...random."

Reagan tugs on my jacket. "I want to get out of here."

I hold my hand up to suggest Dick back up. "We're leaving, and don't think about following us."

He goes from pleading to angry in seconds flat. "This is all your fault," he spits out and I go still, waiting to see where he's going with this.

"My fault?"

"Yeah, your fault and you're going to pay for this, asshole."

"How is selling your girlfriend out in a card game my fault, and it wasn't me with my tongue down the throat of some random girl."

"It's not like that. I wasn't cheating..." He scratches his head, and struggles for something to say, to make this right for him. "We're on a break, and she doesn't fucking put out." As Reagan gasps behind me, he points a finger at me. It takes all my strength not to snap it. "This is all on you."

Rage wells up inside me and I don't want to be standing here trading barbs with this asshole, not when Reagan needs me. "My responsibility is debatable, but the choices you made when you were on a break—very questionable, and disrespectful, don't you think?"

He gets up in my face, and it takes everything not to knock his perfect fucking teeth out. "My choices are none of your business."

I pull myself up to my full height and stare him down. "When they affect Reagan, they're definitely my business."

"She's not your business."

"She wasn't, but Cochrane, you changed all that." Reagan was never my business. Never. That didn't stop me from lurking in the shadows to make sure she always made it home safely. Where the hell was her douche bag boyfriend then? He doesn't deserve her. He never did. But I'm not involved in her choices. They're hers and hers alone and I've made so many bad ones myself, who am I to judge?

"Let's go," Miranda begs and we both turn.

"He's a fucking hood rat, Reagan. Trash. A goddamn low-life cockroach who doesn't even deserve to be at this school." None of us say anything, which pisses him off even more. "Fine then, go crawl into the gutter with him, see what life is going to be like without your parents' support. It's me they want you to marry. Rocco might be a star here on campus, but in the real world, he'll fail and only drag you down with him. But go. Go have some fun with a gutter pig, and when you come crawling back to me, it better be on your knees. With your mouth open."

Wow, just fucking wow. If Reagan didn't need me right now, I'd tear Cochrane to shreds. Maybe that would prove I am gutter trash, from the wrong side of the tracks. An animal. But it'd be worth it.

I throw my arm around Reagan's shoulder, and while she's tiny, tonight she seems much smaller, more fragile. She's strong, that much I know, but no one deserves any of the things her boyfriend has done to her and said to her, all in the span of a week.

We walk in silence, and every now and then she makes a tiny sobbing sound. We reach her house, and Miranda unlocks the door. Once inside, Reagan and I head to the living room.

Miranda hangs out by the archway as we make our way to the sofa. "I think we could all use a drink."

She disappears and I gesture for Reagan to sit, but she stiffens and turns to me, a fierce determination on her face, and for a second, I think she's going to rightfully kick me to the curb.

"I'm leaving," she announces.

I gulp. "No, no. I'll leave."

She blinks at me several times, and I'm not sure my words are registering. "Reagan, I'll leave. I'm making things worse for you. I never should have come here in the first place."

"Why did you?"

Because I really like you.

"I don't know."

She steps up to me and takes my hand. "I'm leaving. I'm going to the cottage tonight, instead of next weekend. Dad invited you as well, remember?"

"I know, but what is it you want?"

"I want you to come with me."

12

REAGAN

My heart is lodged somewhere in my throat as I sit beside Rocco in the passenger seat of my Volkswagen. Rocco keeps casting me glances, and while I'm upset, it's strange, because I'm not crushed, or broken-hearted. I care for Cochrane. We've been together for a long time. We planned to have a life, a family together. Now, well... now that dream has sailed, or rather, sank spectacularly. The question I keep asking myself, however, is why did it take seeing his tongue down another girl's throat for me to realize we don't belong together? Shouldn't I have come to that conclusion after he sold me to Rocco? But it's more than that. It's the cruel things he said to Rocco. It showed me a part of him I'd never seen before. How could I possibly go back to a man like that?

In my peripheral version, I notice Rocco cast another anxious glance my way, and my pulse jumps a bit each time he does. He's worried about me, and that fills me with a new kind of warmth.

"I'm okay," I say.

"It's not you I'm worried about," he jokes as he squirms a little in his seat. "I have a reputation, Reagan. I'd never live it down if one of the guys caught me driving this little ladybug."

I laugh, and it brings a smile to his face. He's trying to cheer me up and I appreciate all his efforts.

"It's a Volkswagen Beetle, not a ladybug. Besides, even if it was a ladybug, those things are fierce. They can bite, you know."

He grins, slides his hand across the seat and captures my hand. He gives it a little squeeze and I rest my head against the headrest and close my eyes, a wave of exhaustion overcoming me. Must be the adrenaline dump.

"Normally I'd tell you to rest, but if you don't give me directions, we might end up back in Chicago."

I chuckle, and peel open my eyes. "Just get us on the highway, and then we can go from there." There's a moment of silence and then I break it. "Rocco."

"Yeah?"

"Thank you."

"For what?"

"For being here tonight, and for…freshman year. Why did you follow me home like that?"

"The campus isn't safe for a girl walking alone, especially at night."

I consider that. "Did you follow all the single girls home?"

A little shiver goes through me and he turns the heat on, which I greatly appreciate. I love that he notices all the little things.

He jabs his thumb into his chest. "Let's just say campus security should have been paying me."

I laugh at that. "Kingston is lucky to have a guy like you."

I'm lucky to have a guy like him.

"If you're trying to sweet talk your way into my pants, it's working," he says, his voice low and teasing, but there's something else there—a truth beneath his words? Does Rocco want to sleep with me? God, I really shouldn't be so happy about that. "You're the sweet talker, not me." I go quiet again. After a beat, I whisper, "I'm sorry."

"What are you sorry about?" he asks.

I shake my head, my heart aching at all the cruel things Cochrane said to him. "You don't deserve to be talked to like that. Cochrane is wrong. You're none of those things." He stares straight ahead, and I take in the lines of his profile. "I guess I know why you two don't get along. I used to wonder why you were never at any of the Wolf House parties, or why you never went to any of Cochrane's gatherings. I mean, you two were roommates. You were just never around."

"Now you can't get rid of me."

I smile at him when he casts me a fast glance. "Maybe I don't want to." I turn and stare straight ahead. "I feel like a fool. How could I have ever been with a guy like that?"

"This isn't on you. He just never showed you that side of himself, and maybe you should just be thankful that you found out sooner rather than later."

"Yeah…" I say and let my words fall off. I'm not sure what my parents are going to say about the whole thing. They love

Cochrane. They're best friends with his parents and they've been planning our wedding for as long as I can remember.

We sit in silence for a long time, both lost in our thoughts, and I give directions once we come to our exit. He pulls off the highway and I guide him down the side roads until we reach the gravel road leading to our lake house.

"This is kind of in the middle of nowhere," he says as he turns on the high beams and slowly follows the curvy path. Most of the cottages are closed up for the upcoming winter, and ours will soon be as well. I'm just glad it's open now, and we're able to escape the city, college and real life for a while.

"Did we miss it," he says when we come to the end of the road.

"Nope, that's us right there." I point to the left, to the cottage at the end of the lane, perched high with a view of the lake from every window.

He gives a low, slow whistle. "It's gorgeous."

I swallow, a niggling guilt inside. I've been so privileged my whole life and being with Rocco, who's had nothing...I don't know, I'm a little embarrassed.

"Hey, what's wrong?" he asks.

I crinkle my nose. "It's extravagant, I—"

"Don't ever apologize for what you have, Reagan. Your parents work hard, and they deserve all their successes."

I smile at him, appreciating the fact that he's not calling me a princess, a spoiled brat, or any of the other names I've heard over the years. "Thank you," I murmur, and with this incredible new closeness blossoming between us, I lean across the seat and kiss his cheek. His eyes go wide as his hand flies to his face like I might have just slapped him.

"I'm sorry," I say quickly. "I don't know why I did that." I hold my hands up. "I just felt so close to you a second ago, but I never should have done that without asking." God, what was I thinking?

His throat makes a gurgling sound as he swallows. "Don't be sorry." Before he can say anything more, joking or otherwise, I grab the door handle and open it. I wince against the bright interior lights and hop from my car. Rocco sits inside for a second. From the look on his face, my kiss shocked him, and he's likely trying to figure out what to make of it. I'm not sure he can, when I can't figure it out myself.

I stretch my arms out and turn toward the water, watching the waves lap gently against the shore. The creaking dock makes me smile. How many times did that sound lull me to sleep when I was younger?

"Hey," Rocco says, coming up beside me. "Want to take a swim?"

"It's freezing."

"I think I might need that right now," he says and I'm about to ask why until my brain kicks into gear, and I understand. It takes everything in me not to giggle like a school girl, and not to glance down at his crotch.

"How about we take our things inside first?" I suggest. He walks to the back of the car, grabs our duffle bags and backpacks. "I can take something."

"Got it." His voice is low, deep, almost tortured. "Just get the front door for me."

He closes the trunk and I fish my keys from my pocket and hurry to the door. I open it and swing it wide for him. He enters and I flick on the lights, and he looks around, admiration in his gaze. I try to see the wide expanse through his view, and take in the two closed bedroom doors, the one open bathroom door, the wide living room that flows into the kitchen—which also has a door to the outside—the rooms separated by an island.

"I love it. I don't think I'm ever going to leave."

"I know. I love it here too, Rocco."

He drops the bags, and turns to me, his body close, crowding mine, yet oddly enough, I want to get closer.

"You spent a lot of time here as a kid?"

"I did."

"Do you have a treehouse?"

I laugh at that, even though his treehouse story fills me with such sadness. No kid should ever have to seek comfort and refuge in a treehouse.

"No, but maybe we can build one."

"That would be fun." He glances around. "Which room is mine?"

"You can take my old room." I point to the first door. "I'll sleep in Mom and Dad's."

He snatches up the bags again and deposits them in each of the rooms. He comes back out and I take two beers from the fridge and hand him one. I hold my bottle up to him, and he eyes me.

We clink bottles. "What are we drinking to?"

"To Cochrane." He angles his head as he's about to take a drink, his eyes dancing with questions. "When you think about it, if it wasn't for him, we wouldn't be here together," I say. His bottle pauses halfway to his mouth, and his expression changes, becomes darker. "I just mean, I'm glad I found out who he was."

Okay, it's clear I want something to happen here between us, but each time I allude to it, he freezes up.

"How about that swim?" I suggest and set my bottle down, backing away from him, needing a reprieve from his scent and gravitational pull. The air feels cooler the second I put distance between us, and he glances at his bedroom door.

"Are you okay with me swimming in my boxers?"

"If you're okay with me going in my bra and panties." Oh God, what is it about the word panties that sends heat charging through me? Of course, I've said panties before in front of numerous other people and it's never pulled that kind of reaction.

"I'm probably not okay with that, but what can you do, right?"

For a second, I consider what he means. Does seeing me in my underthings turn him off, or is it the exact opposite? I glance at him. Warmth, need and...desire? Is that what I'm seeing in his eyes? If that's the case, the guy is all kinds of contradictions tonight. Cold one minute and hot the next. I'm making it clear where I stand. I guess he's having doubts. With everything that's happened over the last week, I can't blame him.

"Let's go then." I push open the door and the cool air washes over us. I shiver. "Are you sure you want to do this?"

"What is it with you always being cold?" He casually throws his arm around me as we walk to the water, like two good friends who hang out all the time.

"I don't have all that muscle to keep me warm like you do, Rocco."

He laughs. "You don't have to get in if you don't want to."

I can't help but wonder. If I get really cold, will he take me to the shower again, hold me against him?

Is that what you want, Reagan?

Yes.

It's exactly what I want.

"No, I'm not going to chicken out and let you tease me about it for the rest of my life."

"There's nothing chicken about you. You're a lot tougher than you realize."

Beneath the full moon, which is illuminating a path of light across the lake, I spot admiration in his eyes.

"Why do you say that?"

"For one, you're struggling through a degree you don't want, and find extremely hard, but you check in each day and do what has to be done."

"Can I ask you something?"

"Only if I get to ask you something back."

We reach the dock, and it wobbles beneath my feet. "How did you get into football? I mean…" I totally forget what I'm saying when he reaches over his back and peels his shirt off, exposing a wall of muscle and scars. My hands itch to touch each one, to kiss them better.

"Up here," he says and he's grinning like a fool when my gaze lifts to his. I shake off the arousal. "I had a coach in high school." He unzips his pants, and tugs open the button. I struggle to find my words. "I guess he saw potential in me. He taught me to use my hands for good instead of bad."

Oh God, my stupid brain takes that moment to consider how much I'd like him to use his hands—good or bad—on my body.

"That's really nice," I say.

"If it wasn't for him, I don't know where I'd be today. I certainly wouldn't be here on a football scholarship, about to go swimming with you." He goes quiet for a long time, staring out over the lake, and I can almost feel the struggles he's gone through. My heart hurts for that young boy. "It was the first day of high school, and I'd been in a couple of brawls before first bell. Fighting. It comes naturally. Coach Phillips really changed my life, Reagan." He laughs. "Don't get me wrong. He was hard on me. Hellishly hard. I needed that, though." His eyes lift slowly, reach mine. "He was like the father I never had. I owe him so much. You would really like him. He'd like you too."

I want to ask him about his own father, his mother. I'm sensing it's a subject he doesn't like to talk about, so I don't. "I'd like to meet him."

He nods slowly, still lost in thought. "Can I ask you something?"

I shrug. "I guess."

"Do you think you'll regret living the life your parents want for you instead of the life you want?"

I blow out a breath. "That's quite the question."

"You don't have to answer. It's just that football isn't just my ticket to a better life. It's my passion." He puts his hand on his chest, near his heart. "I think I'd lose a piece of me if I lost football, you know. That's what painting is for you." This time he puts his hand on my chest. "In here, it's your passion...your heart."

"I've always done what was expected of me by my parents—"

"And Cochrane..."

"Yeah...there's... there are certain expectations, when you're from the world I live in. I...I'd love to open my own gallery someday, Rocco. My parents appreciate art, but they don't think it's a good future for me." I wave my hand around my luxurious cottage. "This and school. They've given me everything, pay for my school and housing, and it feels wrong to just go off and be frivolous with my life, you know."

He takes one of my hands. "I understand."

There is nothing in his eyes to suggest he's humoring me. He might not have grown up with privilege, but that doesn't mean he doesn't understand that there are still pressures. Like he said, rich or poor, everyone has problems. He stands there a moment longer, watching me. I think he's going to comment some more, and I wait for the argument that I should do what I want, be who I am. It doesn't come. My gaze drops, takes in his near naked body, and my hand lifts without thought. Something moves in a nearby bush and it snaps me back, drags me out of this trance I always seem to be in when he's around. My arm drops.

"Are you doing this or what?"

"Doing what?" I ask, my lust-imbued mind a scattered mess. Did he know I was going to touch him? Is that what he's asking?

"Are you going to strip down to your bra and panties?"

Panties...

Kill me now. "Yeah, of course." I reach for the hem of my shirt, and he turns to give me privacy. That's when I realize I didn't give him the same courtesy. "Sorry, I didn't turn when you undressed."

"You don't need to be sorry." With that he runs to the end of the dock and jumps in. Cold water splashes so high a few drops reach me.

I toss my shirt and jeans to the dock, and decide to cannon ball as well. It might be the only way I'm getting in that ice-cold water. I come up, and search for Rocco. "Where are you?" I ask.

"Marco."

I spin, treading water and laughing. "Oh, we're playing that game, are we?" I swim away and call back. "Polo."

"Marco." His voice is closer now, and I swear the energy from his body is warming the water around me.

I swim away, even though I'm second guessing that choice. Let's face it, I want to be caught.

"Polo."

I turn back around, and Rocco is nowhere to be found. "Where are you?" I call out. Catching me off guard, bubbles form in the water in front of me, and he pops up. I scream and splash him, and he slides his arms around my waist before I can get away. Not that I'm really trying.

"I win," he says.

With his body meshed against mine, his mouth close enough for me to taste him, I'm pretty sure I'm the winner in this situation. "Have you cooled off?" I ask for lack of anything better to say.

He stares at me long and hard, and I wish I could read minds. Whatever is going through his head is causing him a great deal of torture.

"Yeah, cooled off," he says, his hands leaving my hips as he flips to his back and starts floating.

I do the same, and float beside him. "It's gorgeous tonight."

He moves his hands, creating small ripples in the water—not to mention in me. Never in my life have I wanted to touch myself as badly as I do now. Correction, never in my life have I wanted someone else, and that someone else is Rocco, to touch me as badly as I do now.

"See that cluster of stars over there?" I point. "That's Cassiopeia, named after the vain queen Cassiopeia in Greek mythology. Apparently, she liked to boast about her unrivaled beauty."

"That's because she never met you."

I laugh. "Wow, you say you're not good with words, but you're on your game tonight." I glance around. "Do you have a play-book around here you sneak peeks at?"

"Smart ass." He laughs and tugs on my hair.

I go back to stargazing and sigh. He might say the nicest things to me, but I'm not naïve enough to think he considers my beauty unrivaled.

"I used to love coming to the lake at night. Normally I'd lay on the wharf and look at the stars. I downloaded a bunch of astronomy books. Then I'd study the star clusters and see if I could find them in the night sky."

"You're kind of a nerd."

His humor catches me off guard and I laugh, my body sinking a little with the movement, and I take in water. I go back to treading water and start coughing.

"Jesus, Reagan." He comes to my aid quickly and propels me back to the wharf. He jumps up and pulls me out of the water with him. I cough and cough to clear my lungs, and he stands there tapping my back to help dislodge the water. When I finally clear it, he exhales. "You scared me. I thought I was going to have to perform mouth to mouth, and I really suck at it."

I'd bet a million dollars he doesn't.

A shiver wracks me and he drags me to him. "Let's get you inside and warmed up."

"We could light a fire," I suggest.

"A shower first. You need to warm up fast. I never should have dragged you into the lake with me."

"You didn't drag me in. I wanted to go."

We get inside and he hurries me into the bathroom. He turns on the shower and adjusts the temperature. "Come on."

I step into the shower with him, and in typical Rocco fashion, he puts me under the spray, letting me hog all the hot water, but I'm not having any of that. He's cold too. I wrap my arms around him, pull him in with me.

Our bodies mesh, align, and a needy noise I have no control over crawls out of my throat. He takes a fistful of my hair, tilts my head back to look into my eyes and goes still.

"Are you choking?" he asks.

"No."

"You made a strange noise."

I swallow. Hard. "I know."

"Are you okay?"

"I don't think so."

He lets my hair go and inches back, as my entire body burns with a deep need for him. I've never experienced anything like it. It rips through me, tears at me, demands to be noticed.

"Reagan..."

"Rocco."

He swallows as I pull him back toward me, letting him know in no uncertain words what I want from him. He takes a deep breath, then another, and he lets it go, air hissing from his lungs like a deflated balloon

"Rocco," I whisper again, the desire in my voice evident, even to my own ears.

"I can't." My heart speeds up. Blue, tortured eyes meet mine. "I can't be your rebound, Reagan. I just can't."

"It's not like that."

"I don't want to be that guy." He puts his big palm over my heart, half of his hand covering my breast. "You're hurting. We make bad choices when we're hurting, and I don't want you doing something you're only going to regret come morning."

"I'm not looking for a rebound tonight, Rocco, and even if I am making bad choices, I want this with you tonight. I want to be held, and touched…" I run my finger over his bottom lip. "I want to be kissed."

His face twists, clearly tortured. The thickening between his legs tells another story, though. He wants this as much as I do, and that excites me. Thrills me. I've never wanted—needed—to be desired like this before.

"Fuck, Reagan."

"Yeah, please."

He goes completely still, understanding exactly what I want. I stand there waiting. Will he flee, or will this be the man I give my virginity to?

She coughs, and I put my palm on the sides of her head. "Are you okay?"

"I think I might have some water still in my lungs. I might have to take you up on that mouth to mouth."

I stare at her long and hard. I want her. There's no doubt about that. Reagan and I, though, we're different people from different worlds. She's a good girl who will eventually go back to Cochrane, or someone else from her class of society. But those are the rules put in place for her, and unfortunately for me, and for her, she's not the type of girl to smash them. Tonight, though, I could give her what she wants. What she craves. It's wrong in so many ways, but fuck it.

I slide my hand around her neck and dip my head. The second my lips land on hers, I forget every reason why this is a bad idea. She whimpers, and I slide my other hand around her waist, pulling her body tightly against mine, rubbing my hard cock against her soft body, my craving for her intensifying. She slides her hands over my chest, exploring, touching, caressing, and I groan into her mouth. I have no idea why her touch warms me from the inside out. Christ, I've been touched by numerous women. Never before have I come this close to shattering.

I turn the shower off, wrap her in a towel, and take her to the bed. She sits on the edge, her big hazel eyes wide, a mixture of desire and fear lingering there. It's the fear I need to address before this goes any further. I drop to my knees in front of her and slide my hand around her neck.

"You're a virgin, Reagan."

"I know."

"Why?"

Her eyes widen at the question as water drips from her hair, traveling to the tip of her nose. I brush it away and wait for her to answer.

"I wasn't ready for sex."

I brush my thumb over her soft cheek, and she leans into it. "You think you are now, or is this about Cochrane?"

"It's about me wanting you, and hoping you want me too." she says honestly, and my heart does some strange somersault. So many times in life, I've been tossed away, unwanted and unlovable, but right now, in this moment, this beautiful girl wants me. I've been beat up and bruised—never broken. Deep inside, however, I am positive this is the one girl who could break me.

"I want you." I glance down at my bulging shorts. "That's pretty obvious." Her soft chuckle curls around me, but it's her palm on my face that's like a warm hug to my heart.

"Tonight. No regrets," she whispers.

I grip her hair and bring her mouth to mine. I kiss her, softly at first, until she's moaning and running her hands all over me, unable to get enough. I deepen the kiss, slide my tongue into her mouth. Her sweet flavor explodes on my tongue and I know that I'm done for. I break the kiss, and she sits there, eyes half open, mouth still poised for mine as I back up. She blinks, a measure of worry flooding her eyes. My heart jumps.

"Reagan, let me know right now if this is what you want. I've wanted you for a long time now, and I'm not sure I'll be able to stop once I had a taste of your sweet body."

"Rocco," she says quietly. "I want this. I want you."

Air leaves my lungs and I resist the urge to scream from the rooftops as I slide my fingers into my boxers and tug them off, dropping them onto the wood floor of her bedroom. With my dick free, I take it into my hands and stroke. She watches, eagerness all over her face.

She blinks up at me. "I want to touch."

"I don't want to know about your sex life with Cochrane." Christ, thinking about her in his arms, his bed, fills me with white hot rage. "But, just how experienced are you?"

"Come here."

I step up to her and she opens her mouth for my cock. I slowly feed it to her and groan as she takes me deep. The heat of her mouth wraps around me and standing becomes a much harder skill. "Fuck, Reagan."

She mumbles around my cock. I can't understand a word she's saying. I move my hips, my hard as steel cock sliding in and out of her pretty mouth.

"That is so good." With her sweet lips stretched around my girth, she cups my balls and my body tightens. She worships my cock like it's her goddamn job. Jesus, if I don't put a stop to this, I'm going to be done before I'm even started. I pull from her and she frowns in protest.

"I wasn't done," she murmurs, and tries to reach for me.

"I nearly was."

She laughs, and grins up at me. "I've never really enjoyed that before."

My heart sinks. "Reagan, you didn't have to do that if you didn't like it. I don't want you ever to do anything you don't want to do. You have a say in all this."

"That's it, though. I did like it with you. I love the sounds you make, the way you swelled even more when I took you deep. It makes me happy to make you happy."

I cup her chin gently and something inside me breaks a little. "You're killing me, you know that?" She smiles, clearly liking that. "Let's get you out of these wet things." I drop down again, reach behind her back and unhook her bra. She shimmies out of it and tosses it away. My gaze falls to her gorgeous, full breasts, and her perfect pale pink nipples.

"Killing me," I moan softly, and put my hands on her thighs as I lean in for a taste. I run the soft blade of my tongue over her pale sweetness, and her nubs harden even more. "You are so perfect." Her hands go around my head and she grips my hair, holding me to her breasts as I take my fill, biting and licking and sucking. She moves against me, her hips wiggling on the bed as her body begs mine for more.

I treat her other nipple to the same pleasure before going straightening up. I soften my voice and whisper, "Lie back."

She does as I ask, and I touch her thighs, push them a little farther apart to get a glimpse of the white lace covering her pussy. I take a breath to get myself together. I still can't quite believe she's gifting me with her virginity.

"Are you scared?" I ask, my fingers toying with the band on her panties. She goes up on her elbows to see me.

"I used to be. Maybe that's why I was never ready."

"Why aren't you afraid now?"

"Because it's you. You would never do anything to hurt me. Not purposely, anyway."

My throat squeezes so tight I'm sure I'm going to black out. The way she trusts me completely...fuck, I don't take that lightly.

I stroke her sex through her panties and she moans. "I promise to make this good for you, and if it's not good the first time, we'll just keep doing it until we get it right."

Her smile is soft and sexy as she gives a slow nod. "I like the idea of that."

I trail my thumbs over the lace keeping my mouth from her pussy, and she quivers beneath my touch.

"Do you touch yourself, Reagan?" I ask.

For a second I don't think she's going to answer. "Yes," she admits.

"That's good."

"Why?"

"That way you know what you like. It's important we both know what you like, and dislike."

"Do you touch yourself?" I give her a look that suggests she's dense and she laughs. "Right, never mind."

I like talking to her like this, open and intimate. With my heart thumping a little harder, I tug the lace down, exposing her silken curls, and my cock jumps. Fuck, all the girls today shave, but I love her like this. "I'm really going to enjoy getting to know all your likes."

"I am too," she murmurs as I kneel, brushing my lips over her pussy as I tug the material down even more. I push her legs together, and drag her panties over her feet and toss them away. I take numerous deep breaths as I gaze at her nakedness. I could almost fucking sob.

"You're beautiful."

She reaches for me and I grip her thighs, my fingers holding her carefully as I slide up and give her clit a slow, leisurely lick.

"Rocco," she murmurs, and I grin. Yeah, getting to know all her likes is going to be a hell of a lot of fun.

"Like that, babe?" I ask.

"Yesss...."

I lick her some more, tasting and teasing her, my brain registering her every moan and movement, aiming to get it just right. I slowly slide a finger into her, and her tight pussy clenches around me. My cock jumps, eager to slide inside, but fuck, how am I not going to hurt her? I work my finger inside her and find all her sensitive spots as I swipe my tongue over her heated clit. She's moaning, something soft and incoherent, as I eat her.

I slide a second finger into her and she gasps as I fill her. I take my time stretching her, warming her muscles, working her into a frenzy.

"That's it. Move your hips, Reagan. Take what you need from my fingers. This is all for you."

She moves a little faster, riding me a little harder, and a keening noise breaks from her throat as she bursts around my fingers. Perfection. Total fucking perfection. It's the only way to describe the way her body is moving in pure bliss. Her juices soak my hand and chin as I lap at her, wanting every last drop of her sweetness.

She's panting, her hands tugging on my hair as I slowly inch my fingers out, knowing so much more about this sweet girl.

"That was...Rocco." She shakes her head, like she's trying to settle her scattered thoughts.

"I'm going to make you come like that every time I touch you." We might have agreed to one night, no tomorrows, but for the next twelve hours or so, I'm going to give her so many climaxes her head is going to spin.

"It's never been this good before," she whispers.

Anger and pleasure hit at the same time. I hate that Cochrane didn't take care of her properly—I also hate that he ever touched her. Yet pleasure threads through me to know I'm the guy who can make this good for her. I slide up her body, my cock between her thighs.

My mouth finds hers and I kiss her, our tongues playing and reacquainting. Her breasts press against my chest, her nipples so hard, I'm sure they could score my skin.

I break the kiss and press my lips to her eyelids, her nose, her cheeks and chin. "I need to be inside you."

"I need that too."

"You ready for me?" I ask, wanting to make sure she's still in this game.

"I am."

"Protection?" I ask.

"Oh God!" Her eyes go wide, sheer disappointment living right there in her pupils, and that's when it occurs to me just how much she wants this tonight—with me. "I'm not on the pill."

"It's okay, I have condoms."

She relaxes. "At least one of us was prepared for this."

"I wasn't prepared for this, Reagan. Not one fucking bit." My heart pounds in my chest as I reach into my bag, and pull out a box of condoms. I turn back to her. "Were you?"

"If you're asking if I wanted this to happen, if I've been wondering in my head how we'd be together, the answer is yes. I just didn't know where your head was or what you wanted."

I point to my head. "This head is telling me all of this is a bad idea." I grip my cock and stroke myself. "This head is telling me to go for it. I guess we know which one is doing the talking tonight."

She crooks her finger. "For a guy who isn't good with his words, I actually think you're doing too much talking."

I laugh at that, rip into the box of condoms and pull one out. She watches in fascination as I sheath myself. "Middle of the bed," I command softly.

She slides to the middle and opens her legs. I do love a girl who knows what she wants.

Love?

Her eyes meet mine, dark and demure, as she grips the sheets.

"Show me." At first she doesn't know what I mean, so I let my gaze travel the length of her, stopping on her wet sex. "Show me," I repeat.

She widens her legs even more and slides her hands slowly down her body, stopping to tweak her nipples as she goes by, then she frames her mons and pulls open her pretty pink lips. I nearly sink to my knees in a trembling mess.

"So nice." Working double time to keep my shit together, I put my knees on the bed, and position myself between her legs. "This first time, we're going to do it the old-fashioned way. I want to see your face, make sure I'm not hurting you." She swallows, and tears make her eyes glossy. "Hey." I touch her face gently. "Why the tears?"

"I guess I'm emotional because this is a big deal to me."

"It is to me too, Reagan. Believe me. I would never lie about that, and I'd never want to lie to you."

"Yeah."

I nod. "I promise, and thank you for wanting this first time to be with me."

I bend over her and find her mouth. We exchange heated kisses as I position my cock at her hot entrance. I inch in slowly, giving her time to expand around me. It takes no time at all, and I've bridged the first tight muscles, which both shocks and arouses me. I slide in a little more, giving her an inch at a time. Her muscles wrap around me, hug me tight, her body completely opening to me, a perfect fit.

I keep a close eye on her face, but there's no pain there, only pleasure. "You good?"

"I've never been better."

"Am I hurting you?"

"It's tight, I feel that, but it's good, Rocco. It's so good."

My heart beats a little faster. If I'm not careful, I'm really going to lose myself in this girl—and I'm not talking physically.

I move my hips a little faster now as my body burns with need. My mouth goes to the hollow of her neck and she pushes her head back as I find a spot that makes her moan. I give her every last inch of my cock, until I'm hitting her cervix, and I rub my pelvis against her clit.

"Rocco..." She scratches her nails over my back, no doubt leaving the best kind of scars a guy can have.

"You feel so good, Reagan."

"So good," she echoes, and I rock my hips gently, pushing deeper and deeper, yet unable to get deep enough. I cup her face, kiss her mouth and pull almost all the way out. She whimpers and I slide back inside her. She's wet and hot, her tight sex gripping me with each thrust. It's insane how close I am. No way am I going to come without bringing her to orgasm again. I can't wait to feel her hot heat surround my cock.

I change the pace, go a little faster, my crown hitting all her sensitive spots. She makes a noise and I lift my head, meeting her eyes. They're barely open as she gazes up at me, and that gorgeous look tells me she's close again, that I'm touching all the right spots.

I rock into her, bang against her clit, and her mouth falls open. "Rocco." She breathes my name into the dim room, and it curls around me, hugs my heart like an invisible fist. "I'm…"

"Yeah, babe. You're right there. Jesus, you're squeezing me." I can't get air into my lungs as she comes around my cock, her heat scorching my last working brain cell. I continue to pump into her, letting her ride out each glorious wave until I reach my breaking point.

"Fuck," I groan as I let go, filling the condom with my seed, at the same time filling her body, wanting to leave a part of myself inside her for a little while longer. It's such a crazy thought I can't even believe I'm having it.

"I feel you," she murmurs and presses her mouth to my neck when I collapse on top of her. I gasp for breath, her soft chuckle curling around me. What on earth does she find so funny?

I inch back to see her face, and she smiles up at me. I arch a brow and she says, "If I'd known sex was going to be that good, I would have been doing it all along."

"I really don't know how to say this without sounding like a misogynistic asshole."

She rakes her nails through my hair. "What?"

"I'm glad you haven't been doing it all along." I shake my head. "That coming from a man-whore. I get it. I have no right to say that." I brush her hair from her face, my humor long gone. "I'm just glad we did this." I let out a breath. "That you did it with me. Not all guys want, or care, about making it good for the girl."

She puts her hands on my face, and blinks dark lashes over watery eyes. "Thank you."

"You just seriously thanked me for sex." I laugh. "I'm the one who should be thanking you."

"Okay, go ahead," she teases, a new energy, a new lightness about her. It fills my soul with happiness.

I slowly inch out, and there is blood on the condom. "How do you feel?"

"Amazing."

"Okay," I say, even though I'm a bit worried. I discard the condom and grab a few tissues from the box to clean her up.

"Rocco?"

"Yeah."

I put the tissue between her legs and she shivers. "I think it was only this good because it was with you."

My hand stills between her legs as old insecurities creep through my brain. The truth is, I feel the exact same way, and I'm past the point of denying how much I like her, how much I want to keep her in my life. But this is Reagan Ellison, beauty and brains with a bright future in front of her. I might be a football star now, but deep inside, I'm not sure I'll ever be good enough for a girl like her.

My body is sore in the most glorious ways. I roll to my side and take in a sleeping Rocco. It's not even morning yet, and I should feel tired, not invigorated. With the blankets around his waist, his arms above his head, I study his solid body, as I feel my arousal rising, racing through me. Sex with him was soft, and tender and gentle. The way he took care of me hit on a different level, a deeper one, and that scares me a little. Or maybe a lot.

I lightly touch his chest, run my hands over his scars. Bending, I lightly press my lips to his chest and kiss him gently. He shifts, moves beneath my hands, and I lift my head, find him looking at me.

"Sorry. I didn't mean to wake you." My voice is hoarse and low.

"You didn't."

I grin at him. "Yes, I did."

He touches my still damp hair, runs it between his fingers. We showered before we fell asleep an hour ago, and we also changed the bedding. I was foolishly embarrassed by the blood, but Rocco wasn't having any of that. It's crazy how he can put me at ease, how we can talk about things like my virginity, the blood on the bed, like it's normal conversation. But it's more than that. There's an intimacy in the way we open up and share, and I'm not sure I'd feel that with any other guy.

"Okay, you did wake me," he admits. "But I don't mind." He bends to drop a gentle kiss onto my mouth.

I savor the kiss, wanting more, wanting everything.

Careful, Reagan. He's not offering everything.

"This is a nice way to wake up."

His warm gaze moves over my face. "Are you sore?"

"No."

He grins at me. "Yeah, you are."

I laugh, a new lightness in me. "Okay, yeah, I am but I'm not too sore to take you again, if you want."

"Like you even have to ask." I chuckle at his totally male answer and press my mouth to his chest and kiss him some more. "But we're not going to."

My head lifts, and that little tingle of worry tightens in my stomach. I know the rumors, heard the stories of the jocks deflowering virgins in some disgusting game they played for points. Though that happened freshman year, and we're seniors. But that doesn't mean I wasn't a game to him. Revenge on Cochrane, perhaps.

No, Rocco is not like that.

Honestly, I hate myself for even considering it, but old insecurities flow through my veins, and they've left their fair share of ruts over time. Like I said, I never knew who wanted to be my friend because of what I had or because they liked me.

"Hey, what's wrong?" Rocco asks.

I put on a smile. "Nothing. If you don't want to—"

"Sunshine," he begins and it's so ridiculous how much I love it when he calls me that. How close it makes me feel to him. "I *want* to. I told you that. You're sore and we're going to give it a bit of time, but believe me, the second you're not sore, I'm back in here." He slides his hand down my body and cups my sex.

I chuckle, the last of my worries evaporating. Rocco's stomach takes that moment to growl. I lift my head to see him. "You must be starving."

"Yeah, I didn't eat after the game."

I sit up and cross my legs. "I'm sorry. You should have been out celebrating the win, and I dragged you into my problems."

"You didn't drag me into anything."

I frown. "Why were you at Wolf House, anyway?"

"You texted me and told me where you were going." Rocco holds up his hand clenched in a fist, unfurling one finger. "One, I didn't want you walking back to the pub alone in the dark." He unfurls the second finger. "And two, I was worried Cochrane was going to give you a hard time and I didn't want you to have no backup if he did."

I frown and pluck at the bedding. "I never thought he was a cheater." A humorless laugh comes out of my throat. "I guess we were on a break, and how am I any better? I just slept with you."

His eyes darken, his brow furrows. "You regret it," he states quietly, and reaches for the blankets to push them off.

I grab his arm. "No, not for one second." He stares at me long and hard, and deep in his brain, I get that he's trying to decide whether I'm telling the truth or not. "I promise."

He gives a slow nod and puts his hand on my cheek. "I couldn't live with myself if I knew you regretted this, Reagan."

"Later, when I'm not sore, I'm going to show you just how much I don't regret this."

He frowns. "Cochrane...are you two going to get back together after our month?"

I swallow. Hard. "You...you really don't like him, do you?"

He scrubs his face. We both know I'm hedging, that I'm not saying yes or no. The truth is, I'm hurt. I can come to terms with Cochrane being with another girl, I guess. We were on a break. The things he said about Rocco, however. I can't get past that. My stomach sours just thinking about the vile names he called Rocco. No one deserves to be treated like that, made to feel lesser. I saw a side of Cochrane I'd never seen before, and the things he said to and about me...shocking as well. Will he unleash that side of himself on me again? Once he has everything he wants, will he start treating me like dirt beneath him, and calling me vile names? If anything, Rocco is the better man. Look where he started and look where he's at right now.

In my bed.

My heart beats a little faster. But what the hell are my parents going to say? Their little girl is not supposed to veer off her carefully crafted path. My stomach tightens even more as Rocco's eyes drill into me.

"How about this," I begin. "How about we don't talk about Cochrane for the rest of the weekend. Let's just pretend we're the only two people who exist."

He smiles, leans in and lightly brushes his lips over mine. "I like that idea." He tosses his blankets off and stands, completely comfortable in his naked skin. I let my gaze rake over him, taking in his scars.

"I can't wait until I'm not sore," I say, wanting him to know I have zero regrets.

He turns, and grins, his playful mood back. He waves his hand up and down his body. "You want some of this."

"Nope."

He angles his head his eyes narrowing. "What?"

"I don't want some, I want it all."

He laughs. "I don't know what I did to you, but I like it."

I search the floor for clothes, and find his shirt. "Mind if I wear this?"

"Nope."

He opens his duffle and pulls out a pair of sweatpants. I breathe in his scent as I smell his shirt and grab a clean pair of panties from my bag. I dress and turn to find him staring at me. A thrill goes through me at the ravenous gleam in his eyes. I don't think any guy has ever looked at me with such yearning before. It's scary, and exciting.

I jerk my head toward the other room. "Let's go find something to eat." He stays close to me as we head to the kitchen, and I open the fridge to find soda, beer, juice and a few condiments. "Drink?"

"Sure." I take out the juice and pour two glasses. In the freezer, I find bread and bacon. There are no fresh eggs, but we can work with what we have. I root out a frying pan. "Check the cupboard to see if there's any canned fruit. Mom always stocks the place with peaches."

"Mmm, peaches." The doors open and close and he sets a can of peaches on the counter. I nuke the bacon to thaw it and toss it in the pan. I'm about to reach for a fork, when he comes up behind me, puts his arms around my waist and looks over my shoulder.

"Bacon. That's a food group, right?"

"It is in my world."

He continues to hold me and I continue to like it. It's so weird, this intimacy between us. My heart beats a little faster when he's around; my body is so aware of him. I don't want to compare, but I'm not sure I ever felt this kind of comfortableness with Cochrane. But I'm not supposed to talk or think about him this weekend.

I sway slightly as I separate the bacon in the pan. Wait, what was that? I push back a little. Yup, it's still there. Grinning as an idea takes hold, I turn the stove off and spin until I'm facing Rocco.

"You want me to cook..." He stops speaking, his words dissolving in the charged air around us. "What are you up to?"

I point downward. "You seem to have a little problem this morning."

"Little?"

"Ohmigod, what an ego."

He shrugs. "What can I say?"

"Okay, let me try this again, you've got a big problem down there."

"You're too sore, babe. I want to wait."

Warmth spreads through me. My God, he's so incredibly sweet it's hard to believe he's for real.

"Agreed, but there is something I want to do in the meantime. Something I want to finish." Before he can say a word, I sink to my knees and take his pants down with me.

"Holy fuck."

I blink up at him, his cock thickening in front of me. I lean in, and his crown taps the dent in my top lip. I take his thickness into my hand. His breathing changes, each hard, labored breath like a stroke over my clit, making me wet. I love seeing him like this. Love the way my touch can reduce this big, scary football player into a quivering mess of need.

He pushes my hair from my shoulders and grabs a fistful. "You want to suck my cock, Reagan?"

I blink up at him, and wet my lips. He pinches his eyes shut for a second, agony all over his beautifully scarred face. "Yeah..."

His eyes meet mine. "You like that, huh? You like it with me?"

Something in the way he's saying that…I don't know, but he needs to hear my answer. It's important for him to know that I like having him in my mouth.

"Yes."

His jaw clenches. "Take my cock into your hot little mouth. Let me watch you suck me off."

My sex pulses at his dirty words, my nipples hard little peaks begging for attention. I lean in, lick the pre-cum from his crown and his growls of pleasure curl around me, giving me confidence in my abilities. I savor the tangy taste of him, breathing in his scent as I take him to the back of my throat. God, I want every inch of him in my mouth, but it's impossible. Still, it's not going to stop me from trying.

He tugs on my hair, his moan of pleasure like praise to my ears and I slide my mouth back to lick his crown, taste his offerings.

"That is so good, babe."

I glance up at him, take in the way his eyes are closing, the muscles in his body tight. I can't believe how close he is. I swallow more of him, going impossibly deeper, and he eases into my throat. Never have I wanted to pleasure a guy like this. I never thought it could bring me pleasure until Rocco.

"I want to taste you so badly." He groans, and I want that too. My body warms all over and my pussy grows impossibly wetter. "I'm going to toss you onto your bed, and put my mouth all over you." He takes a couple fast breaths. "I want to fuck you everywhere. Especially your tits." My nipples harden just thinking about that. I inch back.

"I've never done that before," I tell him, and he nods.

"We're going to do lots of firsts, Reagan."

I smile and go back to pleasuring him, loving the idea of a weekend of sex. And a weekend of first. I might not be able to be his first in the bedroom, but here at the cottage there are other things we can do. We're in my territory now, and that's foreign to him.

"Babe," he tugs on my hair, but I clamp my hands around his legs and hold him in my mouth. I want to taste him. "You want this? You want my cum in your throat?"

I murmur and nod around his engorged cock, each swollen vein filled with heated blood as I suck on him, like my very existence depends on it.

"Fuck, babe..."

His words, so soft and tender, so full of...I'm not exactly sure what the right word is. All I know is he's filled with wonderment. Like he's surprised that I want to do things for him.

"I'm there," he moans, and a second later, he spurts down my throat. I drink him in. Or at least I try to. I stay on the floor until he spills every last drop, and I glance up at him. The second my eyes meet his, catch the warmth and gratitude staring back at me, my heart does a little tumble.

He smiles at me, and runs his hand over my mess of hair. "Hey," he says, and it makes me grin.

"Hey yourself."

"For a guy who doesn't like surprises, I really liked that one."

I wipe my mouth with the back of my hand. "We have the whole weekend, and I think I'm going to surprise you a lot."

"I think I'm going to like that." He frowns. "What about you? Can I touch you?" His stomach grumbles, and I chuckle.

"Rain check?"

He pulls me to my feet, and presses a kiss to my forehead. "I'm going to do the dirtiest things to you."

My entire body quivers. "I'm looking forward to it. Right now, I'm going to feed you."

He pulls his sweats up, and gets me a glass of water. "Drink."

I do as he says, and point to the coffee pods. "Why don't you make us coffee and I'll get this food ready."

I turn from him. When he doesn't move right away, I'm about to glance over my shoulder to question him when big arms circle my waist. He lifts me clear from the floor as he gives me a bear hug. It does the craziest things to my beating heart.

He sets me on my feet, and goes to work on the coffee. I don't need to turn to know he's watching me. I can practically feel his eyes burning into the side of my head.

"Is there something you want to say?" I ask, unable to keep the happiness from my voice, which raises the question, what is it about being secluded with Rocco that makes me so happy? I just caught my long-term boyfriend, my future husband, cheating on me, and my parents are going to flip out once they find out we're no longer a couple. Our mothers have been planning our wedding forever. Yet, here I am, in the woods with Rocco, and I'm very happy.

"I like you."

I turn to him, and while his eyes are filled with delight, there's a seriousness about him. "I like you too, Rocco."

"Good."

Just like that, he goes back to making the coffee and I put the toast down as the bacon cooks. He opens the fridge. "No milk."

"There's powder in the cupboard."

Once he fixes our coffees, I plate our food and set a jar of jam on the table. He looks at it and looks at me.

"I might never leave here."

I laugh. "It's my happy place too. But reality calls."

"Not until Monday it doesn't."

"But it still will." I push down the stupid lump in my throat. What's going on here isn't reality, it's fantasy and that's okay, for now.

He bites into the bacon and moans. My gaze leaves his face, and settles on the biggest scar on his chest. I want to ask. I don't. It's not my business and maybe it's not wise getting too personal with him. It will only make it harder when this is all over.

"My father was a bastard," he begins. "Especially when he was drunk."

"I'm sorry, Rocco."

"Thanks, but it's not your fault."

I look at the angry scar. "He did that?"

"I was twelve, bringing him a beer, like he asked. Tripped over my own feet, and the bottle broke on the floor beneath me. Landed in emergency getting stitches with a drunk father ranting in the waiting room. That's when child protective services started getting involved."

I wince, understanding he's telling me something very personal, very private, something I suspect he doesn't tell too many people. I like that he's comfortable enough to open up with me. I feel the same way about him.

"I'm sorry you got hurt," I softly empathize. "As awful as it was, maybe going to the hospital was a blessing. With child protective services involved, it got you out of that environment."

He laughs, but it holds no humor. "Not really. I was thirteen the first time I went to a home. Things were no better there. Most foster families do it for the money. They don't want or care about the kids." He frowns. "My father was a bastard, but he was still my father. Being taken away wasn't easy for me."

I frown. We had such different upbringings, yet we're here together, right now. Breathing the same air and enjoying the same things. "I'm so sorry you had to go through that."

"It's okay." Dark lashes fall over blue eyes. "I don't want anyone's pity."

I look over his face, note the way the hard angles seem softer this morning. "What do you want?"

15

ROCCO

With the bacon halfway to my mouth, my hand stills, Reagan's question hanging heavy in the air between us. *What do I want?* To be perfectly honest, at this very moment, I want my hands and mouth on her—I want to lose myself inside her—but the real problem is, I might want it tomorrow, or again next week...maybe forever. But that's not going to happen, and I honestly have no idea why I even told her that much about my history. There are a lot of rumors about me, but I've only ever opened up to Alistair.

I toss the bacon into my mouth and try to settle my racing heart as she waits for me to answer. "I guess I want to finish my degree, get into the NFL, and live happily ever after."

Her lips quirk. "Fairy tales. Nice, but—"

"But you don't believe in them either," I say, finishing her sentence.

She shakes her head, and toys with the corner of her toast. "How did you know?"

"We're not so different in some ways."

"You're right."

"I want that for you, Reagan. I want you to have the happily ever after, the house, kids and minivan."

She reaches across the table and squeezes my hand. "I want that for you too."

I nod. In the world I grew up in, fairy tales don't exist, but if she starts living her own life, maybe she can have all the things she wants and deserves.

"What do you want to do after the NFL?"

"The scholarship comes with a degree, and while football is my life, and I don't know what I'd do without it, I'm pretty good in math."

"If you weren't, you wouldn't be here right now."

She's referring to the card game. "If your douche..." I catch myself. No trash talking her boyfriend, or her ex-boyfriend. I'm not even sure she knows where she stands with Cochrane. "If Cochrane hadn't handed you to me, I wouldn't be here." I consider that for a second. "I guess now I can't hate him as much as I used to."

Her lips pinch tight. "Yes, you can. He was horrible to you."

"I hate that he hurt you."

She nods and looks down for a second. "After the NFL, what are your plans?"

I shrug. "I love coding, so maybe something in the tech industry." I lean back and take a sip of coffee. "Or maybe I'll open my own art studio." Her eyes go wide, then she laughs. "What, you don't believe me?"

"No, I don't." She crushes a napkin and tosses it at me. "So you can stop that right now." I catch the napkin and toss it back. "Do you think about having a family or kids?"

"I don't know. I guess not really. Is that something you want?"

She nods. "Cochrane and I talked about it." She snorts. "We had our entire future planned out."

"And now?"

She rolls one shoulder, and shrinks into herself. "And now...I have no idea what the future holds."

"Can I ask you a question?"

"I guess."

"You and me. Us." I point my finger back and forth between the two of us. "Here, this weekend. Is it still what you want this morning, now that you've had time to sleep on it?"

She grins. "It's not like I really slept, but yes, it is, and I'm sorry I brought up Cochrane. It's just you mentioned family, and kids."

Christ, I can't even stand to hear his name on her lips. I'm not sure what I'll do if she goes back to him, and I see them on campus together. I push that thought from my brain. "You'd be a good mom."

She bites into her toast and goes quiet, thoughtful, a little smile touching her lips as she recalls something from the past. "Did you ever have to do that project in high school where you take an egg home and have to care for it for a week. You know, like it was your baby."

I nod and remember the foster home I was in when I was assigned that project. Food was scarce and punishment was harsh. "Yeah, I remember that. I bet you made it through the whole week with that egg fully intact."

"I did. How did you make out?"

I rub my stomach. "I made scrambled eggs."

She stares at me for two long seconds, then breaks out in a belly laugh. "Did you really?"

Her laugh is contagious. "I was hungry."

"You're always hungry."

I lick my bottom lip, my gaze going to her nipples, which are poking against my white T-shirt that does little to hide her gorgeous body. "Yeah, I am," I agree, my hunger for food shifting to a hunger for her. My head lifts, and while I want to take her again, I also want to enjoy our time together outside of bed.

I stretch my arms above my head and she stares at my chest. "Do you have a lot of studying to do today?" I ask.

"I do, but first I thought we could take the kayaks out, and maybe later we can grab the rods and fish from the dock."

"Maybe I'll catch us a walleye for dinner. Toss it on the barbecue."

She smiles at me. "You're game?"

"You bet. I do have one small problem, though." I run my hands through my mess of hair, finger combing it into place as my dick twitches, and my mind races, recalling why it's a tangled mess in the first place. "I've never been in a kayak, and I've never fished." She claps her hands, delight stamped all over her face. "Why does that make you so happy?"

"I get to do a first with you, and don't worry, you're naturally athletic and it's pretty easy."

"I like easy."

She laughs at that and tosses the napkin back at me. "I am not easy."

"I am." I give a wiggle of my eyebrows, and she stands and shakes her head. While she might not be easy, and I wasn't suggesting she was, she is easy to be with.

"You've been with a lot of girls, haven't you?"

"Yeah." Shit, I'm not going to lie to her, but I don't want her to think she's just another notch on the bedpost. I take in the tightening of her body.

"Last night...was I any—"

"Jesus, Reagan. Don't do that. Don't compare yourself with anyone." I drag her into my arms, and brush her hair from her face. "Last night, and what you did for me earlier..." I put my hand beside my head and mimic an explosion. "Mind blowing."

She smiles, her worries easing. "Yeah? It was good for you?"

"Good? No, it was fucking great. I have never come so hard in my entire life. Everything in the way you trusted me with your body, the way you opened up for me, that was all new for me too, Reagan. Last night wasn't just a night of firsts for you." What I don't tell her is that sex with her was the best sex I ever had, and it's probably because I feel things for her that I have no right feeling—and had never felt for anyone else.

With a new lightness about her, she goes up on her toes and kisses me. "Such a sweet talker."

"I'm telling you the truth."

"Uh huh," she teases.

"I am," I say and whack her ass. She yelps and jumps back, a wide smile on her face, and I love that I was the guy who put it there.

"Come on, let's get outside and enjoy the sunshine."

"I'd rather take you back to bed, and enjoy you, Sunshine," I mumble under my breath.

"What was that?"

"Nothing." I toss the last of my breakfast into my mouth. We put our dishes in the sink, and get ready to enjoy our day. Reagan finds some suntan lotion, and after we're greased up, we head to the dock. The early morning sun glistens on the water as we drag the kayaks into the lake. Reagan gives me a quick lesson and I'm a fast learner, so I catch on quickly.

We paddle around the big lake, a comfortable silence between us as we lose ourselves in our own thoughts. We float and paddle until the sun is high in the sky. I have no idea what time it is or how long we've been out on the lake. We left our phones back at the cottage and I have to say, no communication with the real world is rather cathartic. A loud knocking sound ripples across the water, and I glance around.

"Over there." Reagan points and I follow the direction.

"What is it?"

"A woodpecker."

"Let's go see." We paddle toward it, the sound getting louder.

"It's a beautiful bird. Annoying as hell, though, especially at five in the morning, when it's banging against the satellite dish."

I laugh at that. "I'm guessing you're talking from experience."

"Oh yeah."

I take in a deep breath, filling my lungs with the morning air, and letting it relax every bone in my body.

"Nice, huh?" she asks.

"Peaceful."

"Rocco?"

"Yeah."

She comes up beside me. "Thanks for coming here with me."

"There's nowhere else I'd rather be," I tell her honestly. I glance around at the tall trees reflected in the water. "You should paint this."

"I should. It's gorgeous."

"Sanctuary." There's a long pause as I have an epiphany. "Hmm."

"What?"

I take in the peaceful view before me. "I never thought a wide-open space would give me the same feeling as the treehouse."

"Yeah." She smiles at me and we go quiet for a long time, just soaking it in, and letting it soothe our souls. A bird flies overhead and squawks, breaking the moment. "Want to race back in?" she asks.

"Depends."

"On what?"

I wag my eyebrows, and go into playful mode. "What does the winner get?"

She taps her chin. "How about this. If I win, and you lose, I get to do whatever I want with you for the next hour." She points to me. "If you win and I lose, you get to do whatever you want with me for the next hour."

"In no world would that be considered losing for me, Sunshine," I say and her soft laugh wraps around me and strokes my dick.

"You agree to the terms, then?"

"You bet I do." I start to paddle, but she dips the end of hers into the water and splashes me, throwing me off to get a head start. I swipe at my face as her laughter curls around me. "You're going to pay for that."

She's squealing when I catch up to her, and she tries to splash me again, but she's laughing so hard, having so much fun, she starts to wobble and loses her pace.

I pass her by. "See you on the dock, where I get to do all kinds of dirty things to you." My heart pounds a little harder. God, I love seeing her happy like this. I make it to the shore, jump out and drag my kayak up onto dry land. I walk to the end of the dock and stand there with a gloating, shit-eating grin on my face as I think about all the things my fingers and tongue are going to do to her. I shove my hands into my pockets, and admire everything about her—especially the pleasure on her face—as she paddles in.

She points to me. "You cheated."

"You're the one who cheated, not me." I lift my arms and flex my biceps. "It's these guns that gave me the edge," I joke, just to pull a laugh from her, and she rewards me with one. She drags her kayak ashore, and catching me by surprise, she comes running at me and jumps into my arms, her legs around my waist and arms around my neck. I slide my hands around her ass, and hold her to me as her lips find mine. She kisses me, deeply, and my body reacts the way it always does when she's near, or not near. I don't even want to think about how many times I've jacked off to fantasies with her in mind.

A groan filled with need crawls out of my throat, and her lips linger close to mine as she cups my cheeks and says, "I'm so glad you enjoyed kayaking."

"That's not what's making me moan, Sunshine." She chuckles, and it's so obvious that she loves toying with me. "I have to say, I love that we're the only two people in the world right now."

"I love it too."

I open my mouth about to say, *I love you,* but catch myself. What the hell? I guess I must be caught up in the moment, because love has no place in this situation. We have the weekend, not a future. I'd be wise to remember that.

I put my mouth close to her ear, worried she can read what I'm feeling on my face. "I won."

"That's because I let you."

I chuckle, and her body vibrates in my arms. "Is that because you want me to have my way with you?"

"I really like that you're a quick learner."

"What would you say to me stripping you right here on the dock and putting my cock in you?"

Her chest rises with a deep breath, and a flush of heat crawls up her neck. She blinks innocently at me and shrugs. "What can I say? I can't break the terms now, especially after I was the one who set them." Her legs slide down my body until she's standing, and my cock is so damn hard it's straining against my jeans. Tease that she is, she rubs against me, fully aware of my arousal.

"Take off your clothes," I growl.

She draws her bottom lip into her mouth and glances around. We're secluded. Unless someone on the other side of the lake has binoculars, no one can see us. I wouldn't let her strip if I thought there was a chance of anyone else seeing her. I don't want anyone other than me looking at her gorgeous body. She backs up and reaches for the hem of her T-shirt, ready to tug it off.

"Slow."

"Oh," she murmurs. "You want to watch, huh?"

"Yeah."

She wiggles her curvy hips and leisurely drags her shirt up over her stomach, chest and head. I growl with want, and she gives me a demure yet sexy smile in response. Two seconds later, her bra joins her shirt on the dock. She takes her gorgeous breasts into her hands and squeezes them together, and my cock jumps, aching to slide between her creamy cleavage. I am so going to fuck her tits.

"Nice..." I murmur.

She unbuttons her jeans and I rip into my pants, freeing my cock. She grins as I take my dick into my hand and stroke it. It's crazy how hard I am. We fucked last night and she sucked my cock this morning. Nevertheless, I can't get enough of her.

"You have the nicest tits. I might have to fuck them."

She gasps and wets her thumb to run it over one pebbled nipple, and I nearly shoot off in my hand. Turning slightly to shake her sweet ass at me, she kicks off her shoes, slides her tight pants to her feet, and tosses them away. Her fingers go to the band of her panties.

"Stop," I command softly, and she fully turns to me, and arches a questioning brow. I quickly close the distance between us, and slide my hand between her legs. Her heat scorches me, and I love finding her so hot and ready.

"I loved this sweet mouth of yours wrapped around my dick, but you know what I'm going to love even more?"

"What?" she asks, her voice breathless as my finger shapes her lips.

"My mouth." I tug her panties to the side, and push a finger into her. She gasps. "Right here."

16

REAGAN

"Rocco..." I murmur as he does the most amazing things with his fingers. He hits a spot inside me so sensitive, I nearly sink to my knees as pleasure gathers in my core. I briefly close my eyes as birds take flight in a nearby tree. I wasn't ready for sex before—and I am not about to examine that too closely at the moment—but now, I'm ready for everything and anything with Rocco. I want him to do whatever he wants to my body. Things I've never even heard of before.

"Feel good, Sunshine," he murmurs, and presses the butt of his palm to my clit. I move against his hand, shamelessly, ride him furiously. Being with him is freeing, and I like it. A lot.

"So good," I tell him, even though he already knows by the way I'm moving my body, sliding up and down his deft fingers.

"I want my mouth on you," he whispers.

"Yes please."

My response brings a chuckle to his lips, and I open my eyes, my breath catching at the desire and need in his eyes. I'm not sure any guy has ever looked at me the way Rocco does. His finger slides down my body, taking my panties, and I groan in protest when he inches back.

"Don't worry, babe. I'm going to take real good care of you. I promise you that."

He kicks off his pants, and I stand there naked, under the noonday sun, my body a hot, quivering mess of need as he lays our clothes out on the dock. My heart squeezes at his thoughtfulness. If I'm not careful here, I could fall for him and do the one thing Cochrane warned me against.

Would it be so bad to fall for Rocco? We're different people with different goals and different pasts, but here right now, we're the same, and who says we can't have a future?

Oh, just my parents, and society. I'm supposed to do the right thing, marry the right guy. Anything else—anything less—would reflect badly on the family name. The thing is, Rocco isn't...anything less. He's caring, gentle, and is constantly putting my needs first. He has a reputation, a bad one, and he's known to sleep around. Maybe he never shows anyone else the side he's showing me. I've certainly never shown anyone this sexual side of me before.

"You okay?"

I blink to bring myself back, and smile. "I am."

With the gentlest touch, he places his palm on my cheek. "If you don't want—"

"I want, Rocco," I say quickly. "I want this. I want you. I want you to..." My voice falls off.

"Don't be shy. Not with me, okay?"

"I want you to do everything to me."

His blue eyes darken with lust, and his chest rises, his breath suddenly labored. "What's everything, Reagan?"

"That's just it. I don't know. I was a virgin, remember?"

His eyes close for a brief second. They're full of raw lust when they open. "Fuck, like I could ever forget that."

He steps closer, and the intimacy in his touch, combined with the fact that we're both comfortable being naked around each other, sends a new, unfamiliar kind of warmth through my blood. It leaves me lightheaded, almost giddy with joy. I put my hand on his chest, needing the contact. His fast heartbeat matches mine.

"Is there something you'd like to do to me?"

"Christ, Reagan. I want to take you five hundred different ways and make you orgasm a thousand times before this weekend is over." A hard quake racks my body. He reaches out, squeezes my breasts together. "I want to fuck you here, and shoot my cum into your mouth."

I gasp, my nipples hardening beneath his touch. "I...I'd like that too."

"I want you underneath me, on top of me. Jesus, I want you bent over the bed, your hands tied, while I put my cock into this sweet hot cunt of yours."

"Ohmigod."

He grins at me, my shock a dead giveaway that I want all the dirty things he mentioned and all the dirty talking.

"There we go, now we're getting somewhere," he says, and puts his hand between my legs. "I want my tongue inside you. I want you to come all over my mouth." I just stare, my voice lodged somewhere in my throat. "Lay down," he commands in a soft voice. "Spread your legs and show me your sweet pussy, so I can do all the things I want to you."

My legs are wobbly as I walk to the pile of clothes and drop down. I spread my legs wide for him, offering myself up completely, putting my body in his talented hands.

"I'm the luckiest fucking guy in the world," he murmurs, and it sends a thrill through me. With a simple look, a few simple words, he makes me feel worshipped, like I'm the most important woman in the world—to him. At the moment, I don't care if he says the same thing to all the girls he takes to bed. I just want to bask in what we're sharing this weekend.

He drops to his knees, the sun warming our bodies as he leans forward and swipes his tongue over my clit. All the dirty talk has me so turned on, I nearly climax. I don't want to. Not yet. I want this to last forever. He flattens himself on the dock and slides his hands under my ass, bringing my pussy to his mouth for a feast, and feast he does.

He licks and sucks and puts his tongue into me until I'm writhing and calling out his name. It echoes across the water, and can undoubtedly be heard by the neighbors, if they're near the lake. I simply don't care. Not when it's this good. He slides a finger into me, touches that sensitive bundle of nerves and just like that I break.

"Rocco," I call out, my fast orgasm taking him by surprise, judging by the widening of his eyes as he tilts his head to see my face, his mouth still between my legs, drinking me in like he can't get enough. I know the feeling. He stays between my legs, lightly licking me as my body continues to spasm and pulse in the most glorious way. I usually have to work much harder than this for an orgasm—especially with—nope, not going to think of him.

"Babe, you were so needy."

"I know, that's what you do to me."

He grins and slides up my body. "I like that, you know. I also love the taste of you. I'm going to fuck you right now, but I'm definitely getting my mouth on your sweet cunt again."

"You like the taste of me?"

"Fucking love it."

His lips glisten, and I put my hands around his head to draw his mouth to mine. I kiss him deeply, tasting my release on his tongue. I moan, and his body vibrates. He presses into me, his cock hard against my thigh. I crave the taste of him, am about to ask if I can have him in my mouth again, when he inches back. I pull him back to me, needing the physical contact, needing skin on skin.

"Condom. Pants."

He scrambles to pull a condom from his pants and I grin. "What makes me think you had this planned all along?"

"When it comes to you, Reagan, I'm not taking a chance that I'm not prepared. When you want sex, you get sex."

"You want it too, right?" It's a silly question. His erection tells me everything. But I want to hear him say it.

"I've wanted you for a long time, Sunshine."

His words give me pause as he rips into the condom, and as he rushes to sheathe himself, I'm pretty sure he's not aware of what he just admitted to me.

He's wanted me for a long time.

I want to ask how long. The first night he showed up at my place? Or our freshman year when he'd follow me home to ensure I was safe? My heart beats a little faster, and I close my eyes, warm and needy sensations fluttering in my stomach.

He's back on top of me, and I open my eyes to see his face. The second I do, I know I could be in big trouble here. I'm falling for him. I'm falling for bad boy Rocco Gianni and there isn't a goddamn thing I can do about it. Honestly, even if I could, I'm not sure I want to do anything about it. It's insane, really. Up until yesterday, I had a future planned with another guy.

Rocco lays over me and in one swift motion, rolls me until I'm on top of him. "Ooh, I like this," I murmur, my nipples brushing his chest.

"I want you to fuck me, Reagan."

With zero effort, he picks me up and poises me over his thick cock. Controlling the pace, he pulls me down and I can't breathe, can't think, as his crown pushes me wide open. "Rocco," I cry out, a roller coaster of emotions tearing through me.

"Look at me, Sunshine."

I open my eyes, and his are locked on mine as he allows one inch and then another to slowly enter until he fills me completely. My body opens for him, takes everything he's offering, and once he's thoroughly seated within me, my pussy stretched tight around him, he lets my waist go and puts his hands on my tits.

I sit up a little straighter and close my hands over his, rubbing with him, and reveling in the soft moans of want spilling from his lips. I shift, move my hips a little, and his moans grow louder.

"Like that, do you?" I ask.

"Uh huh."

I move, and lift myself slightly, only to fall back down again, and his face twists in total agony. It's fun discovering his likes too.

"Babe," he murmurs. "Babe, fuck."

Hands back on my hips, he holds me down hard and lifts his hips like he's trying to get in deeper. I love it. He lifts me high, until he's almost out, and powers into me. I gasp, but no sound escapes my lips as he hits my cervix, nearly giving me a full body orgasm, something I've only ever read about, and would really, really like to experience.

"Again," I cry out, and he repeats the motions until I'm delirious and unable to form a coherent thought. Every time he pulls me down, my clit smashes against his body, and deep in my core, an orgasm builds, grows, expands, until I'm panting and begging, blinking tears from my eyes. "More."

He continues to drive into me, hard blunt strokes meant for pleasure only. I cup my breasts, and pinch my nipples, sending shockwaves to my sex. "Rocco," I call out, my body letting go. I tumble into an orgasm, the world around me disappearing as I sink into bliss, nothing existing but this guy, and all the wonderment coursing through my body.

"I love...watching you come," he groans.

The breaking in his voice is a good indication that he's not as together as he's trying to portray. His jaw is clenched tight. He's giving it his best effort to hold off until I've ridden out the waves of pleasure.

"Fill me with your cum," I say and his fingers dig into my hips as he goes still high inside me. I concentrate on each hard pulse as he depletes into his condom. I really wish we didn't have the barrier. I wish I could feel the heat of his release in my body.

With his cock still inside me, I fall over him, find his mouth. His hands go around me, one on my back, and one on my head as he kisses me, his mouth practically devouring me like a man starved. The kiss ends and I lay my head on his chest. We stay like that a long time, holding one another, basking in our post-orgasmic bliss as he grows flaccid inside me.

He breaks the quiet. "I need to get rid of the condom."

I chuckle. "Are you saying I have to move?"

"Sorry babe, we can't take a chance on it slipping off."

I groan in protest but lift myself off, and a quiver goes through me as he slides from my body. I reach for my shirt and tug it on, then gather up the rest of our clothes as I follow him inside. He makes a fast trip to the bathroom, and he's gloriously naked and beautiful when he steps out.

As I take him in, his grin, the playfulness in his eyes, his big hands that touched me so gently, worry worms through me. How am I ever going to go back to being the good daughter, Reagan Ellison, after Rocco?

ROCCO

I love being here with her, in her world, experiencing life as she knows it. I'm pretty sure I've never been so content in my entire life. I glance at her sitting on the dock beside me, her hair tied back, her face free of makeup, fishing rod in hand as our feet dangle over the water.

"Did you fish a lot when you were a kid?"

She turns and smiles at me. My heart beats faster. She's so goddamn beautiful and every now and then I pinch myself to see if I'm really here with her or if this is just some dream. If it is, I'm not ready to wake up.

"Yeah. Dad always enjoyed it. It was our time together, actually." She gives me a wink. "I think he might have wanted a son."

"That's really nice, Reagan. I'm so glad you have such good memories."

She reels her line in, and casts it out again, the shiny red lure banging against the bobber before sinking below the surface.

"Do you have any good memories from your childhood?" she asks, her voice low, almost hesitant.

"I don't really remember my mom. I can't recall her face, you know. There are times though, when I catch this specific floral scent..." I stop speaking for a second as emotions clog my throat.

Reagan's hand on mine soothes the demons inside me, gives me the courage to continue. "That scent, and I have no idea what it was...it fills me up." I laugh. "I'm not saying that right, I know. I've never been great with words."

"You're great with words. Don't underestimate yourself."

I grin. "I think those were happy times for me. There's a sense of peace that comes over me. I felt loved."

"That's nice, Rocco."

"Yeah. I'm wrong, though. If she loved me, why would she leave me?"

"I don't know. I wish I could answer that. I guess your dad never told you why."

"Oh yeah, he did. From the time I could talk, he said it was because of me that she left."

She winces. "What a horrible thing to say to a boy. You know that can't be true."

"I don't know what's true, and I'm not even sure I care anymore."

She goes quiet. We both know I still care. "Postpartum can be very hard on women. Did she have parents to go to?"

"I don't know that either. She left, and we never heard from her again. My father never talked about me having grandparents. I just assumed I didn't." I stare at my bobber, and it disappears into the water. Reagan shrieks and shimmies closer.

"You got one. Give a quick tug and reel it in." I do as she says, and she watches excitedly as I reel the fish in. "It's a gorgeous walleye." She nudges me. "Look at you, and all the beginner's luck."

"Not luck, Sunshine. This kid got talent."

"Yeah, you do," she agrees playfully, and leans to kiss me on the cheek as I set the squirming trout on the dock.

"Now we take the hook out, and I can teach you to clean it."

I'm a tough-ass football player, yet as I sit here and look at the fish, the thoughts of killing, and cleaning it, turns my stomach.

"Reagan..."

I lift my head, and find her eyes. I frown. "Maybe we can just take something out of the freezer for dinner." She stares at me long and hard, so long and hard, I'm sure she's going to ask me to hand over my man card, and rightfully so. What she does next takes me by surprise, and tests the strength of my heart as it swells inside my chest.

She throws her arms around me, and holds me to her, her grip tight, like she's never going to let go, never going to go back to the life she was meant to live. I can't think that way though. She's not mine. She never will be. Deep inside, I know I'm not good enough for her.

"Can I tell you a secret?" she whispers into my ear.

"Yeah."

"I never liked killing and cleaning them, either." She settles on my lap, unhooks the fish and gently puts it back in the lake. She turns back to me and slides her arms around my neck. "I love that you don't want to do it, either."

I swear to God, I never felt as close to anyone as I do to Reagan right now. She lightly runs her lips over mine, and her sweet scent fills my senses. "We can see what's in the freezer, and I can drive to the grocery store down the road to get us some fresh veggies for a salad."

"I'll come with you." I hug her to me. "Actually, I'll go. You stay here and get to work on your stats assignment, and if you have trouble, I'll help when I get back."

She pouts at me and it's so goddam adorable, it almost makes me take her again, right here on the dock. "You don't want me to go?"

"You know I do, but you have to get at your stats assignment. You're not going to fail because of me."

She groans. "I hate stats."

"Someday it will come in handy."

She rolls her eyes at me. "Sure, Dad." I kiss her and laugh. "Do you even know where to find the store?"

"I can figure it out. Just make a list of what you need."

I push to my feet and help her up and she goes up on her toes and kisses me. "Fine, but don't be long."

"You going to miss me, Sunshine?"

"There are wild animals in these woods, Rocco."

"The only thing wild you have to worry about around here is me."

She laughs at that. "You might be right."

We take our rods and head back up to the cottage. Inside, I pull her to me as a strange uneasy feeling mushrooms inside me. I have great gut instincts. I had to in order to survive. Something is off here. Something isn't right. I just can't quite put my finger on it.

"You're okay here alone, right? You were kidding about the wild animals?"

"I'm not afraid." Her face twists. "Not much, anyway. But I'll stay inside until you get back. I'll work on my assignment."

I hesitate for a second and she puts her hands on my chest. "Let me make that list for you."

I pick up my phone from the kitchen table. We haven't used them since we've been here. Reception sucks big time. I want mine with me though, in case she needs me for something. She jots a few things down on a piece of paper and reaches for her purse.

"I got this," I tell her, and for a second she looks like she's about to protest. Instead she nods and heads to the freezer.

"Steak sound good?"

"Perfect."

I head out to her car and come to a complete stop. What the hell happened here? "Reagan," I call out. "Can you come here?"

She comes through the front door, and I point at her flat tire, and that uneasy feeling curls through me again.

"Oh great." She comes bounding over and groans, her hands on her hips, like she's in deep thought. "Let me grab my phone, I'll call our car service."

I grin at her. "No, I got this."

She blinks at me. "You can fix a flat?"

I bend down, and run my hand over the tire, until I find the nail. I tug it out. "We picked up a nail."

She nods, not at all surprised. "Happened to Dad this summer, too. There was some construction on one of the cottages."

The tightness in my chest loosens. At least someone hadn't done it on purpose. I shake my head. My mind always goes to the worst-case scenario.

"Dad put a repair kit in my car in case it happened to me, and I couldn't get cell service." She snorts. "Not that I'd know how to repair it myself." I open the back of her car and I'm relieved to see all the equipment I need to repair it.

"It's time you learned."

At first, I think she's going to protest. She doesn't. Instead she nods, and says, "You're right. I should know these things."

That's my girl.

I nod and keep my smile to myself. This girl is tougher than she even realizes. "You taught me to kayak and fish, now I'm going to teach you some life skills."

She sidles up to me like a damn sex-kitten, puts her arms around me, and presses her hand to my cock. "That's not all you've taught me."

My dick swells.

Easy, boy.

I growl to let her know just how much I want her. She always seems to like that. "I plan to teach you more of that, but first this, food, and studying."

"Killer of fun."

I laugh at her playfulness. "You'll be eating those words later, Sunshine."

"Okay, teach me."

I grab the jack from the back of the car and show her how to position it and lift the vehicle. Once that's done, I use the lug wrench to remove the lug nuts.

"That's not so hard."

I nod in agreement. "You're right, it's not."

"Are you going to put the spare on?"

"At first I was." I pull out a plugging tool. "Until I found this." I grab the plugging tool, and position the plug on the end. "This will plug it, and you'll be able to ride on it until it's convenient for you to get a new one. This could hold forever though."

"Oh, nice."

"This is a rasp," I tell her, and shove it into the nail hole to make it round. I push it in and out, until it's smooth and round. "Now we plug it." I shove the plug in fast, and when I pull the tool out, the plug stays.

"I'm impressed."

"You should be," I tease. "Now see, this is an electric air pump. We hook it up to the auxiliary power source in the dash, and pump up the tire."

"You're a man of many talents, my friend."

I wink at her. "Maybe I'll teach you to pick a lock someday."

"You know how?"

"With my eyes closed." She laughs and I add, "It's not really something to be proud of."

"Maybe not, but not many people in my world have the life skills you do. Cochrane..." She winces, and I frown. For a guy we're not supposed to talk about, she sure brings him up a lot. It shouldn't leave a sour taste in my mouth. I'm not normally a betting man, but if I was, I'd lay down money on her going back to him after our month. I'm not really privy to parental pressure. Most foster parents didn't give a fuck what I did, as long as I left them alone so they could collect their check. I won't judge her choices. I just think she could do better, and I would love to see her take charge of her own life.

I show her where to find the auxiliary power, and she watches as I pump up the tire and check it for leaks. Once done, I pack all the equipment and put it away. I turn to find her smiling at me.

"That's probably way more important to learn than stats!"

I put my arm around her, drag her in for a kiss. "Nah, you have a car service, remember?"

She waves her hands around. "Not out here."

"I guess you were lucky you brought me with you, then."

"Yeah, *lucky* is the word." She gives me a sexy grin, and I get exactly what she's referring to.

I slap her ass. "Get in there and study and I'll be back soon."

She pouts and drags her feet as she walks away. I get in the car and start it, waving to her as I head out the long gravel road. I check my phone and drive to the nearest grocery store. I stock up, grabbing real milk for coffee, eggs for breakfast, and once again, that uneasy feeling is back in my stomach as I walk to her car. I check my phone, not that I expect a message from Reagan, not with the shit cell service.

I go a little faster on the way back, wavering around the speed limit. My muscles are tight and ready, and I don't like the fight or flight reaction I'm having. I drive fast down the gravel road, dust kicking up behind her car, and I slam the brakes on the second I see a very familiar Mustang in her driveway.

"Motherfucker.'

I slam the car into park, and jump from the seat. The driveway is full of dust, a good indication that they just got here. Three guys exit the Mustang, and with arms folded, form a wall—a shaky wall. I recognize them from the rowing team.

"Get out of my way," I seethe through clenched teeth. One guy shakes a bit, and I'm pretty sure he just pissed his pants. A bang sounds from inside the cottage and I charge, pushing through the guys. "Reagan," I call out.

Cochrane steps out from the cottage, a cocky grin on his face.

Keep it together, Rocco. Today is not a good day to kill someone.

I try to see past him, but he's blocking the door. "Where's Reagan?" I growl, my hands fisted at my sides. I want to punch him in the face, but she's my first concern at the moment.

"I'm here." She comes running out, sounding breathless, her eyes big, worried. Her hands are twisted together, and my entire body goes tight.

I swear to God, if he laid one hand on her, he's a dead man. "Are you okay?" I ask.

She nods at me, but Dick takes a step forward, showing possession as he blocks her from my view and folds his arms. "What she is, is none of your business."

"How is it your business?" I ask. "After you gave her to me in exchange for payment, and cheated on her, how the fuck is she any of your business?"

He looks past my shoulder and nods. As he starts toward me, I angle my head to see his goons closing the distance. I harden myself, prepare. This is a road I've been down before.

"Cochrane, don't." Reagan's voice is full of fear and panic, and it snaps at me—pulls me back to my senses. She grabs Cochrane's arm to try to stop him. He shrugs her off—doesn't hurt her. Christ, if he had, he'd be a dead man. I stare at him and all I can see is red.

"Don't touch her again," I warn in a calm voice that belies that rage.

Cochrane is about to say something to me. Reagan speaks first. "Please don't." Her eyes plead with Cochrane, plead with me, and the beast inside me settles—for her.

No way am I going to have her frightened like this. I need to deescalate this situation and I need to do it now. Not because I'm afraid of an unfair fight. I've been in many of them. But because I can't stand to see Reagan upset. This isn't fair to her. None of this was fair to her. Not Cochrane using her for payment, nor me moving into her place.

"It's okay, Reagan." I try to reassure her in my best calm voice. "Nothing is going to happen here."

Dick grins, like he's won the battle, and he might have. I'll give him this one.

He takes another threatening step toward me, like he's not going to let this go. He's a brave man when he has his friends backing him up. I angle my body, prepared, although fighting in front of Reagan is the last thing I want.

"Why are you here?" I ask.

"She wasn't answering my texts and I figured she might be here. I can't understand why you're here."

"She's mine for the month. Or did you forget that, Cochrane? Did you forget you gave her to me?"

"I never should have—"

"Too late for that."

"I'm going to get the money." He looks at Reagan. "I'll get the money and fix this."

I fold my arms. "Until then, she's all mine."

His nostrils flare. "She's not yours...not like that. She's saving that for me, and I'm going to get her back."

"Is that why you threw it in her face last night outside of Wolf House?"

I glance at Reagan, waiting for her direction, her guidance. I won't say anything she doesn't want me to say. I won't tell him that she's already given her most precious possession to me, and make life hard for her.

"He was...helping me with my stats," she explains quickly.

Cochrane snorts, and his friends all laugh. "What does he know about stats? He won the card game because he cheated."

I stand my ground. "You and I both know that's a lie. If anyone cheats, it's you." Cochrane hates it. He fucking hates it that I'm smarter than he is. Do I take pleasure in that? It's quite possible that I do.

"Just go, Cochrane. Please." Reagan blinks rapidly, and I itch to run to her, to pull her into my arms, but that won't help anything right now. I need Cochrane gone.

Cochrane glares at me before slowly turning to Reagan. "Not until you agree to come back and talk to me. Let me explain everything."

She nods quickly, her chin quivering, fat tears right there at the surface. How can Cochrane stand to see her like this? If he cared for her at all, he wouldn't do this.

"No," I snap. "We had an agreement. She's mine, and she doesn't have to talk to you. Not if she doesn't want to."

"She'll want to."

"Why don't we leave that up to her? This isn't you demanding, this is her deciding."

He grins and turns to Reagan. "Will you talk to me?"

"Yes," she complies so quickly, it nearly knocks the wind out of me. "Whatever you want. Just go. I don't want a fight."

My heart thumps. Fuck. She didn't have to agree to that. Not for me. I can take these guys, and if I can't, I'll take the beating to save her from having to cave to any of douche bag's demands. Then again, maybe she wants to talk to him. Maybe it has nothing to do with me. As those old doubts and insecurities rip through me, Cochrane gives a humorless laugh.

"He's not who you think he is, Reagan."

"Cochrane, please, just go," she begs.

"Whatever he's told you. Whatever he's said to you. It's all a lie. He's a lie. Everything about him is a lie." His eyes narrow in on Reagan. "Tell me you didn't fall for any of his bullshit."

"I...didn't."

I clench down on my jaw so hard, I nearly break a bone. I take a small step toward him. A cry rises in Reagan's throat, and I go still.

Cochrane steps down off the deck and stands directly in front of me. Tension fills the air. "I'll get the money, and you can go fuck yourself." His voice is low, threatening, meant for my ears only.

I lower my voice to match his. "A deal is a deal. You gave her to me, and there is no changing the terms now. Keep your fucking money."

For a second, I think he's going to throw a punch. Instead, he snarls something under his breath, his body brushes mine as he steps around me, a winning grin on his face. I close my eyes to keep my shit together. I open them to find Reagan staring at me, relief on her face.

"See you later, Reagan. I look forward to our talk. Make it soon, or you'll be sorry. You both will be."

The car doors slam shut behind me, and it takes every ounce of strength to hold myself in check. The way Reagan is hugging herself helps me with that. I stand still until they drive away and then I rush up the stairs and pull Reagan into my arms.

"Are you okay?"

"I...don't think so."

18

REAGAN

I take in the hardness in his eyes, the untethered hatred living there. "What did he whisper to you?"

He rubs my arms and shakes his head. "Nothing important."

I take deep gulping breaths and try to hold it together. I hate conflict, absolutely hate it. Yet ever since the night Cochrane handed me to Rocco to cover his payment, I've been faced with a lot of it. Earlier I ran out the door, thinking Rocco was back, that something else was wrong with my car, only to find Cochrane and his four buddies pulling up. My heart nearly burst clear from my chest. He'd only just gotten here, and he immediately started questioning me on why I'd ran away to the cottage. I guess he conveniently forgot about all the vile things he said last night. A hard quake moves through me at the memories. I was too dumbfounded to answer, so he started in on where my car was, when Rocco showed up. I wasn't sure whether that was a good thing or a bad thing. Stupid tears fill my eyes, and a ridiculous choking sound catches in my throat.

"It's okay," Rocco says. "Nothing bad is going to happen to you."

"I…I was worried about you." I sniff, and my tears soak his T-shirt. I glance up at him, hating that I'm probably all swollen and puffy. "I didn't tell him we were sleeping together. Not because I didn't want him to know, but because it was four against one and I didn't want to see you hurt."

"I wasn't worried about me. I was worried about you." His voice is deep and rough, like he's trying to calm the storm inside him—inside me.

"I only agreed to talk to him to get him to leave."

"Reagan," he cups my cheeks and wipes the tears from my face. "Fuck." He pulls me against him, and I instantly find comfort in his strong heartbeat.

"I'm sorry."

"You don't need to be sorry. Cochrane's the one who should be apologizing. He never should have shown up here and put you in a situation where you felt forced to agree to his terms."

"He wants me back."

His body goes so tight, it worries me. "Can't blame him."

"He always gets what he wants, Rocco. Somehow or some way, he always gets what he wants."

I lift my head, take in the anger on his face. Blue eyes full of murder latch onto mine. My heart speeds up, a new kind of fear careening through my blood. "Don't go after him."

The tight muscles on his jaw ripple. "I'm not afraid of him."

"You should be. We both should be." He doesn't speak, which frightens me all the more. "Please, Rocco. Don't go after him.

Don't do anything to get yourself in trouble. I don't want you to lose your scholarship. None of this is worth that."

He mumbles under his breath, something that sounds like, "You're worth it." He drops a kiss onto my head, his strength wrapping around me, a security blanket I never want to leave. He continues to hold me until I stop shaking, and says, "I'd better get the groceries from the car."

"Okay."

I stare after him, my body cold at the loss of his heat. He walks slowly, like he's trying to gather his thoughts and pull himself together. My heart continues to crash as he scoops up the bags, carries them inside and drops them on the counter. With his back to me, his shoulders tight, he stays quiet as he unloads them.

"I got everything on the list." He turns to me and holds up a sketch pad. "I found this." He gives a casual shrug, like it's nothing. It's not nothing to me. It tells me how thoughtful he is, that he was thinking of me while we were apart, that he's encouraging my hobby, my passion. I can't find the words to tell him how much I appreciate it, and decide they're not needed.

"You probably brought one with you." He frowns. "It was stupid."

I step up to him, go up on my toes and put my arms around him. I press my lips to his, and he's hesitant. "Maybe this..." He takes a sharp breath. "I don't know..." He pauses as he tears his gaze from my face and glances around the posh cottage. "...is all stupid too."

"Don't." I kiss him again. It's possible he's right. What we're doing here is stupid and reckless and damaging. I cup his head and bring his lips back to mine. He groans into my mouth, and I taste the rage in his body on the tip of his tongue.

"Reagan...I don't think."

"I want to." Eyes filled with uncertainty meet mine, and I try to make light of it and say, "You once told me you either fuck or fight, and since you still contain all the rage inside of you—to protect me—I suggest you take it out on me."

"I'd never take my rage out on you. I'd never do anything to hurt you." His palm on my face is so gentle, wraps around my heart and squeezes so hard, I'm not sure it's something I'll ever be able to come back from. I don't know what tomorrow brings, but today, it's just us. "You know that, don't you?"

I nod. "I do, Rocco, and I can honestly tell you that I have never wanted anything or anyone more than I want you at this moment."

His chest rises and falls rapidly. "You should have what you want." I smile at him and he picks me up, setting me on the kitchen island. "Bedroom. Too. far." I laugh as he talks all caveman-like but it turns to a moan when his mouth finds mine, a little rougher than he's ever been before as he channels all his energy into fucking me.

"Take me, Rocco. Take me hard."

"Fuck, Reagan," he growls, and deepens the kiss, ravaging my mouth as he slides his hands under my T-shirt to cup my breasts. He tugs my bra cups down, freeing my aching breasts and he pinches my nipples.

"Just like that," I tell him. My encouraging words send him spiraling, and the next thing I know, I'm flat out on the kitchen island, and his blue eyes are blazing with raw hunger as he roughly tugs my yoga pants to my ankles. There's a new need, new fierceness about him, going at me like it could very well be our last time. I can't think about that right now, though. Right now, all I can do is lose myself in this man.

He tosses my pants away and reaches over his back to tear his shirt clear from his body. I admire his scarred nakedness, and my body reacts to the rugged male before it. I reach for him. "Fuck me, Rocco. Fuck me hard."

He grabs my legs and drags me to the end of the island. They dangle over and he spreads them, taking a good hard look at my sex, wide open and ready for him to do anything he wants to me. The rough pad of his thumb scrapes over my clit, and I put my hand on my mouth to stifle a scream.

"Hands by your sides," he commands and it surprises me. He wants me to scream, wants me to give myself to this every bit as much as he is. He circles my sopping wet clit, and bends to take it between his teeth.

"God, yesssss," I cry out and he grunts his approval.

One thick finger finds its way inside of me and I grip the edges of the island. "Legs over my shoulders," he orders, and I lift my shaky legs, doing as he asked.

He finger-fucks me on the kitchen island and I stare at the ceiling as it spins around me. A second finger joins the first for a snug fit, and he whips at my clit with the sharp blade of his tongue. Heat races through me, grips my core, and pleasure deepens between my legs until I'm coming all over his face.

"Rocco," I cry out. Intense pleasure engulfs me and I barely hold myself up by my elbows to watch what he's doing to me.

The sight of him between my legs, licking, finger-fucking me, is the hottest thing I've ever seen.

His head lifts and my juices glisten on his chin. My eyes meet those of a wild animal, ready to ravage, and my heart beats faster, ready to be his victim.

"You want to fuck?" he asks.

"Yes."

He lightly strokes me. "You want me to ruin this gorgeous pussy?"

"I do."

He angles his head. "You sure about that, Reagan? You sure you want me to ruin this pussy for any other guy?"

I gulp air, and hiss the word, "Yessss."

He stands there for one second, then another, and I fear he's going to walk right out the door. What he does instead sends heat charging through me. He pulls me up into a sitting position, drags me off the counter, and presses his lips to mine, keeping his protective arms around me to keep me upright. His kisses are hard, brutal, but beneath his roughness there is something that curls around my heart and rips my soul wide open. I'm falling for this guy. Hard.

"My pussy," I moan. "It's all yours, Rocco. I think it's always been yours. That very first day you followed me home from campus, watched over me, I was yours."

He turns me, my back to his chest, and slides one hand around to the front of my throat, and pulls my head back until it's pressed against his chest. His breath is warm on my ear when he whispers, "You're fucking mine, Reagan."

"I'm yours, Rocco."

He buries his face in my hair, and I reach around to touch him. He pushes his cock against me, and I wiggle, begging for him to fuck me. He grips my T-shirt and tugs it over my head, and with a fast movement, removes my bra. I stand there, my back to him, completely naked, completely open.

"These are mine," he growls and takes my breasts into his hands, squishing them all to hell.

I draw a shaky breath as he brands me with the heat of his hands. How could there possibly be another after Rocco? "Yours."

He takes my hands and places them on the island, and I stand there, every nerve in my body alive as my harsh breathing mingles with the sound of his zipper releasing. Hands that could hurt so easily, press against my back until my breasts are pressed against the island, my nipples so hard, I'm sure I'm going to score the countertop.

I whimper when he taps his cock against my ass cheek. "You want this?"

"I do. I want it. I've always wanted it and I'll always want it."

He teases me some more, lightly running the crown over my ass, leaving dampness behind. "Please, Rocco. Take me. Own me. Ruin me."

Soft curses reach my ear, followed by a condom opening. Strong, yet warm hands grip my ass cheeks and he spreads me, opening my drenched sex up for him.

"Mine," he growls and in one fast thrust, he's deep inside me, pushing all the air from my lungs and leaving me gasping for breath. "This what you want, Sunshine."

"It's everything I want."

He pulls almost all the way out, and drives in, hard blunt strokes that give equal amounts of pleasure and pain. I don't tell him about the pain. I want to feel everything with this guy.

He curls one hand around my waist, the other on my back, holding me against the counter. "You are so tight and hot."

His hips move, piston forward as he drives his thick cock in and out of me at a pace that zaps all my synapses. There is no way I can even think. Hell, I can't even breathe.

"Yes, yes, yes," is the only word in my vocabulary so I continue to repeat it. He curls into me, his warmth sizzling through my body and I claw at the island countertop as a powerful orgasm rips through me.

"Jesus," he moans, as my muscles clench hard around him. "I'm there, babe."

I gulp for breath. "Let me feel you."

He hands hold my hips impossibly tighter, and I cry his name with each hard pulse in my body. His groans fill the room, and he collapses over me, peppering wet, hot, open-mouthed kisses to my back. They seep into my skin and curl around my heart.

He inches back, his cock sliding from my body. He pulls me up with him, and I turn to face him. He cups my cheek and his lips find mine.

"Did I hurt you?" he asks, worry lacing his voice.

"No."

"Liar."

I chuckle. "It's what I wanted, and it's what you needed."

"How do you know what I need, Sunshine?"

"Because we're more alike than either of us ever knew."

I grip the steering wheel and cast a glance at Reagan. She's fiddling with the sketchbook on her lap, curling the pages and trying not to look nervous. The effort is wasted on me. Cochrane showing up at the cottage yesterday and making demands upset her. Here I thought I couldn't hate him more. She never should have been involved in the first place, and it does beg the question, once they talk, will he convince her to go back with him, under some mistaken obligation that lives inside her, or will she stay with me?

"Because we're more alike than either of us ever knew."

The words she said after I fucked her on the counter ring in my ears. Are they true? Does she really believe that? There's one thing I do know. Reagan and me, we've come to a certain place together, and while I told her she was mine, I'm pretty sure I'm kidding myself—she was never mine to begin with. Yesterday she also told me I should be afraid of Cochrane, and in a way, I am. He and Reagan have a long history, and he can hurt me through her. That's the power he has over me. I can't tell her what to do. I won't. I just hope she realizes who he is and who he isn't, and what should be held onto and what should be let go. It's not an easy thing to learn. I held the belief that my father would change. That he would rescue me from foster care. It took years for me to learn it was harder holding onto that belief than letting it go.

I reach across the seat, and take her hand in mine. "You okay?"

She gives me a feeble smile. "Yeah, you?"

She's not okay. Neither am I. "You know you don't have to talk to him if you don't want to." She doesn't need for me to say that and maybe I'm only doing it because I want her to tell me she doesn't want to see him, that she hates him as much as I do. But she has feelings for him. How could she not? They've been together for years.

She gave herself to you, Rocco.

This is all so fucked up on so many levels, and I never should have started something with her that I couldn't finish. The only thing that can come from this is hurt and loss. The story of my fucking life.

"It's okay. I'll be okay." Her voice is quiet and I'm not sure if she's trying to convince me of that, or herself.

"Do you want me to go with you?"

She frowns and rips at the paper. "I don't think that's a good idea."

"Doesn't matter. If you want me there, I'm there. Just say the word."

She puts her hand over mine. "You're the sweetest."

I laugh. "Don't tell that to the guys in Burnside. They'd give me a Burnside beating to pound that shit out of me."

Her smile is so soft, so full of warmth, I once again wonder what the fuck I'm doing.

"Do you ever go back? To visit?"

"No. I cut ties with the place a long time ago. Most of my friends from back in the day, I think they're still there. We're all different now." I go quiet for a long time, then add, "It's hard to get out."

"You got out."

"I got out through the foster care system." I stare straight ahead, and flick my signal on to pass a car. "It wasn't always easy, but I guess it was a blessing in disguise. Who knows where I'd be or what I would have become?"

"I think no matter what, you would have made something of yourself, Rocco."

I grin at her, loving her belief in me. I haven't had a lot of that over the years. "You think?"

"You're the strongest guy I know, and have an inner drive I envy."

"You're the strong one, Reagan."

A sound of disbelief crawls out of her throat. "No, I'm not. I fold to what everyone expects of me. I'm the good girl who always does the right thing."

I go quiet again and visualize what it was like for her growing up with her parents, her life always under the microscope. "Funny, your life was spent following rules, and mine was spent breaking them."

She settles her hands over her sketchbook. "Like you once said, no matter rich or poor, everyone has problems, just different problems. That's pretty insightful, Rocco."

I grin. "That's me, insightful." I grip the steering wheel tighter, and hate with everything in me that she's not living her dreams. "I like your father, and I get that your parents only want what's best for you, and I get that's hard, Reagan. I really do." I'm not going to try to talk her into going against what was ingrained in her, her whole life. It's her fight, and it's not my place to do that. I don't want her to resent me in any way. It comes down to this, I was good at football, but I wouldn't be on the football field, headed for a career in the NFL, if I didn't dig deep and fight for it. You have to fight for what you want. It has to come from within.

"Rocco?"

"Yeah?"

"What do you think Cochrane meant when he said we'd both be sorry?"

I shrug. "He can't do anything to me." For the last few days, I've been telling myself that, but now, after Reagan told me he's a guy who gets what he wants, and knowing she's my weakness, I'm not so sure. One thing I do know. If he hurts Reagan to get to me, he's a dead man.

"Yeah, you're probably right, and I don't know what he could possibly to do me other than..."

Her words fall off and she turns her head to look out the passenger side window. "You can't leave me hanging like that, Sunshine."

"I just don't want him to hurt you."

I bring her hand to my mouth and kiss it as my heart thumps against my chest. "I like that you're worried about me, but you don't have to be."

We both go quiet, lost in our own thoughts as we drive home. I pull off the expressway and get behind an elderly couple out for a Sunday drive. I make light of it and ask, "Think that'll be us someday? Two old folks with nothing to do but take a Sunday drive down memory lane."

She laughs. "Yeah, except we'll be on that old bike you love, I'm sure."

"Don't you dare diss my bike." I tug my hand from hers and feign hurt.

"Oh, come on, you can't honestly say it's not old."

"Old isn't the word. It's vintage."

Her soft laughter fills the car, and I'm happy to see this lighter side of her. Cochrane showing up was hard on her heart and her head.

"Fine, vintage. What do you love about it so much, anyway?"

I slant my head and arch my brow. "One, she never talks back."

She blinks at me. "Are you saying I talk back?"

I nod and shake my head at the same time. I'm sure it's an attractive look. A bobble head at its best. "Well…"

She whacks my chest. I grab her hand and bite her fingers, and her chest rises. Is she remembering the hard way she asked me to take her, how much we both fucking loved it? The thing is, though, she asked me to fuck her, and fucking is what I know. What I do. Never in my life have I let my heart get involved. Call me a chicken shit, call me whatever the hell you want. It can't be anything worse than any names thrown at me in my past. I'm scared with Reagan. I don't let people in, but with her, she climbed over that impenetrable wall without even trying.

My whole life, I've never been enough. Not for my father, not for my mother. Reagan makes me feel like I am enough. Even so, that small boy still exists inside of me, that boy knows better than to get to close. Now I'm at a crossroads. Do I listen to him, or do I bury him in the past? What do I hold on to, what do I let go?

We finally make it back to her place and the second I pull into the driveway and see my bike, my anger flares like a blow torch. I stare, unable to still my murderous thoughts, or form a coherent sentence. There is a part of my brain that recognizes Reagan's gasp, recognizes that she's saying something to me in a frightened, panicked voice.

I blink, my head spinning, my thoughts a chaotic mess. I have no idea how long I sit there staring at my bike, how long Reagan has been tugging at my arm as I grip the steering wheel so hard, I'm sure I'm going to snap it from the base. I take one breath, then two, forcing my brain to settle. As soon as it does one thing becomes perfectly clear.

Cochrane is a dead man.

I open my door, step from Reagan's car, and she's right there, running around the front of the vehicle, standing in front of me, pleading with me not to do anything stupid, anything that will get me kicked out of school. Miranda comes running from the house and my gaze flies to hers. Her eyes are big, desperately worried and I hold her gaze. She doesn't need to speak. From the looks of her, she knows who did this, maybe even saw it with her own eyes.

"I'll get it fixed for you, Rocco."

I finally register Reagan's words, and her panic invades my anger, pushes it back a little. I drag her into my arms, fist her hair and hold her close to me. I love that bike. Fucking love it.

You love Reagan more.

That thought hits like wayward fireworks, sending sparks through my body and my brain.

I love Reagan.

I take numerous breaths to calm myself down as Reagan trembles in my arms. A bike can be fixed or replaced, I remind myself as I meet Miranda's eyes again. "Are you okay?" I ask her, giving her a once over, knowing Cochrane and his goons would try to intimidate her. If she told them we were at the cottage, I wouldn't hold it against her.

She nods. "I'm okay," she says quietly.

"They did this while you were here?" I question and look over my wrecked bike again. The lights and mirrors are smashed. The switch gear is busted, and the gas tank has been beat to shit. No way will I ever find an original, but with a little luck, maybe someone can pound out the dents.

"I called campus security." My gaze flies back to Miranda.

"Chad?"

"Yeah, you know him?"

"We go way back."

Reagan looks at me like I might have had a bad run in with him. She'd be wrong. I met Chad when I moved here and let him take my bike for a ride. We became friends, and he especially liked it when I helped out, making sure the single females got back to their dorms safely when he was swamped with other things. I'm basically an honorary security guard.

"They were gone by the time campus security got here. I filed a report." She swallows. There's more she wants to say, but doesn't know how.

"What?"

"It was dark." She gives an apologetic shrug.

"None of this is your fault, Miranda. None of it."

"It's just...I couldn't positively identify any of them. It was Cochrane, though. It was definitely Cochrane and his friends. Security said they'd question them, but without a positive identification..." Miranda comes down the steps, and puts her hand on Reagan's back. "Are you okay?" she asks.

Reagan nods and turns to her friend. I put my arms around her waist, pulling her back against my chest, and Miranda smiles at me as I protect her best friend.

"He came looking for you Saturday morning. I didn't tell him where you were."

"He found me. He found us."

Miranda's eyes go wide. "He went to the cottage?"

"Let's get inside," I say, and glance over my shoulder.

Reagan spins to face me. "What about your bike? We can't just leave it out here."

"I'll push it back to my place. We have a shed I can store it in."

She eyes me, like she's worried I'm going to go looking for trouble. The thing is, trouble came looking for me. I didn't start this thing, but damn if I don't want to finish it. "Let's get inside," I say again, and nudge Reagan. We head up the steps and both girls head to the living room as I lock the door behind us. Reagan pulls her phone from her pocket when it buzzes.

She takes a breath. "It's Cochrane. He's asking when I want to meet up."

I don't react. I don't say anything. She sets her phone down, and Miranda meets my eyes. It's clear she hates Cochrane every bit as much as I do.

"Are you both okay if I go and take my bike to my place?"

Miranda nods, and Reagan says, "We're good, but please don't do anything—"

"I won't."

She eyes me, and I drop a kiss onto her forehead, find her shaking. "Why don't you head up to your room and try to get some sleep? It's been a long weekend."

"Are you...coming back?" she asks.

"Yeah, I'm coming back." It might be in one piece or it might be in a dozen, but one way or another, I'm coming back.

20

REAGAN

I stare at the clock, my heart crashing against my ribs as the minutes slowly tick by. I toss restlessly, my ears waiting for the sound of sirens, or something...something to indicate Rocco is in trouble. I never should have let him leave. I should have kept him here with me, distracted him in this bed. But he's not mine. He doesn't have to listen to me, and I can't tell him what to do. After seeing his bike like that, he obviously needed alone time. I just hope he stays alone. If Cochrane knew what was good for him, he'd hole up in Wolf House and not poke his head out until classes finish in April. What he did was so incredibly wrong, and unforgiveable.

The door downstairs creaks open and I sit up in my dark room, my heart thudding to the beat of the footsteps climbing up the stairs. They pause outside my door. I swallow and wait, and I don't even want to think about how happy it makes me when I hear the light knock.

"You awake, Sunshine?"

His rough and raspy voice slides over my skin, and I rub the goosebumps from my arms.

I flick on my lamp. "I'm awake."

"Can I come in?"

I actually laugh at that. After our time at the cottage, he's asking permission? I suppose I did tell him my room was out of bounds. I shake my head, but the truth is, I love him a little more for checking with me first. Honestly, it's insane how fast things changed between us, how I handed myself over to him—no holds barred.

"Yes."

My door opens slowly, and become acutely aware of the man standing there, his big frame eating up the entrance and overwhelming me in the most amazing ways. Every cell in my body vibrates with want.

"Are you okay?" I ask, and look him over, relieved that he's not bleeding or broken. He closes the door behind himself, and his scent fills the room as he steps closer. "You went looking for him, didn't you?"

He stands over me, and goes quiet for a long time. "Would you hate me if I said yes?"

I pound the bed. "Yes."

"I guess you'll have to hate me then."

"You promised."

"No, Sunshine. I never promised. If I did, I wouldn't have gone looking. I don't break promises."

"Did you find him?"

"No." He tugs on the hem of his shirt. "Can I get in?"

I nod and my body warms as he peels off his shirt and proceeds to get completely naked. I lift the covers and he crawls in beside me. I suddenly forget that I'm angry he went searching for Cochrane. His warmth reaches out to me, and soothes the cold living inside me.

"Then you'll promise me you won't go after him?" He hesitates. "It's not that I'm protecting him. I just don't want this to escalate. I don't want you to lose your scholarship. We can get your bike fixed. It might even be covered by house insurance."

"Not if I don't live here."

"I don't know, we'll see. What I do know is what Cochrane did was wrong and unforgiveable, but your bike, it's not unfixable, you know?"

"Are you going to meet with him, talk to him?" he asks, his voice tired and low as he turns to me and goes up on one elbow.

"I don't know. I'm just as mad as you are, Rocco. He's never been accountable for anything. Maybe he needs to know that there are consequences for his actions."

He pushes the blankets down, exposing my T-shirt. He runs his fingers over the goosebumps forming on my arm. "Maybe he needs a good beating."

"Roc—"

"If he says one word to you that you don't like, if he lays one unwanted finger on you that you don't want, he's a dead man."

My chest expands, loving the way Rocco wants to protect me. It's crazy, but so damn romantic. "Rocco, please."

"Please what?" he asks, his voice low and deep, as he slides over me. He traces my lips with his thumb. His gaze moves over my face, and his cock presses against my legs. He licks my bottom lip, a groan of pleasure filling the room. "Please kiss me right here? Is that what you're begging for, Sunshine?"

"Oh, I get it. You can't fight so you want to fuck."

"Yeah, you get it, Sunshine. Nothing gets past you, does it?"

For a second, I think he's kidding me. That this is about something else altogether. I want to believe that. I really do. But a couple times now, he's brought up the money and mentioned he wouldn't be here if Cochrane had just paid him. I don't want to think about that right now. Not when he's looking at me like he's desperate for my kisses, my touch —that if he doesn't get them, he might combust. My heart dances a little, hoping that's true.

"Nothing gets by me," I lie. Everything gets by me and I have no idea what we're doing here, only that it feels right, and I want to keep on doing it.

I part my lips for him and he kisses me. His hard body presses down on me, and this, right here, right now, is exactly where I am meant to be.

"We have a problem, Sunshine," he grumbles, and buries his face in my neck. His breath scorches my skin as he kisses me and I moan in sheer delight. It's been fun discovering each other's sensitive spots, and I love that he's a quick learner.

"What's the problem?" I ask quietly, not really worried he's going to say something bad. He's hot and aroused, and wants me as much as I want him.

"You have too many clothes on." He winks at me, and positions himself between my legs. "Let's fix that."

He tugs my pajama shorts to my ankles and tosses them away. He looks almost feral as he growls and spreads my legs. Dropping down, he slides his hands under my ass, and brings my pussy to his face. My God, I love when he licks me like that. It's hot and sexy and takes me to the edge so goddamn fast it leaves my head spinning.

"Yes, Rocco. I love that," I tell him.

He doesn't lift his face, and instead mumbles into my sex. "Me too."

He eats at me, sucks my clit and slides two thick fingers into me. Just like that, I shatter around his deft touch. The nicest thing about coming beneath his tongue is the sounds of pleasure it pulls from him.

"You needed me," he mumbles from between my legs. He's not asking me that. I actually think he's telling himself that, like he needs to somehow convince himself of it.

"I needed you, Rocco."

His head lifts and there is a new kind of intensity about him when his gaze meets mine. "I need you too, Reagan."

My heart stops beating as he climbs up my body, stalking, hunting, seeking what is rightfully his. His muscles are tight, as he slides them under me and gathers me into his arms. A wild animal, yet so gentle.

I put my mouth to his ear. "I want you inside me."

His muscles ripple beneath my hands as I run them around his back, lightly scratching his skin. My entire body quakes, my thighs are slick with my juices as I squirm and try to force him inside, even though we don't have a condom.

He presses a kiss to my breasts. "Yeah, babe. I want that too. Let me get a condom."

"I don't want that."

He goes perfectly still, his gaze moving over my face, a check in of sorts. "You're not protected."

"I know." God, what the hell am I doing? "It's what I want."

"Reagan."

"Please, Rocco."

He curses, and lightly runs his thumb over my cheek. "You know I'd give you anything you fucking wanted, but we can't make a mistake here."

A mistake.

Stupid tears fill my eyes. I know he's not saying I'm a mistake...I just don't know, I'm a hot freaking mess of emotions all of a sudden. "You're right. I know. I'm just... emotional, I guess. Everything that's happened over the weekend, and your bike..."

He swallows, and while he's portraying calm, the rippling of his jaw as he clamps down tells me he's every bit as affected by all this as I am. It's like were on a goddamn rollercoaster that's about to run off the rail, and while we're having fun, we know we can only crash land.

"Why don't you get on the pill?" he says slowly. "Then I can take you the way you want."

"Okay."

He lays over me a little longer, doing another check-in, and when I smile to let him know I'm okay—although I'm pretty sure I'll never be okay again—he goes to his pants, finds a condom and puts it on.

Two seconds later, he's inside of me, and I block my mind to everything but the pleasure he brings. I move with him, our bodies linked as one, our arms holding and hugging as our hearts beat against each other.

We don't speak. Instead we just feel and enjoy. His mouth goes to my ear.

"Reagan..."

"Yeah?" I manage to get out as my pleasure peaks.

"I love...this."

I gulp, my heart stilling in my chest. For the briefest of seconds, in the small pause, I thought he was going to tell me he loved me. "I love this too."

He moves inside me, hitting all the right spots, and I let go, soaking his pistoning cock. "Fuck yeah," he growls and throws his head back and lets go. I ride out each glorious pulse, and he holds me tighter, squeezing the air from my lungs, but I don't care. I can't seem to get close enough to him, either. "I don't ever want to stop doing this."

"Me either," I say. His head lifts and eyes that hold so many questions lock on mine. I don't want him to ask. I don't know any of the answers. I don't know anything at all, other than what I feel for him.

He presses his lips to mine and doesn't vocalize what's all over his face. He slides out of me, disposes of the condom and grabs a few tissues. As soon as he finishes wiping us down, there's a noise outside my window and we both freeze for a second.

"Stay there," he says and walks to my window to glance out. He stands there for a long time, staring out into the dark night. His body is stiff, ready for battle, and my heart jumps into my throat.

"What is it?" I tug the blanket up to my neck.

"Nothing."

He comes back to my bed, crawls in and pulls me to him. I rest my head on his shoulder and put my hand on his pounding heart. "Sleep," he orders, and pulls the blanket over our heads, forming a tent. Something's different. Something is wrong. What did he see out that window? I'm not sure, and while he's with me here physically, he's withdrawing. This tent—his treehouse—his way of keeping himself safe. Is he afraid of me hurting him? Is he afraid of hurting me?

I lift my head to see him. "I'm going to call my Dad."

"Right now?"

I chuckle. "No, tomorrow. I'm going to tell him your bike was damaged when we were away checking on the cottage. I feel responsible."

"Not your fault."

"Dad will want to pay for the damages."

"You don't have to do that, Sunshine. Don't you know I'm going to be in the NFL? Money won't be a problem."

"I bet. But you can pay me back when that happens, if it's important to you. Although you don't have to. None of this is your fault." He laughs, and I frown. "What's so funny?"

"Money. Betting."

"What's so funny about those things?"

"Cochrane owing me money because of a bet is what got us in this mess." I freeze and he stops. "Wait, that didn't come out right." He shakes his head.

"Do you wish he would have just paid you?"

"Yeah...no...I mean..."

He doesn't finish and I don't press. I lay back down on his chest, and squeeze my eyes to keep the tears back. For some unknown reason, Cochrane's words come back to haunt me.

"He's not who you think he is, Reagan."

Maybe I should talk to Cochrane and find out exactly what he meant by that.

Practice ran late and I should be tired. I am tired, but there is this uneasy energy inside me. Reagan hasn't talked to Cochrane yet. Not that I know of. Worry mushrooms inside me. What kind of lies will he spill about me? Will she believe them and go running back to him? Angsty and jittery, even though my body is exhausted, I head into Reagan's house. It's dark and quiet, and she's probably fast asleep. If my bike wasn't busted, I'd go for a long ride to push back the edginess prowling through my veins.

I quietly go upstairs, not wanting to wake anyone. I stop outside Reagan's door, my mind racing. Yeah, I'm going to make something of my life. But will I ever be anything but the thug from the wrong side of the tracks? What I should do is walk away. I'm not what she needs. I'm not even sure I'm what she wants. Sure, we're having fun in bed, but sex and relationships are two different things. It's possible that I'm just a goddamn wimp, too afraid of opening up and having her walk out of my life, straight back into the arms of Dick.

Light fans out from beneath her door and my heart jumps. She's been waiting up for me. I knock softly, and she welcomes me in. I open the door and find her in her bed, warm, flushed, so damn sexy it's all I can do not to take her. Maybe I should take her. That would help with easing the strange restlessness inside me.

"Did I wake you?"

"No, I was awake." She pats the bed, and I cross the room. "How was practice?"

"Good." I brush her hair back, lean in and press a kiss to her forehead. "How was your night?"

She waves toward her computer. "Same old, same old."

I grin, and glance out her window at the dark night. It was just last night I was sure I spotted Cochrane and his goons creeping around the property. I should have gone after him, should have pounded as many of them as I could. Maybe he heard I was looking for him, and came for me instead. Why didn't I go out? Oh, because Reagan didn't need that. She didn't need to see a brawl. No, when Cochrane and I get into it, she'll be nowhere in the vicinity.

"Want to get out of here?" I ask.

She frowns, and angles her head, looking at me like I might have a snake growing out of mine. I chuckle quietly. "It's not that late."

"What did you have in mind?"

"Normally on a night like tonight, I'd go to my cave, but since Dick broke my bike, I guess I'll have to settle for a walk. Want to join me?"

She pushes her blankets off, showcasing her curvy body in her pajamas. No matter what this girl wears, I'm always going to want her.

"Stare much," she teases as she turns her back to me and pulls on a bra and sweater, following those up with panties and jeans. She puts her hair up in a ponytail and sticks a few bobby pins in to tame the wayward curls around her face. She is so fucking adorable I could sob. I am seriously the luckiest guy on the planet to be here with her. Even if it can't be forever.

You want forever.

"Why are you hiding?" I ask, stepping up behind her. "I've been inside you, remember? I know exactly what you look like and taste like." I pull her hair to the side and kiss her neck. A quiver goes through her and I like it. I like the way she reacts to my touch.

"How could I forget?" She turns to me, her eyes bright with desire. "You were my first, remember, and a girl never forgets her first."

I stare at her, an odd little ache in my heart because the thought of her having a second, or third, doesn't sit well with me. I put my hand on the side of her neck, brush my thumb over her cheek and lightly kiss her.

"I'll never forget either, Sunshine." She smiles up at me. "Ready?"

"Yeah." Her eyes are dreamy her lips still poised as that one word slips from her lips.

"Do you want my jacket?"

She nods, and I tug off my team jacket and put it over her shoulders. I'm only in a T-shirt, but my body is hot from tonight's practice. I take her hand in mine and we head outdoors. The refreshing night air falls over us and we both take a minute to breathe it in. We walk along the sidewalk, hand in hand, with no destination in mind. Before we know it, we're on the football field.

"Want to make out under the bleachers?" I tease.

She laughs. "Yes, but no."

I pretend I'm throwing the ball. "Too bad I didn't have my ball. I could teach you a few moves."

"That actually would have been fun."

"Yeah?"

"Yeah, I like learning your moves."

I scratch my head as she gives me an innocent look. "Are we still talking about football?"

"We are and you know what?" She throws her arms around me. "I love how passionate you are about football. I am so happy that you get to live your dream every day, Rocco."

A movement in the distance draws my attention. I look over her head, stare into the dark night, but my gaze comes up with nothing. Maybe it was just an animal.

As I scan the campus, I notice one of the buildings. An idea hits. It's not a great idea. In fact, it's a very very bad idea. I'm going to do it anyway. I break from the circle of her arms, and capture her hand.

"Come on."

"Where are we going?"

"You'll see when we get there."

"Haven't we already established that I hate surprises?"

"No, we established that I'm the one who doesn't like surprises. But trust me enough to know you're going to like this one, right?"

"I do."

My heart squeezes tight at that. She trusts me and that will always live inside me, very close to my pounding heart. We hurry across the wide football field until we're at the back door to one of the campus's buildings.

"What are we doing at the art gallery?" she asks, her voice a hushed whisper.

"What does one normally do at an art gallery, Reagan?"

She whacks me and I feign hurt. "Smart ass."

"I thought we'd enjoy some art."

"But it's closed."

"Not to us." I pull a couple pins from her hair and drop to my knees. She gasps.

"Rocco, we can't break in. We'll get in trouble."

"Nah, actually we won't. I know campus security quite well." I wink at her. "Did a guy a favor once."

"Chad?"

"Yeah, you remember me mentioning him."

She puts a hand on her hip. "What kind of favor? Don't tell me he's one of the bad guys? Corrupt campus security."

"You clearly watch too many crime shows." I laugh, and shove one of the pins into the lock, moving it around until I find what I'm looking for. "No. I helped him get a girl, once."

"A girl, really?"

"Yeah, one of the ladies that works in the cafeteria."

"My, aren't you the nice guy?"

"Been called a lot of things." I turn and wink at her. "But can't say as I've been ever called that."

"You are though, Rocco."

My throat tightens at the way she looks at me, and I'm so far gone when it comes to her. I might be out of her league, I might not be accepted into her circle, but goddammit, I am in love with her, and I have to stop being such a chicken shit. I'm about to stand, drag her into my arms and once and for all tell her exactly how I feel.

"Hurry," she says, when voices reach our ears. I shove the other pin into the lock. "How are you doing that?"

"Like this." I move her in front of me, and she sinks to the cold ground with me. I take her hand and put it on the pin. "Move it until you feel a latch."

She works the lock for a second, then goes perfectly still. She glances at me over her shoulder. "Maybe I shouldn't be doing this."

"Don't worry," I say to ease her worries. "If we get caught, I'll take all the blame. Just so you know, I'd never do anything that would put you in harm's way or in a bad situation." I clench down on my teeth, and resist the urge to say like your douche bag boyfriend. "I'll say I kidnapped you and forced you to go to the art gallery."

She chuckles. "Yeah, that's believable."

"If you spin a good enough story, you can make anything sound believable."

She eyes me and lifts her chin a bit, but there's a playfulness about her. "Why do I get the sense you're talking from experience?"

"Probably because I am."

She opens her mouth like she's about to ask something when I move my hand over hers, and click open the lock.

"We're in."

I stand and pull her up. Once we're inside, we leave the lights off and I pull out my phone to turn on my flashlight app. I know for a fact that there are no alarms. It's not like we're at the Guggenheim or anything. This is the Kingston art gallery, where students show off their masterpieces.

"Do you have any of your work in here?" I ask as we tiptoe through the building, our bodies close, constantly touching.

"No, of course not."

"Too bad." I shine my light on the wall and light up all the art. "Yours would look good right there."

"Is that why you brought me here, Rocco? So I could envision what my art would look like on these walls? To show me that I'm not on the path I'm supposed to be on? That I should live my own life instead of the one everyone expects of me?"

"Wow, I just thought it would be fun." I'm making light of it, but she's bang on. "I didn't know you were going to read all that into it."

"You're far more transparent to me than you think."

She goes quiet again, too quiet, and I shine my light on her, find her face flushed, her eyes watery. Shit, I shouldn't have done this. I've crossed a line. "Reagan—"

"Thank you. You're right. I do like this surprise." She gives a big sigh. "No one's ever cared—"

"They care, Reagan. Don't mistake them wanting you to get a good education that will lead to a secure career as not caring."

She nods, understanding exactly what I'm saying. Her gaze drops to the floor. "You're right. They do. They just don't understand."

"Maybe it's up to you to make them understand. That's totally up to you. If that's what you want to do." I'd like to tell her I have no horses in this race, but that would be a lie. I totally care about her, and her future. I want her to live the best possible life.

With me.

She goes silent for a second, and when she lifts her head, my light shining right into her eyes, she winces. "Can you stop blinding me?"

"Sorry."

I shine the light on the wall again, and we walk closer to the displayed art. We both go quiet as we examine the paintings. We move quietly through the rooms, and stop when we come to the sculptures.

"Great sculptures, don't you think?" I lean against the statue of a woman, purposely placing one hand on her breast, acting all innocent. "Have you ever done one?"

She laughs. "Are you twelve?"

"What?" I look at the statue and jerk my hand back. "Where did that come from?"

She whacks me and her laugh curls around me. "So juvenile."

"I bet that's what you love about me."

She goes quiet when the word love spills from my lips and I mentally scold myself. Just because I'm in love with her doesn't mean she's in love with me. She has a goddamn boyfriend who's waiting for our month to be over so he can have her back.

Fuck me.

"I didn't mean—"

"I don't bet or gamble," she says quietly. "Especially when people are putting things on the table they should never be gambling with."

If she's talking about her heart, I get it. I am two seconds away from putting mine on the table, and I'm terrified. Terrified of getting hurt, terrified of her walking away. Terrified of her never knowing how I really feel. If I don't take this chance, I'll end up spending the rest of my life wondering what if. Which is worse.

"You like a sure thing, huh?" I ask.

"I do."

I'm a second away from telling her I'm a sure thing when a door creaks open and lights in another room flick on. "Shit, we need to get out of here."

22

REAGAN

I stare at my phone, checking the time again. My God, will this class ever end? I should be focusing, but my mind keeps drifting back to last night, to the art gallery. I smile, hardly able to believe we broke into the place. But Rocco told me it was safe, and deep inside, I really feel like he'd do anything and everything to protect me. It's a strange feeling. A nice one.

That thought leads to Cochrane, and my bliss disappears. I'm enraged that he and his friends busted up Rocco's bike. I know he's waiting for me to talk to him, and I'm wondering if I should calm down before I do that.

The lecture finally ends, and I pack my things up and head out. The sky is gray, rain on the horizon as I exit the building and start back toward my place. A group of giggling girls catch my attention and I glance over to find them hanging off Cochrane's friends. I pick up my pace, until Cochrane's voice stops me.

I go perfectly still, my phone clutched in my hands. I turn, and as he races toward me, I brace myself. I guess now is as good a time as any to have it out with him.

"Hey," he calls out as he catches up to me.

"What do you want?"

He frowns. "Come on, Reagan. Don't be like that."

"Like what?"

"I told you I was sorry about the other night. I was drunk, and stupid and you were with Rocco..."

"You were the one who put us together, Cochrane, or did you forget that?"

"It was a stupid mistake." He glances past my shoulders.

"Was busting his bike up a stupid mistake too?"

His gaze shifts, his eyes narrow. "What are you talking about?"

I've known Cochrane for years. Does he not think I can tell when he's freaking lying to me? "Are you seriously going to stand there and deny it?"

He reaches for my hair, takes a strand between his fingers, and the second he touches me, bile punches into my throat. "Don't touch me." I jerk back, and his face hardens.

"What the fuck, Reagan? You better get your head on straight. We have a future together. You might be slumming—"

"I am not slumming."

He stares at me, his eyes cold, arctic blue. Anger moves into his eyes, and for the first time in my life, I'm afraid of him.

He takes a threatening step closer, and from my peripheral vision, I note his friends have stepped forward as well. Why do they think he needs backup against a girl? I cross my arms as my heart crashes against my ribcage.

"Are you fucking him?" My throat tightens. "Jesus Christ, Reagan, you better not be fucking him."

"I'm...what I do is no longer your business. We're done."

"We're not done. Not by a long shot."

I take a step back and he follows me. "We are done." I swallow. "I want you to stay away from me."

"Not going to happen."

"Cochrane—"

"No, Reagan, you're mine. If you don't come to your senses, bad things are going to happen."

"Are you threatening me?"

He shrugs. "I'm just saying."

My pulse jumps in my throat as he looms over me, his words and body setting alarm bells off in my brain. What the hell did I ever see in him anyway?

"Come back to me, Reagan, or very bad things will happen, and the fault will be all yours."

I spot movement in the distance, but I'm afraid to take my eyes off Cochrane, afraid that he'll see it as a weakness if I do, and he'll think he's won.

"I talked to my folks the other day. Our families are all planning Thanksgiving together. Come on, Reagan. You know they won't be happy about any of this and you don't want to upset them, do you? Especially over the holidays."

Goddammit, if there's one thing he's good at, it's hitting me where it hurts.

"Dad's already invited Rocco and they won't take no for an answer from him," I shoot back through clenched teeth.

Anger flares in his eyes. "Rocco is an asshole. He's only with you to get back at me." I stare at him, and he laughs. "What, you don't really think he likes you, do you? He fucks anything with two legs and a hot pussy." Rage burns through my blood, and I'm seconds from making a fist and swinging it. "He's a dirt bag, Reagan. Deep inside, you know that. I mean, what could he possibly see in you?" I jerk back as if he's slapped me. His face softens, and he reaches for me again, changing tactics as he backtracks. "What I mean is, you're not really his type. He's just trying to get something from you." Once again, he hits where it hurts. Growing up, I never knew who my real friends were or if they were just looking for something.

"I...I..." I stutter, my brain too wired with worry to summon a response.

"Why don't we just forget all of this? Pretend it never happened. Go back to the way things used to be."

Before I even realize what's happening, Rocco is right there, standing between Cochrane and me. He nudges me back with his body, in a protective move.

"Pretend what never happened?" Rocco asks.

"Back the fuck off, Rocco. This is between Reagan and me."

"Seems to me like she doesn't want to talk to you." He turns to me. "Do you want to talk to him, Reagan?"

I shake my head.

"Look at that. Seems I know her better than you do."

Cochrane takes a step forward, his friends stepping closer, and Rocco braces himself.

"Stop, please," I say, and tug on the back of Rocco's jacket. "He's not worth it."

In the distance, a security vehicle drives by and slows. Cochrane rubs his face and steps back. He smirks at me when I glance around Rocco's shoulder.

"You don't know anything," he yells at me, his eyes as hard as his voice. "But you're soon going to." I suck in a fast breath and step closer to Rocco, seeking his heat and comfort. Cochrane just shakes his head. "Hey, sorry to hear about your bike."

Rocco goes tense as Cochrane provokes him, and in that moment, I almost want Rocco to fight him, and that thought is coming from the girl who hates confrontation.

Rocco shrugs. "Shit happens. I'm sure whoever did it will regret it."

Cochrane stares at Rocco, and I hope he takes his words seriously. I'm not sure what Rocco will do, but I don't think he's going to let Cochrane get away with it.

Cochrane steps back. "See you, Reagan."

I don't speak. I just stay pressed against Rocco as Cochrane steps up to his friends, and they all clap him on the back.

Rocco turns to me, his gaze moving over my face. "You okay?"

"Yeah."

"What was that all about?"

"He's trying to convince me to forget what happened and to go back to him." I frown and glance down. Rocco touches my chin and lifts it.

"What?"

"He said you...basically he said you were just fucking with me to get back at him." I swallow as old insecurities grip my throat.

"What did you say?"

I stare at the guy who has been nothing but kind, gentle and protective of me. "I think Cochrane is an asshole."

"Something we agree on." He laughs.

"I actually think we agree on a lot of things."

"Yeah, we do, Sunshine." He throws his arm around my shoulder, and starts walking me toward home.

"You don't think he can do anything to hurt us, do you?"

He stiffens for a brief second and relaxes again, but it's forced as I stare at him. "Nah, he's just all talk." He drops his arm, and jogs backward. "Come on, I have something I want to show you."

"I've already seen it," I joke, some of the tension draining from me as his enthusiasm curls around me, and hugs me tight.

He laughs. "Funny girl." He turns and starts jogging beside me. "Come on, pick up the pace. I don't have all day."

"Aren't you supposed to be in class right now?"

"Keeping track of me, are you?"

I roll my eyes at him and pick up my pace. We reach our place—our place—and he opens the door to usher me in. He captures my hand, leads me up the stairs to my bedroom. "So I was right, you do want to show me...something."

He laughs, and pushes open my door. "I hope you don't mind that I came in here when you weren't home. I know how protective you are of your room."

I step inside and my heart thumps in my chest. My gaze moves over to the easel set up by my window, along with printed photos of the ocean, taken the night he drove me to his private cave off the highway. "What..."

He shrugs. "I thought maybe you could do some paintings for the art gallery. There was a bare spot on the wall. We can sneak in again and hang your painting to fill it."

I laugh, warmth and lightness invading my body and soul. "You're crazy." I throw my arms around him, and find his lips with mine.

"You like it, huh?" he asks after I kiss him.

"I love it."

I love you.

"Show me how much you love it," he teases.

"Don't you have somewhere to be?"

"Yeah," he murmurs, and puts his hand between my legs. "Right here."

He lightly strokes me through my yoga pants and my body burns from the inside out. I reach for the button on his jeans and free it. He angles his head, clearly intrigued by what I'm doing. Grinning, and deciding to show him just how much I love my new easel, and how much I love him, I sink to my knees and chuckle quietly when his soft curses reach my ears.

"I was just kidding, babe. You don't have to show me anything."

I glance up at him, take in the tightness on his face. "Oh, but I want to."

"Fuck," he grumbles, as I tug his pants down and free his cock. "Who am I to stand in the way of a girl who knows what she wants?" I laugh, and his cock settles on the crook in my top lip. "Babe," he moans, pre-cum dripping from his slit as he grows thicker.

I run my hand over his hard length and hold my tongue out.

"Holy fuck." His curses fill the quiet of the room as his cum drips and lands on my tongue. "That is the hottest thing I've ever seen."

"Maybe not," I say, as I think about the way I want him to take me today.

"I don't know what that's supposed to mean, but I can't wait to find out." He grips my hair and holds it from my face as I open my mouth for him, relaxing my throat so I can take him deep. He jerks forward and feeds me his cock, and I grow so wet between my legs, I'm pretty sure I'm going to come just from pleasuring him.

I suck him hard, take him deep and his groans send waves of heat through me. He rocks into my mouth and I cup his ass, wanting every inch in my mouth but knowing it's impossible. He hardens even more, and while I plan for him to come in my mouth, there's something we need to do first.

I back away, and his cock remains pointed at my mouth as I go back on my heels. "Babe, you're killing me." The heat and need in his voice thrills me, and I push to my feet, take him into my hand for a long stroke before I back up. He stands there like a wild animal as I strip before him, tossing my clothes to the floor and turning to crawl onto my bed. With my ass pointed at him, he curses and I turn and crook my finger.

He rips his clothes off and he's on me in an instant, his body over mine, his cock pressing against my leg as he devours my mouth. I love how needy he is, love the untamed desperation about him. I know that feeling well.

I push on his shoulders and he lifts his head, his eyes full of questions. Deciding to show him, I reach down, coat my fingers with my juices and rub them between my breasts to lubricate myself.

"No fucking way."

I press my tits together to form a tight channel. "I want you right here."

He rakes his hands through his hair. "You are so goddamn beautiful and full of surprises." He puts his knees on either side of my torso and shimmies up, his hands braced on the headboard behind me. He powers forward and slides between my breasts.

"You feel so damn good."

"I want you to come in my mouth."

"Yeah, babe. You want to taste me?"

"I want all your cum inside my body," I tell him and I swear his cock expands another inch.

He pumps his cock between my breasts. Everything about this is all for him. It's for me too; I'm enjoying the tortured yet pleasured groans rising in his throat. With each forward thrust, I take him into my greedy mouth, and his thrusts become almost manic as he chases his release. I love that I can do this to him.

With each hard, blunt stroke, meant for his pleasure, he lands in my mouth, and I love everything about this moment we're sharing, from the realness, and the rawness, to the sheer, deeply moving intimacy.

His body goes still, his groan reaching my ears as he shoots into my waiting mouth. He glances down, watching intently as he releases, and I drink him in. "So goddamn beautiful," he groans, and I hold him to me, wanting every last drop. He pulses and spasms and when he's drained, he pushes off the headboard, and falls over me. Big, warm hands brush my hair from my face, and his smile is soft and sweet.

"I guess that's showing me." He laughs. I'm about to move, get out from under him so he can get to class when he captures me and holds me down, lowering his mouth to my pussy. "Now it's my turn to show you."

I laugh, loving that idea. "Who am I to stand in the way of a guy who knows what he wants."

23

ROCCO

I finish my passing drill and Coach blows his whistle. I tug my helmet off and glance around the bleachers, searching for Reagan, even though I know she's in class. Still, I can't help but hope to see my girl out there watching and cheering me on.

We all head into the locker room and get showered and changed. Alistair steps up to me as I'm pulling on my team jacket.

"Any news on getting your bike fixed?"

"Yeah, I got a couple calls in, and I'm waiting to hear the quote."

He nods, and knows better than to offer me money. "You know if you need anything…"

"I know." I pat him on the back. "Thanks, man. I got this covered." I don't really. I'll have to find a way, though. I made my high school coach a promise to take care of her and I'll find a way somehow. I tug my phone from my pocket to see if there are any missed calls or messages from Reagan. I smile when I see her text, telling me she'll catch up with me after class.

"Reagan?" Alistair asks.

"Yeah." I can't seem to wipe the stupid grin from my face.

"Rumor has it Cochrane is pissed and out for blood."

"He should have thought of that before he put her in my hands."

"You like her, don't you?"

"Yeah, I do. A lot." I take in his frown. "What?"

He shrugs, but I stare at him. He's got something to say. "Out with it."

"I don't know. I just...she's not the kind of girl you usually go for and I don't trust Cochrane one bit. He could make things difficult for you."

"How?" It's a question I already know the answer to. But if he fucks with Reagan, I'll break every fucking bone in his body.

"Be careful, that's all I'm saying."

I nod and I'm about to tuck my phone away when an email pops up. I open it and quickly read the message from the Dean of Science. "What the fuck?"

"What's going on?"

"The Dean wants to see me."

"What for?"

"I don't know. Maybe it has something to do with my scholarship. I might have forgotten to send a form in last month." I make light of it despite the sudden storm swirling in my gut. I've been in the Dean's office before, for paperwork and career talk. This feels different, though. This feels bad. I shove my phone in my pocket, and try to shake off the burst of nervous energy in my blood. I scoop up my bag and head toward the door.

"Text me and let me know, okay?"

I nod, my mind on a million things. "Yup," I agree and head out the door. With the sun shining today, lots of students are out on the lawns studying, and I keep my head down and make a beeline to the administration building. I step inside and the scent of pine cleaner fills my nostrils, and amplifies the dread inside me. Why do I feel like I'm walking into the executioner's office?

I take a breath and shake it off. It's nothing. Nothing at all. I'm just here to sign a paper. I head down the hall and stop outside the Dean's office. His door is cracked, and it's opens slightly as I knock.

"Come in," Dean Blakely says.

"Hey." I enter his office and find him sitting behind his colossal dark mahogany desk, which is always littered with files, paper coffee cups and books. He usually has a smile for me. Today, not so much. The dread in my stomach mushrooms, and my heart picks up pace as he gestures toward the chair across from his desk.

"Have a seat, Rocco."

I close the door, leave my football bag by the door, and drop into the seat across from him. I keep my mouth shut as he checks something on his computer. He presses a few buttons, and sits back in his chair, the leather squeaking under his weight.

"I've heard some disturbing news."

Fuck me. Twice.

"Oh yeah, what's that?" As I sit there looking at his frown, his gray bushy eyebrows knitting together, I continue to tell myself this is nothing. But that's a lie born out of self-preservation, because right here, right now, this is about to change my trajectory. Every instinct in my body tells me so.

"I heard there was some gambling going on, and you were involved."

I take a couple deep breaths, brace my elbows on the arms of the wooden chair and steeple my finger. "Who told you that?"

"That's confidential."

"If someone is talking about me, I think I have a right to know."

He picks up a pen and taps it on his desk. What does he have to be nervous about? I'm the one getting thrown under the bus here.

"Let's just say, the information came to me from a very reliable source, and if it's true, you could be in very big trouble."

"What kind of trouble?"

He squirms a bit, and tugs at his collar. Whatever he's about to say, he's either uncomfortable doing it, or he's been put in a situation where he has no choice. What the fuck has Cochrane done?

"There's been an investigation at Wolf House. Your name came up repeatedly."

I shake my head. Of course it did. Cochrane has pull there, just like he has pull here in the Dean's office. My guess is Cochrane's daddy and Dean Blakely go way back. Isn't that the way it is? The rich protect the rich. Isn't that why Reagan landed in my arms—to protect her asshole boyfriend.

"If this is true..."

"I'm the only one named? No others are being implicated here?"

He picks up a piece of paper and reads it. "There is another name." My heart jumps into my throat and cuts off my air. Please don't say Reagan. Jesus Christ. I can understand Cochrane dragging my name through the mud, but is he that much of a bastard that he'd ruin Reagan's name too? Ruin her education, her future? "I take it you know Reagan Ellison?"

Holy fuck. Cochrane is a dead man.

DEAD.

My hands shake and I tuck them under my legs as sweat breaks out on my body. What the fuck am I supposed to say, or do? "I know her, yes."

"Apparently, she's involved in some payout scheme. She gave herself to you in lieu of payment of sorts. That's very unorthodox and could result in a suspension, for her and for you." His head lifts, his eyes zeroing in on me. I catch the worry there. This man knows he can ruin careers, and I suspect it's to save his. "If that's true, I will need to speak to her."

As the room spins—my life, Reagan's future—flashing before my eyes, the lie easily spills from my lips. "She's not involved in any of this. You don't have to talk to her."

"I don't know about that."

Jesus fucking Christ. Is this really happening? Did Cochrane really throw us *both* under the bus? He's every bit as guilty as I am, yet I'm the one here in the office, about to lose everything I spent years fighting for.

"If I take full responsibility, will you leave her out of this?" That's when it hits me. This is what Cochrane wanted all along. The fucker knew I'd take full blame and protect her. I shake my head. Well done, Cochrane. Well-fucking-done. Looks like he won this war after all.

Dean Blakely nods slowly. "I could take that into consideration." He leans forward, and links his fingers together. "She comes from a very well connected family. Her father is a donor to the new wing of the library. We probably don't want to drag her into this scandal."

"Yeah." I get it, I get exactly what everyone with more power than I have is doing.

"You should probably keep your distance, don't you think? You know, for her sake."

With my words lodged in my throat, I nod, grab the back of my neck, and dig my fingers into my tight muscle. At least Reagan won't be fucked over because of my fight with Cochrane. I shake my head and glance at the ceiling. I once asked myself what I'd do for love. I guess I now know the answer. Reagan and I, though, we never stood a chance and I guess there is a part of me that always knew it. The Dean's chair shifts and my gaze flies to his as my anger once again flares.

"You know I'm not the only one, right?"

He tugs at his collar again. "The others will be dealt with."

I lean forward, not ready to let this go, and maybe there is a part of me that just wants to see him squirm some more. "What others?" Shit, I hope Andrew isn't in trouble. He's the only one from Wolf House that I like.

He shuffles papers on his desk and avoids my direct gaze. "I'm afraid that's confidential."

"What happens to the person who came to you with this information?"

"That person will have different consequences of course. They are, after all, the person wanting to right the wrongs taking place at Wolf House."

A humorless laugh crawls out of my throat. When Reagan said Cochrane had a way of getting what he wanted, she wasn't wrong. "You know this is fucked up, right?" I ask, unable to contain my temper. He bristles before me, shocked at my blunt language.

"Rocco, I'd appreciate a little respect."

"Why are you doing this?" I grip my hair and tug. "What does Cochrane have on you?"

His throat makes a sound as he swallows, like he's surprised, but the truth is written all over his face. "That's enough, young man."

I laugh. "Why? Why can't I say what I really feel? What else do I have to lose?"

"Your scholarship."

I go still. "Are you saying you're not taking that from me? I get to stay here?"

"No, I'm not taking it from you. You can finish your degree."

I push to my feet, and put my hands on his desk. "Then what are you taking?" I don't know why I'm asking. I don't want to hear the answer poised on his lips like a sharp blade ready to pierce my heart.

"You're being pulled from the football team. I'll have a talk with Coach Myers and will explain all this to him."

My blood drains to my toes as he confirms what I already knew. I stare at him and he fusses with the papers on his desk, indicating the meeting is over. This might be over, but it's not over between Cochrane and me. Oh no, it's not over by a long fucking shot.

I move around the chair, snatch my duffel bag and walk out of his office. The hall narrows in on me as I work to get my anger under control and step outside. I stalk across the campus, scanning everyone and everything I see. My phone pings, and I ignore it. My only focus is on finding Cochrane and giving him a Burnside beating. No one deserves it more.

I search the campus, but it's now late afternoon, so he's probably back at Wolf House having a celebratory drink. The guy finally fucked me over. Why I was such a threat to him is beyond me. Maybe he knew I had a thing for his girl all these years. Maybe he only put her in my arms to finally show me that I was nothing—would always be nothing. But I wasn't 'nothing' to Reagan. I was her everything, and she was mine. That shit was—is—real. I guess in the end, I really did prove to him that I could make her fall for me.

Was that my goal? Is that why I moved into her house? To take her from Cochrane and show her I was the right guy for her? Talk about everything blowing up in my face.

"Rocco."

I turn at the voice, and Miranda comes into view as she hurries my way. My heart stalls when I see the worried look on her face.

"Is Reagan okay?" I hold my breath. He better not have gone after her, hurt her or upset her in any way.

"It's not Reagan I'm worried about."

"She's good, then?" I ask, the panic in me subsiding slightly. Reagan's been through enough, and I'm not going to be the guy—won't be the guy—to tell her what Cochrane did, how he was willing to throw her under the bus, again, just to win. One thing I know about Reagan is she's a fighter, smart enough to figure out she's better off without Cochrane in her life.

Miranda looks me over, and I get what she sees. A goddamn animal on a rampage. It will take the Falcons entire defensive line to stop me from fighting Cochrane, and I'm not even sure that will be enough.

"I'm fine."

"Yeah, you look it." She reaches out to put her hand on my arm and I flinch. "Do you want to talk about it?"

I plan to talk about it, with my fist. "I have to go, Miranda."

"Rocco, please, you look like you're ready to murder someone and I can only guess who that someone is. I don't like him any more than you do."

"Then you shouldn't be trying to stop me."

"I'm stopping you for you. Because I care about you and your future."

I laugh, and it comes out sounding like an animal caught in a trap with no way out—except to chew off its own leg. Come to think of it, that seems to be a fitting description for my life. Fucked.

"I have no future, Miranda."

The worry in her eyes deepen. "What are you talking about?"

I swallow, and shift my bag on my shoulder. I shouldn't say anymore, I've said enough, yet the words, "It's over. Football is over. No chance of the NFL now," spill from my lips.

She pales before me, her lips practically trembling. She glances around, searching for the same man I'm after. "What did he do?"

"Does it even matter now?" I start to walk away and she reaches for me.

"Rocco, please don't."

"Go home, Miranda. None of this has anything to do with you, and I've dragged enough people into my life as it is. I don't want to see anyone else get hurt."

Confusion moves over her face, and of course it does. How could she possibly know the extent Cochrane would go to even hurt Reagan just to get back at me? It's my fault, really. I never should have gone to that fucking card game, never should have shown up at her place, demanding a room. Stupid. Stupid. Stupid. And you can't fix stupid, right?

I walk away and glance back over my shoulder, but Miranda is on the move, running in the opposite direction. I pick up my pace and start jogging toward Wolf House. My chest swells with all the rage welling up inside me as I cut through the parking lot and head toward the impressive front entrance to the stone building. Blood boils in my veins, a cauldron over-flowing, ready to erupt, when I find Dick standing outside laughing with his friends. I drop my bag, and his head lifts, like he was expecting me, as I close the distance between us. He grins at me, and it only stokes the anger inside me.

"What the fuck do you want, Rocco?" he asks, and cracks his knuckles.

I'm ready. Come at me, asshole. I take in his friends as they close in. It's not going to be a fair fight, but there's definitely going to be a fight. Maybe I want the beating. Maybe I want the pain. Maybe it will take my mind off the hurt of losing what was never mine to begin with.

"Fuck with me, but you don't fuck with her," I growl through clenched teeth.

He snorts. "I have no idea what you're talking about."

Blind rage grips me, and I'm fucking done talking. I pull my arm back, and take the first swing. I punch his jaw, making it a good one because I'm sure it's the only one I'll get in. I knock him into the arms of one of his friends. They push him to his feet as someone jumps me from behind and Cochrane comes at me swinging. He hits my jaw and as pain rockets through me, so does a high-pitched female scream.

Reagan.

24

REAGAN

Miranda puts her arms around me, holding my shaking body as fists fly, four against one. Rocco is pulling himself up off the ground, only to receive a boot to the ribs as he rises. Guys and girls come running from Wolf House when they hear the commotion. Rocco tries to turn to see me, but a punch to the face, delivered by Cochrane, stops him.

He curses and somehow manages to shake off the guys holding him, but can't break free from the circle of people. Cochrane is bouncing around him, laughing, his fists in the air. Rocco spits blood, and when Cochrane attacks, Rocco lands one solid punch on Cochrane's jaw, sending him flying backward.

"Stop!" I scream again and grab my phone ready to call campus police, although I can't. Rocco can't get caught fighting. He could lose his scholarship and I don't want to be the one responsible for that. "Cochrane, stop!" I scream. "I'll talk to you. Whatever you want."

Cochrane grins at me as his buddies help him to his feet. He rubs his jaw and twists his mouth. "Yeah?"

"Yes," I agree, anything to stop this barbaric fight, where there can be no winner. I knew this was a long time brewing, and Miranda scared the hell out of me when she found me on campus and told me we needed to get to Wolf House asap. She was too breathless from running to tell me why. Not that I needed her to. I'm smart enough to figure things had come to a head with the two guys in my life. We both ran here as fast as we could, and now, I'll do anything to put a stop to this unfair fight. "Leave him alone."

"I can fight my own battles, Reagan," Rocco says, his blue eyes dark and cold. "Go home."

His words are harsh and cut me a little, but I'm sure he's not trying to hurt me. In fact, he's probably trying to protect me. I hold my hand out to him.

"Let's go."

He stares at me for a second, and I instantly know...I instantly know this is going to be really bad. His eyes hold love as they look at me, but there's a stark emptiness lurking there too. A hurt that goes deeper than I've ever seen before. A hurt that no one can heal. A choking sob gurgles up from the depths of my throat, and Miranda hugs me tighter. She knows this is bad too. The air is thick with volatile emotions. I can taste them on my tongue.

"Leave, Reagan," Rocco says through clenched teeth.

Tears flood my eyes as everyone stares at me, some with phones in their hands to document the moment. No doubt this incident will be all over social media before the next punch is thrown. "Rocco..."

"Come here, Reagan," Cochrane orders and his friends part, giving me a direct path to him. Rocco spits blood again and averts his gaze. Does he want me to go to Cochrane? What the hell is going on here?

"No." I back up, and Miranda backs up with me.

Cochrane's laugh is a twisted bark of cruelty. "Don't cry for him, Buttercup."

"Don't call me that."

He smirks, and I'm suddenly frightened of him, of what he can do...of what he might have already done. "No, you'd prefer it if I called you Sunshine, like this loser?"

My gaze flies to Rocco, waiting for him to react, to fight Cochrane, to protect me. He does nothing and my heart sinks to my stomach. My throat closes so tightly it's hard to breathe and the scene before me blurs even more through my tears.

"I don't want you to call me anything."

He snorts, and the hairs on my neck stand. "You have no idea, do you?"

I need to run as much as I need to stay, to hear what he's talking about, even though every instinct I possess tells me I'm not going to like it. "What are you talking about?"

"You think Rocco really liked you?"

My gaze slides to Rocco. I find him watching me, murder in his eyes, but then it fades, like he has no hope, like the fight has gone out of him. My legs go weak, and I rely on Miranda to keep me standing.

Cochrane shakes his head and looks at me with pity. "Why do you think I warned you not to fall for him?"

"I don't...know."

He laughs and it scrapes down my spine, and a cold shiver wracks my body. I hug myself to ward it off. It's been a long time since I felt such a bone deep cold. Rocco always had a way of warming me. I can't actually remember the last time I was cold inside.

Cochrane turns to Rocco. "What was that you said about spreading your Rocco charm?"

"Shut the fuck up, Cochrane."

"No. She should hear what you said. You know, when I said she was too smart to fall for a guy like you and, oh, shit what was your response?" He scrubs his chin like he's thinking. "Oh, right, I remember. He asked if I was sure about that." Cochrane whistles. "I don't know about you, Reagan, but that sure sounds like he was calling you stupid. Unless of course you didn't fall for him. Then you're smart, like I said you were."

"I..." What the hell is going on? His words bounce around inside my brain, and I glance at my feet, trying to sort things through.

"Come on, let's go." Miranda tugs at me. "You don't need to hear any of this."

I lift my head. Rocco still won't look at me. Why won't he look at me?

Oh, because what Cochrane is saying is true.

"You're going to want to hear the rest of it, Buttercup."

I sniff and go still, waiting for him to continue as the world goes dark around me. Phones record everything playing out and I wish the ground would open up and swallow me whole, because Cochrane was wrong, and Rocco was right. I am stupid.

"It was all a game, Reagan. He wanted you to fall for him to get back at me. I told him not to touch you. He agreed, but said he couldn't be held responsible if you touched him first, or if it was his dick you wanted when the month was over."

I gasp at the crudeness, and anger propels me forward. I push Cochrane's friends out of my way and stand before Rocco. His head is down, and blood is dripping from his nose.

"Look at me."

His head lifts, and I don't know what to make of it. The way he looks at me with warmth, compassion and love robs me of my last breath, but there's a hardness there too. "Did you say that, Rocco? Did you say all those horrible things?"

His shoulders tighten, ever so slightly. If I didn't know him as well as I did, I wouldn't have noticed. Wait, what the hell am I saying? If he said those things, then I don't know him at all, do I?

"Answer me!"

"Yes." His blue eyes go harder than I've ever seen them.

"Told you," Cochrane says.

A growl crawls out of Rocco's throat. "Shut the fuck up."

"Yeah, shut the fuck up, Cochrane."

A smile touches the corners of Rocco's mouth as I tell Cochrane to fuck off.

"It's okay, come here, Buttercup. I'll make everything better for you. You know you belong with me."

"Then why the hell did you hand me over to Rocco! I don't ever want to see you again, Cochrane. We're done. For good."

"That's my girl," Rocco whispers under his breath and I'm not even sure I heard him correctly. Tears flood my face, and that softness is back on Rocco's as I sob almost uncontrollably. I've never felt such pain in my chest before. It hurts to breathe, to talk...to simply stand here.

A bloody hand captures my arm and he pulls me to him until my ear is near his mouth. "Do one thing for yourself, Sunshine." I'm about to pull away. He has no right to tell me to do anything. Not after playing with my heart. How could I have fallen for him? How could I have loved him? "Keep painting."

And right there is my answer. He wants me to keep painting. But none of this makes sense. How could he be playing a game with me, yet tell me to keep painting, like he actually cares? He doesn't care. He couldn't. I was a game to him.

"Shut up," I shout, my entire body shaking, not knowing what to make of any of this. "All of you just shut up." A girl comes closer with her phone and I snatch it from her hand, smash it to the ground and stomp on it. She's about to protest, but takes one look at my face and backs off. Yeah, I get it. I look like a deranged lunatic, and yes, they should all be afraid.

I step up to Rocco again, and put my face right in his. "I hate you. I hate everything about you. I'm glad Cochrane wrecked your bike...and your face."

Anger is making me lash out. Pure unchecked rage. I've always kept my cool, my temper. I have always been the do-gooder, the rule follower, letting my parents guide me down a path I never wanted to go, because oh, you know me, I hate confrontation. Hate it! Yet here I am, my face not even an inch from Rocco's and I'm shouting loud enough that those on the other side of campus can hear me, while everyone has their phones out to capture my manic display. This is what heartbreak has done to me. This is what Rocco has done to me. Honestly, I'm not even sure who 'me' is anymore—especially without him.

"Cochrane was right about you all along. You're a rat. Trash and I never should have crawled into your gutter."

He glances at Miranda. "Take her home. Please."

I want to yell some more. I want to pound on his heart and make him hurt as much as I do, but I'm exhausted, my limbs weak.

"Reagan," Miranda says gently, giving me a little tug. I stumble away from Rocco and Miranda puts her arm around me.

"I don't ever want to see either of you again," I spit out, before I sniff, and go quiet, my heart shattered into a million pieces that will never be the same again. I loved Rocco. Correction, I love Rocco. Why the hell did I go and fall for him? I consider all the things we've done together. Is any girl immune to that kind of charm? But that's all it was. Rocco was charming me, and knew exactly what he was doing to get back at his enemy. Here I thought I was a pawn for Cochrane, only to find out I was a pawn for Rocco too. That's all I was to them. Neither valued me as a person. I was simply a tool for them to hurt one another with.

"Let's get you home," Miranda says.

"Fuck that. I'm going to the Growler. I'm getting drunk and picking up the first guy I see."

She opens her mouth to tell me how stupid of an idea that is, but I glare at her, in no mood for a lecture.

"I'm stupid."

"You're not stupid. I don't even know what's going on, Reagan. None of this makes sense."

"Maybe alcohol will help."

"Yeah, maybe," she agrees, to humor me. Alcohol isn't going to make any of this better, but maybe for a little while it will help numb the pain inside me. We go straight to the pub, and I sit at the bar and order four shots of tequila. I push two over to Miranda.

"You don't have to if you don't want to," I tell her.

"Yeah, I do." We click glasses and we both swallow the shot in one gulp. We slam our glasses down on the counter, like we used to do freshman year, glance at each other and laugh. Well, will you look at that? I can still laugh.

It's Tuesday, so the place isn't busy. There's no band, but there is music and there are a bunch of guys at a table. They're young, maybe freshmen. Perfect.

I take another shot, and so does Miranda. I order more and get us a couple of beer chasers. Sitting on my stool, I swivel and throw my head back, letting the alcohol burn through my body. A song comes on that I love and I grab Miranda's hand and drag her onto the floor. We start dancing, and instantly draw the attention of the frat boys.

Never in my life have I done anything so reckless or foolish, but you know what? It feels good to forget about life for a while…forget about obligations, responsibilities…broken hearts.

Miranda and I dance, and I can tell she's trying to stay sober to watch over me, and maybe that's a good thing. I'm a light-weight when it comes to alcohol and can already feel the effects of the shots.

"I love you, Miranda, and that is not the tequila talking."

She grins. "I know you do."

"I need another shot."

"Pretty sure you don't," she murmurs, but follows me to the bar anyway. I take a couple more shots, and back to the dance floor we go. I'm being stupid, but whatever. We already estab-lished that I am. This back and forth from the bar to the dance floor routine carries on for quite a while. Over an hour later, I sway to the music, only to realize it's not Miranda grinding up against me. Nope, it's one of the frat boys. I turn to him, and put my arms around his neck.

"Hey," I say in my best seductive voice. I laugh, almost hyster-ically, because I don't even have a seductive voice, although Rocco sure seemed to love the way I talked and opened up to him in bed. Lies. All freaking lies. I probably wasn't even very good. I laugh hysterically again.

Frat boy arches a brow, but goes back to grinding against me, because getting in my pants is far more important than me being bat-shit crazy.

I blink, my eyes are so damn heavy, all I want to do is close them for a moment. With my arms around the boy, I put my head on his chest, and I'm not even sure my feet are on the floor.

"Okay, that's enough."

That voice. It's Rocco's. But it can't be. Why would he be here? Strong arms slide around my waist and pull me from frat boy. I whack at the hands holding me. "That's enough, Reagan." Warmth spills over my body as Rocco puts his mouth to my ear, and equal amounts of anger and love surge through me.

"Leave me alone." I glance at the frat boy. "Aren't you going to help me?"

He shakes his head and goes back to his friends, and even though I'm drunk, I realize he's making the right choice. For himself. Not for me.

"I'm taking you home." I spot Miranda watching us while she nibbles on her bottom lip, a nervous gesture that's a dead giveaway.

"Did you call him?" She doesn't answer, but instead she follows us outside. "We are no longer friends," I tell her as Rocco scoops me up into his arms. He carries me to my house at breakneck speed, and the whole time I struggle, pound on his chest but it doesn't slow him down or faze him. I hate that he's so muscular, that nothing I can do, that not even my fist can penetrate his heart.

He carries me inside, and I'm not sure what he just said to Miranda, but she follows us up the stairs and stays in the hall when he sets me on my bed. He drops down with me and for a brief second, compliments of all the alcohol, I forget what he did. I snuggle into him as he pulls the blankets over our head, and makes a safe fort.

"Nice," I mumble.

He places a soft kiss onto my forehead. "Get some sleep, Sunshine."

Sunshine.

My memories fill back in. "You don't get to call me that anymore."

He crawls out of our secure fort. "I know."

"I hate you, Rocco."

"I know that too," he whispers as he walks across the room and quietly closes my bedroom door behind himself.

I push the blankets off and stare at my door, my tears falling hard. "I love you."

I close my eyes, and the next thing I know, it's morning. I peel one eye open and try not to move. Did someone get the name of the linebacker who took me to the ground? No, I remind myself. It wasn't a Falcons linebacker. It was the team's tight end who tore my feet out from underneath me and ripped my heart in two.

I groan loudly, and a knock sounds on my door. I try to sit up, but the room spins, so I flop back down, and put my arm over my eyes. "Come in."

The door inches open and Miranda peeks her head in. "Hey. I was waiting to hear you wake up."

"Ugh." Wait, she was the one responsible for calling Rocco.

"You okay?"

"No. I'm mad at you."

"I know. Can we talk, though?"

"Only if it's not about Rocco, or Cochrane, or anything else that involves my heart." I glance at my easel. "We can talk about painting." I frown. "No, we can't." Air leaves my lungs in a whoosh as I shrink into myself, wanting nothing more than to throw the blankets over my head and hide from the real world. "Rocco bought me that easel."

"Yeah, that's what I want to talk about." She takes a seat on my bed, everything about her serious.

"Miranda, please—"

"Something isn't right, Reagan."

I give a very unladylike snort. "Yeah, tell me about it."

"No, I mean it." She frowns, and shakes her head. "None of this makes sense and I stayed up all night thinking about it." She picks at my bedding, and I can almost hear her brain spinning. "I ran into Rocco when he was looking for Cochrane. He wanted to kill him."

"They wanted to kill each other."

"I know, but he was so angry, he said some things to me he probably never meant to say."

Now she really has my attention. "What did he say?"

"Something about football. He said his football career was over."

My heart lurches. Oh God, no! It's all he ever wanted, all he ever fought for. This can't be happening. I might hate him right now, but I love him too and want only the best for him. Don't even ask me to understand that.

"Why?"

She shakes her head. "I really don't know, but my guess is it has something to do with Cochrane, and...you."

"Why would I have anything to do with him losing a career in football?"

"Cochrane wanted you back. You didn't want him. His father has a lot of pull, Reagan." I go quiet, barely able to fill my lungs as I consider all the things Cochrane could have done to destroy Rocco. "I think he's behind all this."

I roll away from Miranda and stare at the white wall as I remind myself of yesterday's conversation. "He said mean things. He didn't even deny it."

"Yeah, but we all say mean things when we're mad, don't we?"

I swallow, and my insides squeeze as I consider all the cruel things I shouted at Rocco as he just stood there beaten and bloodied and took every single barb.

"Yeah..."

"Maybe he's pushing you away because he's afraid...or maybe he's protecting you. I really don't know."

Rocco had a horrible upbringing, and to this day he has a lot of demons. "People have always left him. I wasn't going to leave him."

"Then maybe he was protecting you."

In all the time I've spent with Rocco, he was there for me. Helping. Protecting. Encouraging. That does not sound like a guy who was playing a game with my heart. "From what?"

"Does it matter?"

"I...guess not."

"All I know is what I've seen with my own eyes these past few weeks. You've blossomed, Reagan, and I've never seen you happier. I think you two should have a conversation."

"But it was all a lie." I groan and pound the bed, clinging to the hurt from yesterday, the cruel things he didn't deny. "Our relationship, it was a lie, Miranda."

"What if it wasn't? You know better than I do that Cochrane gets what Cochrane wants. That he plays dirty."

"Yeah," I say, my breath coming a little faster now as worry for Rocco pushes back the anger I've been holding close.

"I called Rocco from the pub because you needed him, and you know what he did, Reagan?"

I go quiet for a second, then say, "He came running."

"Would a guy who was fucking with you do that?"

I turn to my window and wince at the light filtering in. "No."

"Right. So like I said, none of this makes sense. He's pushing you away for a reason. Even if he did say those things in the beginning, and maybe he did mean them, things changed, and you two fell in love."

I blink through the tears blurring my vision, my heart jumping in my chest. "You think he's in love with me."

"Of course, he is." She takes my hand. "He's protecting you... from something."

Panic fires every nerve ending in my body. "Oh God, Miranda. Oh God." My throat gurgles as I roll to my back. "All the mean things I've said to him. Why would he ever talk to me again?"

"Because he loves you."

25

ROCCO

I step outside my house, and not even the early evening sun does anything to lift my spirits. Not much can. Fuck, it's been three days since I lost my girl—although she was never really mine to begin with—and I don't even have a bike to jump on and go for a ride to clear my messed-up head.

I take a deep breath as cars drive by, horns honking as everyone heads to the football field to watch tonight's game —that I won't playing in. Fuck me. I guess I can look on the bright side of things. I get to stay in school, get to finish my education. That's something. It's just that none of that feels important if I don't have the woman I love to share it with.

I pull my keys from my pocket and open the lock on the shed. The second I pull open the doors, my heart falls into my stomach. No. Fucking. Way. Anger floods me. Cochrane destroyed my bike and then took everything from me. Now he's gone and taken the crumpled bike too.

I stare into the empty shed, and my hands fist at my sides. If I go find him and give him the beating he deserves, the only thing I have left will be taken away from me. Maybe it's worth it, though. Maybe I was never meant to be anything, to have anything in this life.

I slam the doors shut and the bang reverberates through me. As my teeth rattle, I turn and head down the sidewalk, toward Wolf House. I keep my head down as partiers yell from their vehicles. I'm sure everyone on campus knows I've been kicked off the team by now, and I'm sure the rumor mill is doing its magic. What will they say about me this time? Do I even care? Honestly the only one I care about is Reagan. What she thinks matters. But I pushed her away, and in the heat of the moment, she said cruel things about me. Things I deserved after hurting her. But I couldn't let her get dragged down with me. I'm just glad she saw Cochrane for who he really is, and there will be a better guy out there for her somewhere.

I pick up my pace when the sound of my bike revving reaches my ears. I spin so fast, I nearly do a faceplant. Who the fuck is riding my bike? From the distance, I can only tell it's two people. A big man on the front, and someone smaller on the back. I stand there as they come closer, and the second I realize who it is, the world goes a little fuzzy.

The bike stops, and Mr. Ellison takes off his helmet and gives me a smile. "She rides nice, son."

"How...what's going on?"

Reagan climbs off the bike behind him and my heart hurts when I look at her. I love her so fucking much, all I want to do is run to her, pull her into my arms and tell her everything will be okay. But that's a big fat lie, now isn't it, and I really only ever wanted to be honest with her.

"Reagan," I begin and swallow around the lump in my throat. "What's...going on?" My gaze goes to my bike. It's running smoothly, and even the gas tank has been replaced.

"We fixed your bike."

I shake my head. "You didn't have to do that."

"I wanted to, and remember you once said to me, *who am I to stand in the way of a girl who knows what she wants?*"

I nod. "I remember." Of course, we were talking about sex. I glance at her father, a little uncomfortable. My thoughts should not be going to the bedroom and all the fun things we did while he's standing there.

As if reading my sudden unease, he smiles at me. "I think I'm going to take in the football game," he says.

Reagan gives him a hug. "Thanks for all your help, Dad. We'll meet you there, okay?"

She'll meet him there. Me, I'm not going anywhere near the field.

"Reagan?" I question when she turns to me. "What's going on?"

"Dad helped me fix the bike." She waves toward my ride. "He called in a few favors to get it done quickly."

"Thanks, but you didn't—"

"I didn't mean those things I said," she blurts out, her eyes wide and worried, her cheeks pink. "You're not a rat, you're not trash, I was never slumming, and you do belong here at Kingston."

I take a breath and let it out slowly. "I'm not mad at you, Reagan." I'm mad at myself for dragging her into my shit. Then again, I guess Cochrane was responsible for that. I'm just glad I got to spend time with her. Got to know her... touch her. It's those memories that will help me get through life.

"I said those things to hurt you."

I nod in understanding. "I know."

"You hurt me."

My heart thumps and I pinch my eyes shut. "I'm so sorry. I never meant to hurt you."

"I know." My eyes fly open. "I once told you, I knew you'd never do anything to hurt me. Purposely, that is. I guess I momentarily forgot that when Cochrane told me you said mean things, and you never denied it."

"I did say those things." My gaze moves over her face, waiting for her to react, and when she doesn't, I continue with, "I was just trying to piss Cochrane off after the card game. He took everything out of context."

"Why didn't you defend yourself?"

"Because...because we can't be together, Reagan." I step back, working to put physical and emotional distance between us. "Maybe in some fucked up way, I thought if you hated me, it would be easier. I don't even know if that makes sense. I'm sorry. Sometimes I'm not great with words. I usually let my hands do the talking."

"Yes, you do, and I like the way they talk." She takes my hand and puts it on her waist. I quickly tug it away. "Reagan, we can't." My gaze goes to my bike. "Wait, how did you get my bike from the shed?"

She gives me a wicked grin. "I learned how to pick a lock from the best."

A laugh bubbles out of me, and she laughs with me. It eases some of the tension in my body. "I wouldn't go bragging about that."

"Why not?"

"It's not brag-worthy."

"Maybe not, but you are." She takes a step toward me.

Her sweet scent wraps around me and it takes every ounce of restraint I possess to keep from reaching out to her. "What are you talking about?"

"I had a long talk with my parents." She glances down for a second. "About...everything."

I brush my hand over my face, unease inside me. Jesus, if she told her father what I did, the things I said, why would he fix my bike and ride it to me. "You told them about us?"

"Yes, and Cochrane, the card game—"

Panic bursts inside me and the need to run and run and run until I can't run away from all this anymore pulls at me. "Reagan, you shouldn't have done that."

"Then we talked to Cochrane's parents."

"Holy fuck. Just go, go be with your dad and pretend you never met me. It's what's best for you. You don't want to get any more involved in this than you are." I try to back up, but she grabs my arm.

"Involved in what? Getting you back on the team, and outing Cochrane for lying to his father to get back at you...and back at me."

She pulls me back to her and I stumble. "What the hell?"

"I had a long talk with Miranda. I was so confused at first, I wasn't able to see through the hurt, but when I calmed down, I asked myself, how can a guy who was so sweet, gentle, caring and considerate, a guy who really cared about my future, play with my heart just to take down his enemy." I blink at her, my pulse practically climbing out of my throat when she adds, "I came to the conclusion that he can't."

"Reagan...you don't understand." Wait, did she just say I was back on the team? I shake my head. That doesn't matter right now. All that matters is that she doesn't get dragged down with me.

"I understand everything. My parents and Cochrane's parents are best friends, and believe it or not, the Montgomery's are decent people. Between us all, we put two and two together. Cochrane's father only knew half the story when he went to the Dean. Cochrane spun him a story and he thought he was doing the right thing. When my father visited his old friend Dean Blakely, and filled him in on the other half of the story, he reinstated you. You're back on the team, Rocco, and while Cochrane won't be punished by the college, he has his father to answer to, and that's enough."

"Reagan, I can't believe any of this."

"It's true, and during that long talk with my parents, I told them I wanted to switch to the art department."

"Oh no."

She laughs. "It's okay. I showed them my art, and the painting of the ocean through your cave was their favorite."

"You painted it?"

"Yes, and I want you to have it."

I'm so touched, I can't even find words to thank her.

"Thank you for helping me find my way. Now it's time for you to get back on the path you were meant to be on." A car goes by and the horn blares. She smiles at me and glances at her phone. "The game is about to start and I'm not sure they can win without their tight end."

My throat is so tight as tears pound against the back of my eyeballs. Reagan believes in me. In us. "Reagan...I...I love you. I've always loved you. The second I saw you freshman year with Cochrane, I loved you."

She puts her hand on my face. "I know, and that's why you made sure I got home safely from night classes. The reason you made sure all the other girls on campus got home safely is because of this." Her hand falls from my face and she places it over my heart. "You pushed me away to protect me. I realize that, and I appreciate it. How could a girl not love a guy who would sacrifice everything for love?"

My heart nearly jumps out of my chest, and I have to ask, because if I'm hallucinating, and she didn't just tell me she loved me, I might have to destroy something. "You love me?"

She laughs. "Of course I do."

I pick her up and spin her around, hardly able to believe this is happening. I set her down and brush my thumb over her lip. "You're not going to be in any trouble, are you?"

"No, but you are if you don't get this…" She pauses to pinch my ass. "tight end on the field in the next few minutes, you're going to be in trouble."

I glance past her shoulders, my heart racing. "Thank you."

"You don't need to thank me, but if you want to later…" She gives me a wink. "I'll let you."

I grin and kiss her again. She breaks it and pushes me. "Get on the bike and get moving. Your gear is already in the locker room, thanks to Alistair."

"He knew you were up to this?"

"Yeah."

I grab the helmet her father left on the bike. "I'm going to kill him for not telling me."

She puts her hand on my cheek and I lean into the softness. "How about not doing that. When it comes to fight or fuck, I'm rooting for the latter."

I stand there grinning at how far we've come together, how lucky I am to have an incredible woman like her in my life. "Now get out there and get a touchdown for me."

"I will." I jump on my bike and she kisses me.

"A touchdown for the team, and a touch down there for me, later." Jokingly, she points downward. "Although I must warn you, I might want two."

I laugh, a new lightness inside me as love fills my heart, and I let it. "Who am I to stand in the way of a girl who knows what she wants?"

"Go get 'em, Rocco."

"I will, Sunshine. I will. Then I'm coming for you."

Reagan

Two Years Later:

I used to think woodpeckers were gorgeous majestic birds until one decided that the corner of the cottage was the best place to jackhammer with its beak at five in the morning. Groaning, I peel one eye open and then another. I turn to find Rocco sleeping quietly, his arms over his head, his chest rising and falling quietly. I smile, my heart so full of love for him.

The thing is, every day I find myself falling deeper and deeper in love with him. After college, he went on to play for the NFL, and I couldn't be more proud. All his hard work paid off. Me? I switched majors and needed to take a few extra years to finish my arts and design degree. But that's okay. It's also good that I have those business courses behind me. They're going to come in handy when I finally get my gallery up and running, and start selling my paintings and art by other upcoming artists. One piece I'll never sell, though, is the one in the cave, right when I was beginning to fall in love with Rocco. That's a special one that no one sees but us.

I grin, thinking back to when Rocco broke us into the college gallery. I know what he was doing, what he was trying to prove, and I love him all the more for it. It helped me face my parents and fight for what I really wanted. Since then, Mom and Dad have really changed their outlook on life, accepting my path, and completely excited about the announcement Rocco and I made to them last week.

The cabin vibrates as the woodpecker goes at it, getting on my very last nerve. I shake my head, hardly able to believe Rocco can sleep through the racket.

Not wanting to wake him, and a little jealous that he can sleep through that noise, I push the covers off and step into the main room of our family cottage. Rocco and I came here as soon as summer hit, even though he bought a huge house near Kingston after signing with the NFL. He wanted a place for us, something close to my school, so I could finish up my degree. I do love the privacy here, surrounded by trees, and the lake, and *some* of the birds. Miranda is coming to visit later, and I'm looking forward to seeing her. She's working for a station near Kingston, allowing us to stay close as she put her journalism degree to work. I love that she's still finding drama in everything. But she's a true friend to me and Rocco.

I put on a pot of coffee and step outside. Clapping my hands hard, I glance at the noisy woodpecker. "Go away," I holler, and it flies away. But it lurks in a nearby tree, waiting until I leave so he can get back to his hammering. My efforts are futile! My diamond ring glistens in the sunlight, and I smile. The first thing Rocco did with his signing bonus was buy me an engagement ring, and we married right after his first season because he refused to wait.

I breathe in the morning air and take in the little ripples on the lake. A breeze blows in and a little shiver goes through me. But I'm not really cold. Not anymore. Not with Rocco in my life. I walk around to the back of the cottage and glance at the majestic tree house Dad and I built to surprise Rocco last year when he came back from his first NFL season. He laughed so hard, picked me up and spun me around with childlike enthusiasm. While Dad never understood the secret Rocco and I share, he didn't question my desire to build a treehouse at the cottage. No doubt he assumed I wanted it for children down the road.

I walk to the treehouse, run my hand along the ladder, and take the five steps up into it. I grin as I glance at the walls, completely covered in my art. Rocco insisted we hang them so we could make our little treehouse a home. One wall is still bare, though.

"What are you doing up there?"

I poke my head out as Rocco climbs the ladder, his hair mussed from sleeping. He's never looked sexier, and my body sparks, wanting him inside me again.

"Woodpecker woke me."

He shakes his head. "I'm going to kill that thing. You need your sleep."

I laugh. "No, you're not. He's just a woodpecker doing what woodpeckers do." He stands beside me, crowding me, over-whelming me. My heart beats a little harder in my chest.

He slides his arms around me and his early morning erection presses against my stomach. "In that case, I'm going to take you right here, right now, because I'm a man about to do what men do."

"I think I like that idea." He frowns, like he's suddenly remembering something. "Rocco, it's fine." No matter how many times I reassure him, he's still a little worried.

He drops to his knees and presses a kiss to my baby bump, and the moisture that floods his eyes every time he does that brings tears to my own eyes.

"I can't believe I'm going to have my very own family, Reagan." His voice is broken and hoarse, filled with want and need and so much love it wraps around me and squeezes me tight.

"We're having a family," I say, recalling Mom and Dad's reaction. They were over the moon excited of course, and making a million plans for the baby. One plan I won't let them make however, was on our child's future. Rocco and I will teach and guide our little one, but whatever our child wants to be in life is up to them.

"Thank you, Reagan," he chokes out. "Thank you for this." He gently caresses my tummy.

I run my fingers through his hair as tears pour down my face. He's been thanking me a lot since I told him we were pregnant. "Thank you," I say in return. "I can't even imagine where I'd be or what I'd be doing if it weren't for you. Well, yes I can, and I'd be miserable." Staying with Cochrane would have been a mistake, a life lost and ruined. Mom and Dad definitely saw that after the way he manipulated the poker game situation and got Rocco kicked off the college football team for a short time.

"Are you happy, Reagan?" He tugs me down and presses his lips to mine. It's a deep, love-imbued kiss that steals my breath, and fills my heart.

"I have never been happier," I tell him, even though he knows that. But sometimes he asks anyway, that lost little boy still residing inside him. But that boy grows stronger and braver under my care, showing up less and less as our love continues to grow deeper and stronger.

"I hope we have a boy and he looks just like you."

"We don't want that, Sunshine." He laughs. "We want a girl who looks just like her beautiful mother."

I warm all over. "Such a sweet talker."

"It's the truth." He brushes my hair from my face and looks over my shoulders. "No matter what we have, I can't wait to make art with them and fill that wall. When that's done, this treehouse really will be a home."

"A family of three…"

The corners of his mouth turn up playfully. "For now."

"You're determined to keep me pregnant, aren't you?" I laugh. For the last year, he's been telling me he wants a dozen kids, which might be ten too many for me.

"I'm determined to do whatever makes you happy, Reagan." He brings my lips to his and lightly grazes his mouth over mine. "No one deserves happiness more than you." The truth is that he's the one who deserves happiness, and I plan to do whatever it takes to put a smile on his face every day and maybe we'll end up having twelve kids. Seeing him so happy makes me happy, and I love that Mom and Dad fell in love with him too. How could they not? He's kind, compassionate and spent years watching over me, when I wasn't even his. Rocco Gianni is definitely one of the good guys and I'm the luckiest girl in the world.

I press my lips to his. "Now what was that you said about a man doing man things?"

"Are you sure it's okay?"

I love how much he worries about our little baby, and I know he's going to be overprotective, but a good dad. The best dad. "Well, if you don't want to," I tease.

"Oh, I want to, Sunshine. I want to strip you naked and put my hard cock inside you and make love to you until the sun goes down and you're seeing stars."

"I always see stars when you make love to me, day or night." I grin. "I love you, Rocco, and just so you know, you're as good with your words as you are with your hands."

Thank You!

Thank you so much for reading Keeping Score, book three in my End Zone. I hope you enjoyed the story as much as I loved writing it. Please read on for an excerpt of The Play-maker, book one in my Players on Ice series.

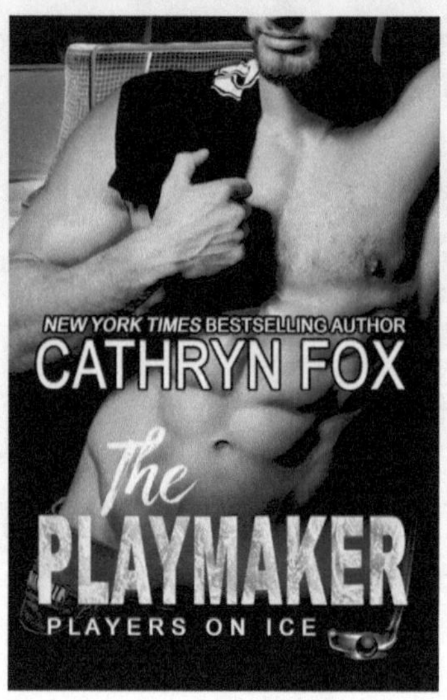

The Playmaker

"I LOVED this book. I enjoyed how their love story came together and look forward to reading the next book in this series." Mary, Amazon Reviewer."

I didn't want to ask him for a favor.

He was the cockiest hockey player I knew.

And my brother's best friend.

But I needed to learn about the game, and he was down with a concussion.

I didn't realize he had an agenda of his own.

One that involved showing me his off-ice plays.

I should have said no.

Should have kept things in the central zone.

But one sweet taste was a game changer, and the only words on my lips were yes.

Until a lifetime of secrets spilled out...

The Playmaker

Happy Reading,

Cathryn

THE PLAYMAKER

Nina

Fat drops of spring rain pummel my head, wilting my curls as I dart through Seattle's busy traffic to the café on the other side of the street. My best friend, Jess, is inside waiting for me, undoubtedly hyped up on her third latté by now.

I step over a pothole and search for an opening in the traffic. I hate being late, I really do. I totally value other people's time, but when the email came through from my editor, asking me to write a hot hockey series, my priorities took a curve. I've worked with Tara for a couple years now, and I know her like—pardon the pun—a well-worn book. To her, hesitation equals disinterest. She's a mover, a tree-shaker, and it wouldn't have taken long for her to offer the opportunity to another author. She wanted a quick reply and I had to give it to her.

I got this!

Yeah, that was my response, but what did I have to lose? I've been in such a rut lately, thanks to my fickle muse, deserting me when I needed her most. I swear to God, sometimes she acts like a hormonal teenager. I need to whip her into shape so I don't lose this gig. The royalties from a series will help make a sizeable dent in the bills that are piling up high and deep.

High and deep.

I laugh. One of those self-derisive snorts that crawls out when you'd really rather cry. Yeah, that pretty much sums up the *I got this* response I emailed back. High and deep, like a big steaming pile of—

A car horn blares, jolting me from my pity party. With my heart pounding in my chest, I step in front of the Tesla and flip the guy off. I safely reach the sidewalk and once again my mind is back on my job, and off the impatient jerk in the overpriced car.

I step up on the sidewalk and lift my face to the rain, the cool water a pleasant break from this unusual spring heat wave we're having. Pressure fills my throat. The hum of traffic behind me dulls, leaving only the sound of my pulse pounding in my ears. Panic.

Why the hell did my editor think I, former figure skater turned romance novelist, would want to write a series about hot hockey players? Yeah, sure my brother is an NHL player, but that doesn't mean I'm into the game. I hate hockey. No, hate is too mild a word for what I feel. I loathe it entirely. But you know what I don't loathe? Eating. Yeah, I like eating. Oh, and a roof over my head. I really like that, too.

I draw in a semi self-satisfied breath at having rationalized my fast response.

Except my reply was total and utter bullshit. I don't *got this*. In fact, I...wait, what's the antonym of *got this*? All that comes to mind is, *you're screwed*. Yep, that pretty much describes my predicament.

Why didn't I just stick to figure skating?

Because you took a bad spill that ended your career.

Oh right. But seriously, a hockey series... Ugh. Kill me. Freaking. Now.

I reach the café, pull the glass door open and slick my rain-soaked hair from my face. I quickly catalogue the place to find Jess hitting on the barista. Ahh, now I get why she picked a place so far from home. I take in the guy behind the counter. Damn, he's hotter than the steaming latté in Jess's hand, and from the way she's flirting, it's clear he'll be in her bed later today.

I sigh inwardly. It's always so easy for her. Me? Not so much. Men rarely pay me attention. Unlike Jess, I'm plain, have the body of a twelve-year-old boy, and most times I blend into the woodwork.

I pick up a napkin from the side counter and mop the rain off my face. Doesn't matter. I'm not interested anyway. From my puck-bunny-chasing brother to all his cocky friends, I know what guys are really like, and when it comes to women, they're only after one thing, and it isn't scoring the slot. I roll my eyes. Then again, maybe it is.

And of course, I can't forget the last guy I was set up with. What he did to me was totally abusive, but I don't want to dredge up those painful memories right now.

I shake, and water beads fall right off my brand-new rain-resistance coat. At least something is going right for me today. Semi-dry, I cross the room and stand beside Jess.

"Hey, sorry I'm late."

Jess turns to me, smiles, and holds a finger up. "I'll forgive you only if you're late because you were knees deep into some nasty sex, 'cause girlfriend, it's been far too long since you've been laid."

Jesus, what ever happened to this girl's filters?

Thoroughly embarrassed, my gaze darts to the barista, who is grinning, his eyes still locked on my friend, looking at her like she's today's hot lunch special and ignoring me like I'm yesterday's cold, lumpy oatmeal.

Ugh, really?

"Non-fat latté," I say, and scowl at him until he puts his eyes back in his head. I might be an English major but I have a PhD in the death glare. Truthfully, I'm so sick of guys like him, one thing on their minds. Then again, Jess only wants one thing from him, so I really shouldn't have a problem with it. Why do I? Oh, maybe because Mr. Right, my battery-operated companion, isn't quite cutting it anymore, and it's left me a little jittery and a whole lot cranky.

Jess is right. I *do* need to get laid.

Jess's lips flatline when she takes me in, her gaze carefully accessing me. "What?" she asks, her mocha eyes narrowing.

God, sometimes I really hate how well she can read me. "Nothing."

She straightens to her full height, and I try to do the same, but she dwarfs me, even without her beloved two-inch heels. I square my shoulders, but it's always hard to pull off a high-power pose when you're only five foot two, and teased relentlessly about it.

"Come on," she says, and guides me to a corner table. I peel off my coat and plunk down. Jess sits across from me. "Spill."

I point to my forehead. "Do I have 'idiot' written here?"

She looks me over, and cautiously asks, "No, why?"

My phone chirps in my purse, and I reach for it. Great, it's my editor wanting to set turn-in dates. "How about never?" I say under my breath.

"Uh, Nina. You're talking to your phone. You better tell me what's going on."

"You're not going to believe what I just agreed to."

"Do tell," she says and leans forward, like I'm about to spill some dirty little sex secret. If only that were the case.

I grab my phone and hold it up, showing her Tara's message. "I just agreed to write a hockey series," I say, and toss my phone back into my purse, mic-drop style—without the bold confidence.

Jess pushes back in her chair, clearly disappointed. She lifts her cup, and over the rim, asks, "I don't see how that makes you an idiot."

My mouth drops open. Jess and I have been friends since childhood. She of all people knows how much I hate hockey. "Are you serious?"

She shrugs. "You're a writer."

Mr. Sexy Barista brings me my coffee and he shares a secret, let's-hook-up-later smile with Jess. "And...?" I ask when he leaves.

"Writer's write and make things up. I know you hate hockey, but what does that have to do with anything?"

"I can't come up with a plot, or write about the game, if I don't know anything about it."

She shakes her head. "And I can't believe your brother is a professional player and you never once paid attention to the game."

"I was busy pursuing a professional skating career, remember?"

She reaches across the table and gives my hand a little squeeze. "I know. I'm sorry."

My tailbone and neck take that moment to throb, a constant reminder of a career lost.

I didn't just lose my dream of skating professionally the day my feet went out from underneath me, I lost my confidence, too. A concussion will do that to you.

Good thing I majored in English in college. Once I hung up my skates, I began to blog about the sport and sold a few articles. I joined a local writers group, and after talking to a group of romance writers, I tried my hand at one. Much to my surprise, it actually sold. I went from non-fiction to fiction, in every sense of the word. Happily ever after might exist between the pages, but it certainly doesn't in real life. At least not for me.

I take a sip of my latté, and give an exaggerated huff as I set it down. Jess instantly goes into problem-solving mode when she sees that I'm really stressed about this. As a brand-new high school guidance counselor, she can't help but want to fix me.

"Okay, it's simple," she begins. "You have to learn the game."

"How am I supposed to do that?"

"Turn on the TV and watch."

"I can watch a bunch of guys chase a stupid puck around a rink all I want, I still won't be able to understand the rules."

"How dare you call my favorite sport stupid."

"Jessss…" I plead. "What am I going to do?"

She crinkles her nose. Then her eyes go wide. "I've got it. Shadow your brother."

I give a quick shake of my head. "No, he's on the road, and he won't want me hanging around."

Jess goes quiet again, and that hollowed-out spot inside me aches as I think about Cason. I miss my brother so much and wish we were closer. Cason and I grew up in a family where there were no hugs or words of affirmation. I know Mom and Dad loved us, but as busy investment bankers, work consumed their lives. Sure, they put me in figure skating, and Cason in hockey when we were young, but they never shared in our passions, or really supported our pursuits.

I guess I can't expect my brother to display love, when none was ever displayed to him.

"Why don't you teach me?"

"It might be my favorite sport to watch, but I don't really know all the rules. I think you'd be better off getting your brother or…" She straightens. "Wait. I got this," she says, and

I cringe when she tosses my three-word email response back at me. A warning shiver skips along my spine, and I get the sense that whatever she's about suggest, is going to take me right down the rabbit hole.

"What about Cole Cannon?"

I groan, plant my elbows on the table, and cover my face with my hands. "Never," I mumble through my fingers. "Not in a million freaking years."

Jess removes my hands from my face. "Why not? He's your brother's best friend. I'm sure he'll help you."

"Cocky Cole Cannon, aka, The Playmaker. Do I need to say any more?" I reach for my latté and take a huge gulp, burning the roof of my mouth. Damn.

"I know you hate him, Nina, but—"

"Of course I hate him. You remember the nickname he used to use when we were kids—Pretty BallerNina. I was a figure skater, not a ballerina," I could only assume he was mocking me about being pretty too, but I keep that to myself.

"At least he worked your name into the moniker, and hey, it could have been worse. He could have called you Neaner Neaner, like Cason did."

I glare at her and she holds her hands up. "Okay, okay. I get it. But Cole's been home for a month, recovering from a concussion, and his team—the Seattle Shooters, in case you don't know the league's name," she adds with a wink, "are probably going to make it to the playoffs, so you know he's watching all the games. You don't have to like him to ask him to explain a few of the plays, right?"

"I suppose."

Wait! What? Am I really thinking about asking The Play-maker to help me? I reach for my latté and blow on it before I take another big gulp.

"And if you ask me, while he's helping you learn the plays, I think you two should hate fuck."

I choke on my drink, spitting most of it on my friend as the rest dribbles down my chin.

OMFG, how embarrassing. All eyes turn to me. Mortified, I grab a napkin and start wiping my face, but Jess is laughing so hard, I start laughing with her.

"Couldn't you have waited until I swallowed?" I ask.

"That's what she said."

"Ohmigod, Jess. How are we friends?"

She waves a dismissive hand. "You know you love me because I'm hellacioulsy funny."

"I do, just stop cracking jokes when I'm drinking."

She leans towards me conspiratorially, and I brace myself. "I wasn't joking. You and Cocky Cole Cannon should hate fuck. He's as sexy today as he was when he used to hang out with Cason at your house when we were teens." I give her a look that suggests she's insane. She ignores it and wags her brows. "He's explosive on the ice, but do you know why they really call him the Cannon?"

"Because it's his last name."

"Yeah, but that's not the only reason."

Don't ask. Don't ask.

"Okay, then why?" I ask.

"'Cause he's loaded between his legs."

Yeah, okay, I totally set myself up for that.

"You don't know that," I shoot back. My mind races to my brother's best friend, and I mentally go over his form. He's athletic, tall and—as much as I hate to admit it—hot as hell. The perfect trifecta. Could he be packing too? Working with some top-notch equipment?

Jesus, what am I doing? The last thing I should be thinking about is Cole's 'cannon'.

"Come on." Jess grabs her purse. "I'll drive you there."

I flatten my hands on the table. "I'm not going to his house, especially not unannounced."

"Give him a call then."

"No."

She sits back in her chair and folds her arms, a sign she's changing tactics. "And here I thought you liked your condo and food in your cupboards."

I groan at the direct hit.

Her voice softens and she touches my hand. "But you know you always have—"

"Fine." I stop her before she brings up my trust fund. Yeah, sure, Mom and Dad set money aside for me, but I don't want to use it. I want to live by my own means, make it on my own merit. Besides it wasn't their money I wanted, then or now, it was their attention, their love. I moved out years ago and only ever hear from them on my birthday or at Christmas.

I pull my phone from my purse. "I'll text him. If he doesn't answer, we don't talk about this again." I go through my contacts and find his number, having stored it years ago when he called to check on me after my injury. The call had taken me by surprise; so did his concern. Maybe my brother put him up to it. I don't know. Nor do I know why I kept his number.

My fingers fly across the screen, but in no way do I expect him to respond. At least I hope he doesn't. I read over the text. *Sorry to hear about your concussion. I was wondering if you could help me with something.* Then hit send.

I set my phone down and look at Jess. "Happy?"

"Hey, I'm not the one who's going to be homeless."

Point taken. Maybe I should be hoping he *does* text back.

My phone pings, and we both reach for it. Jess gets it first, and from her smirk, I guess my wish just came true—Cole responded.

Careful what you wish for.

"What does it say?" I ask, afraid of the answer.

"It says, sure what's up?" Jess's fingers dance over the screen as she responds for me.

"What are you saying?" I ask, panic welling up inside me. "So help me, if you're telling him I need to get laid…"

The phone pings again and she holds it out for me to read.

"I asked—I mean *you* asked if you could stop by his place, and he said sure."

"I don't know whether to kiss you or choke you," I say.

Jess laughs. "I think you'll be thanking me." She stands. "Come on."

We make our way outside, and the rain has slowed to a light mist as I follow her down the street to her parked car. I hop in and question my sanity. Am I really going to ask Cocky Cannon to teach me the game?

Jess starts the car and the locks click as she pulls into traffic. Guess so.

"You remember where he lives?" I ask. I think back to when he bought the house. He had a big party to celebrate. I was invited but didn't go. Why would I? Watching the hockey players with their bunnies was not my idea of a good time.

"Of course." She jacks the tunes and sings along off-key as she drives. Twenty minutes later, she pulls up in front of his mansion. It's a ridiculously big house for one person. I stare at it, and once again question my sanity.

"Go," Jess says.

"I'm going," I shoot back. I open the door, and smooth my hand over my mess of curls. Why the hell did I do that? It's not like I'm trying to make myself presentable or impress him. We don't even like each other.

I force my legs to carry me to his door, and I'm about to knock when it opens. My breath catches as I take in Cole, standing before me shirtless and barefoot, dressed only in a pair of faded jeans that hug him so nicely.

God, he is so freaking hot—and I never, ever should have come here.

As we stare at each other, like we're in some goddamn Mexican standoff, I can't stop thinking about his 'cannon'. My gaze drops to the lovely bulge between his legs, and a moan I have no control over catches in my throat as Jess's words come back to haunt me.

You two should hate fuck.

Thank you, Jess, for planting that idea in my brain. Christ, I should have choked her when I had the chance.

Oh these two are going to have some fun!! Check it out here! **The Playmaker**

ALSO BY CATHRYN FOX

End Zone

Fair Play

Enemy Down

Keeping Score

All In

Blue Bay Crew

Demolished

Leveled

Hammered

Single Dad

Single Dad Next Door

Single Dad on Tap

Single Dad Burning Up

Players on Ice

The Playmaker

The Stick Handler

The Body Checker

The Hard Hitter

The Risk Taker

The Wing Man

The Puck Charmer

The Troublemaker

The Rule Breaker

In the Line of Duty

His Obsession Next Door

His Strings to Pull

His Trouble in Talulah

His Taste of Temptation

His Moment to Steal

His Best Friend's Girl

His Reason to Stay

Confessions

Confessions of a Bad Boy Professor

Confessions of a Bad Boy Officer

Confessions of a Bad Boy Fighter

Confessions of a Bad Boy Doctor

Confessions of a Bad Boy Gamer

Confessions of a Bad Boy Millionaire

Confessions of a Bad Boy Santa

Confessions of a Bad Boy CEO

Hands On

Hands On

Body Contact

Full Exposure

Dossier

Private Reserve

House Rules

Under Pressure

Big Catch

Brazilian Fantasy

Improper Proposal

Boys of Beachville

Good at Being Bad

Igniting the Bad Boy

Bad Girl Therapy

Stone Cliff Series:

Crashing Down

Wasted Summer

Love Lessons

Wrapped Up

Eternal Pleasure Series

Instinctive

Impulsive

Indulgent

Sun Stroked Series

Seaside Seduction

Deep Desire

Private Pleasure

Captured and Claimed Series:

Yours to Take

Yours to Teach

Yours to Keep

Firefighter Heat Series

Fever

Siren

Flash Fire

Playing For Keeps Series

Slow Ride

Wild Ride

Sweet Ride

Breaking the Rules:

Hold Me Down Hard

Pin Me Up Proper

Tie Me Down Tight

Stand Alone Title:

Hands on with the CEO

Torn Between Two Brothers

Holiday Spirit

Unleashed

Knocking on Demon's Door

Web of Desire

Pinterest http://www.pinterest.com/catkalen/